EX-CON

Scott Hildreth

Published by
Eralde Publishing

Cover Photography Copyright © Darren Birks Photography
Cover Design Copyright © Creative Book Concepts
Text Copyright © Scott Hildreth
Formatting by Creative Book Concepts

ISBN 13: 978-0692516058

DEDICATION

We talked late nights, solved the world's problems, and stood up when we had to regardless of the potential outcome. Here's to standing proud, doing your time instead of letting the time do you, slinging ink (and not going to the SHU for the tattoo gun because we were always one step ahead of the guards), and enjoying NWA every time it came on the radio. All we needed was a second chance. Here's to second chances and to having a cellie who's always got your back.

Deuce, this one is for you, brother.

EMILY

June 6, 2006

Neither of my parents abused me, nor was I exposed to pornography or a perverted uncle at an early age. My sexual desires weren't something I developed; they were part of my being. The night we met I was in a sexual lull and had been there for some time. I was dissatisfied with men in general - for reasons I didn't fully realize at the time - and I had become fed up with even attempting to move forward. I had all but given up on men and sex, and by nothing more than a small streak of blind luck, he entered my life.

I had been in a bar dancing alone, and was disgusted with the behavior of the drunken men who were making comments about my choice of clothes. On that particular night, I was batting roughly .984 for being lightly sexually assaulted by strangers. In hindsight, maybe I should have worn a bra, but if I had I wouldn't have met Jackson, so scratch that thought.

I was walking out - well, stomping out would be a more accurate description. The departure stomp I often used when I wanted everyone to know just what it was I was thinking without actually *saying* it.

I tossed my hair over my shoulder and exhaled a sigh from my soul.

"That's *it*, I fucking swear," I huffed as I turned toward the door.

1

"Don't leave mad," the drunken thirty-something year old former frat boy said as he grabbed my arm and spun me around.

"Let me go!" I demanded as I attempted to pull away.

The music had changed from a dance beat to some lullaby bullshit, and most everyone had walked from the dance floor to their respective tables which were situated twenty or so feet away. Amidst the edge stood my closest possible assistance and he seemed to be immersed in talking to his drunken date.

With his mouth still agape, the drunken asshole who held my arm gazed down at my boobs with wide eyes. After staring for what seemed like forever, he nodded his head toward my tits as he spoke.

"You can't go out in public dressed like *that* and expect a man not to notice," he said.

"Let me go, I mean it," I said as I tried to free my arm from his grip.

My top was sheer, but tasteful. Underneath, I wore a white tank and no bra. In my opinion, I was able to choose whether or not to wear a bra, because it wasn't always necessary. Small "C" cup breasts were affixed to my chest like two stones, and cinching them even tighter to my narrow frame wasn't necessarily required. The temperature in the bar was such that my nipples had been hard for the fifteen minutes I was inside, five of which I chose to pass by dancing.

Alone.

His hand still gripping my upper arm firmly, I had no reason to believe his half-drunken ass was going to release me anytime soon, so I felt screaming was my only way out. I hated to be *that* girl, but I desperately wanted to be left alone. I inhaled a deep breath, paused, and gave fair warning.

And that was the moment when I met Jackson.

"I mean it. I'll fucking scream," I said through my teeth.

"Is there a problem?" a voice from behind me asked.

Thank God.

His tone was deep and calm, yet distinctly demanding of a response.

Frat boy released my arm as his eyes went wide. "No, Sir, there's no problem."

I turned around. My savior was tall, extremely muscular, and what portions of his body weren't covered by the seemingly microscopic leather vest he was wearing were decorated with tattoos. With a very strong jaw covered by a few days growth of beard, he looked rough. The type of rough no man would want to cross. I may have been slightly biased at that particular moment, but describing him as attractive wouldn't have done him justice. He was a far more refined handsome, a man I was certain had no idea he was as strikingly good looking as he appeared to be. As I gawked at him in the same manner I had been ogled all night, I pleaded my case.

"That asshole was trying to pull my top down, and when I tried to leave, he grabbed me and wouldn't let go," I explained as I attempted to catch my breath.

"You dropped this," my savior said as he held my purse at arm's length.

I glanced toward his hand. I didn't realize I had even dropped it. As I reached for the purse and took it from his grasp, he stepped around me and toward my nipple loving nemesis.

Without warning, and so quickly I didn't even realize what was going on for sure, my savior grabbed the man who was harassing me by his wrist. Although he only held his wrist, the asshole seemed to be in excruciating pain. As he winced and buckled his knees repeatedly, the questioning began.

"You know her?" he asked as he twisted the man's wrist.

Frat boy shook his head and winced in pain as he gave his response.

"No…" asshole murmured.

"You've got no right to grab a woman like that," he growled, "No fucking right."

He turned the man's wrist slightly, forcing him to bend his knees even more. As my would-be attacker was almost kneeling on the floor, my newfound tattooed friend gazed down at him and sighed.

"So, did you try and pull her top down?" he asked.

"I…I…just…" dumbass groaned in response.

I leaned toward my handsome friend and whispered *my* response to the question he had asked.

"He tried about ten times. When I decided to leave, he grabbed my arm. I've got the marks to prove it," I shuddered.

He peered over his shoulder. Still holding the man's wrist in his hand, his eyes narrowed slightly and he seemed to grow angry as he visually inspected the red marks on my arm.

As the anger seemed to build inside of him, he pursed his lips and exhaled through his nose.

"You don't need to see this," he said through his teeth as he turned to face the asshole.

"No, I *want* to see it," I responded as I took a step away from him.

A man and a woman approached from the left, pointing toward the boob groping idiot as they walked onto the dance floor.

"I saw him. He was trying to pull her top down since she got here. She was leaving and he grabbed her arm. My wife and I saw it all," he explained as he stepped beside us.

My hero raised the man's wrist, lifting the asshole from his crouched position. Without speaking, he released the man's wrist. Immediately, the asshole raised his hands as if he was ready to fight. In shock that he didn't at least attempt to turn and run away, I stood with my mouth open and stared.

"Respect. You've got a lot to learn about respecting women. Hopefully after I'm done whipping your ass, you'll see things differently. Remember this: *show respect, get respect*," he said.

In a blindingly fast blur, he struck the asshole in the face with his fist. As the shit head did his best to block the punches, my savior continued to beat him. Blood splattered from the jerk's nose and lips, and as he raised his hands to his face, it began to drip on the floor.

"And don't forget it," he grunted as he punched him one last time.

The asshole fell to the floor and moaned.

Oh, God. I really didn't need to see that.

Almost immediately, two bouncers were on the dance floor, attempting to grab both men.

"I'd back off if I were you," my hero explained as he turned to face the two bouncers.

His hands were raised to his chest and he was obviously ready to continue the fight. The muscles in his upper arms flared as he turned to the left and quickly to the right, situating his clenched fists in front of his chin as if prepared to box. After a quick study of my hero, the two bouncers exchanged nervous glances and eventually took a step rearward.

"I'm walking the girl to her car. If either of you try to stop me, you'll look like him when I'm done with you. And you need to call him an ambulance, his jaw's broken," he said flatly as he turned to face me.

5

The pool of blood was slowly growing, spreading across the concrete floor as a reminder of what had happened. As one of the bouncers bent over to help the man up from the floor we turned and began to walk away.

"You alright?" he asked me as he wiped his knuckles on his jeans.

Other than watching you almost kill that guy for grabbing me? Yeah, I'm just fine.

I bit my lower lip and nodded my head.

"I'm Jackson," he said as he bent his elbow and hooked his thumb on his belt, "Grab hold of my arm until we're out in the parking lot."

"Em…Emily. Or Em…just uhhm…call me Em," I stammered.

As if I had no choice, I followed his instructions. I shifted my purse to my opposite shoulder, slipped my arm through his, and walked by his left side as we maneuvered past the whispers, stares, and extended fingers recognizing him as the man who'd fought a stranger to save a girl from being humiliated - or something potentially much worse.

We exited the bar and began to walk through the parking lot. The fact I didn't know him wasn't bothersome at all, and in fact, I felt rather comfortable walking with him; almost too comfortable. I tossed my head to the side as I recognized my car.

"I'm the silver Camry, right over there," I said.

"So, why'd you do that? You know, beat the crap out of that guy?" I asked as we stepped alongside my car.

"Because it's what he deserved. He had no right to touch you without your approval. And I can guarantee you one thing, the next time he considers acting like that, he'll remember what happened tonight, and he'll reconsider," he responded.

He brushed my hand from his arm as if he was preparing to turn and walk away. I didn't want him to leave. I preferred it not be so simple. Walking through the parking lot with my arm wrapped around his I felt safe, secure, and even drawn to him no differently than if we had been out all night on a date. I realized I didn't have any idea who he was, but there was a big part of me willing, and even more that seemed to be wanting, to take the time to get to know him.

"What do you think about this top?" I asked.

"You look remarkable," he said with a nod, his eyes never shifting from mine.

Standing there in a leather biker vest, covered in tattoos, and with one hand still bleeding, his manner of speaking didn't seem to fit his looks. He was calm, had a distinctly decisive tone to his voice, and spoke differently than I expected a biker to speak. In short, he was intriguing, and I was beyond interested in knowing more about him. No one simply walks into a bar and beats the crap out of a random guy and then walks the girl to the car. He had a story, motive, a reason, something...

And I wanted to hear it.

I placed my hand on my hip and arched my back a little more. "You don't think it's too...I don't know...revealing?"

His eyes never leaving mine, he shook his head slowly. "Sure don't. And it really doesn't matter what you wear. A man doesn't have a right to do what he did."

"Guys are assholes," I breathed as I straightened my posture.

"They sure can be," he said as he glanced over his shoulder.

He seemed either nervous or like he was looking for someone.

"Do you need to go?" I asked.

He turned to face me as he shrugged his shoulders. "Supposed to meet some of the fellas, but they seem to be running late," he said under his breath.

He kicked the toe of his boot against the asphalt as if digging an imaginary hole. As I watched him continue to chip away, I decided to try my luck.

"You wanna hang out sometime?" I asked sheepishly.

Typically I wouldn't have been so forward, especially with someone I didn't know, but resisting my desires seemed to be something I had all but forgotten. After I spoke, the lingering silence which followed led me to believe I had made a grave mistake. As I prepared to swallow my pride and become even more embarrassed by his 'no' response, I slumped my shoulders and waited.

"I don't think that's a good idea," he responded.

"Why?" I snapped back.

The question shot from my lips as if I took exception to his rejection.

To be brutally honest, I thought it was a great idea. I was twenty-one, in great physical shape, and I believed I was a very attractive woman. I was considerably younger than what I guessed him to be, but I didn't care and I felt he shouldn't either.

His mouth curled into a smirk. He shifted his eyes along the length of my frame.

"I don't *hang out* with women. There's not much sense in it. Sooner or later, you'll want to take it further, and it'll never work out," he explained.

"Because?" I shrugged.

He started kicking the ground again, scraping the toe of his boot across the asphalt. After several swipes, he pursed his lips, inhaled through his nose, an exhaled. His lack of response to something I viewed as simple surprised me.

"Well, I'll tell ya," he said as he looked up.

"Sexually, I'm different than most men. I can't be in a relationship with a woman unless she's…" he paused and it seemed a hand had wiped his face with embarrassment.

He began to kick his imaginary hole a little deeper, focusing on his boot as he did so.

"Unless she's…unless she's *what*?" I shrugged.

He tilted his head rearward, rolled his shoulders, and tilted his head to the left and then the right, popping his neck as he did so. After a short hesitation which included chewing on his bottom lip, he inhaled a shallow breath and sighed out the corner of his mouth.

He fixed his eyes on mine. Breaking his stare seemed impossible. I consciously held my breath as I waited for him to continue.

"I'm a dominant. I've got to be in a relationship with a woman who's…" he paused and bit the edge of his lower lip.

"All men are dominant," I scoffed.

The fact he felt the need to tell me he was dominant seemed ridiculous. To think he believed I was a woman who would want to wear the pants in a relationship, especially after he had just saved me from some random douchebag, was laughable. If he wasn't interested, I wondered why he simply wouldn't say so. As I stood wondering what might be wrong with me, he began to explain further.

"Not dominant in the way I'm talking about," he responded as he shook his head lightly.

"What way are you talking about?" I asked.

He shook his head again.

"Wow. I'm a big girl. Afraid you're going to scare me? I seriously doubt it," I scoffed.

He continued to stare down at his boots and shake his head.

"You never know, maybe you and I…"

He glanced upward, sighed heavily, and slowly raised his hand between us, hesitating as it hovered in front of my neck.

"Listen, I'm going to touch your neck. I won't hurt you," he said.

I shook my head lightly and wrinkled my nose. "Touch my neck?"

He nodded once.

"I'm going to touch your neck to prove a point. We both might learn something from it. Depending on how it goes, we might end up hanging out sometime," he paused and chuckled lightly.

"Remember, I won't hurt you. I promise, and I don't break promises," he assured me.

Touch my neck to prove a point?

I glanced around the empty parking lot. After confirming there was no one watching, for some strange reason I nodded my head in agreement. In hindsight, I was glad I did.

"Okay," I shrugged.

"Don't move," he said in a soft but demanding tone as he reached for my neck, "And remember, I won't hurt you. Not now, not ever."

I nodded my head once again and swallowed heavily in anticipation of what was to come. He leaned forward, positioning his face beside mine, and pressed his lips to my ear. As he inhaled slowly, his hand squeezed my neck firmly.

As his strong hand clutched my neck, my knees went weak and I almost dropped my purse. I had never had a man wrap his hand around my neck, and although I had no idea what point he was trying to make, I enjoyed what he was doing. I closed my eyes and relaxed into his hand.

"You like that?" he breathed into my ear.

I nodded my head as I attempted to swallow.

"When I ask you a question, I'll need you to respond, Emily. I'll ask you again," he whispered into my ear.

He remembered my name.

I swallowed again as my knees wobbled beneath me.

He inhaled, held his breath for a few seconds, and exhaled into my ear. Goosebumps rose along the length of my arm. He massaged the tips of his fingers into my neck, gripping fractionally tighter with each passing second. He was far from choking me, obviously knew exactly what he was doing, and he left no doubt in my mind he was in charge of the situation. I opened my eyes and gazed blankly at the dark asphalt parking lot. Whatever he had done to me was apparent. I was sexually aroused so deeply I had become uncomfortably wet.

"Do you like my hand on your neck?" he asked through his teeth, enunciating each word as he spoke.

His warm breath against my jaw caused the hair on my neck to stand, and a tingle shot along my spine.

The response barely escaped my lungs.

"Yes," I murmured.

His grip tightened slightly. He pressed his mouth to my ear and held himself there for what seemed like a lifetime.

"Close your eyes," he whispered.

"Okay," I squeaked.

"For the sake of this experiment, imagine being naked, Emily. Imagine me tying you up and binding your hands behind your back with a rope. Imagine me securing your bound hands to a steel post in a room, preventing you from escaping. Imagine me having my way with you sexually - for as long as I want. I would do as I wished, and you would

11

allow me to do so, willingly. Imagine that, Emily," he breathed into my ear.

And he released my neck.

I fell forward, stumbled, and almost dropped to the ground. He steadied me in his arms and grinned as he waited for me to either accept or reject his demonstration.

My mind spinning, and aroused beyond the explanation of words, I stared at him in disbelief and blinked my eyes repeatedly.

"Turn on? Or turn off?" he asked.

I glanced down at my crotch. I wanted to tell him to stick his hand in my shorts and find out, but I was too much of a lady to make the offer. Instead, I fixed my gaze on his boots, sighed, and slowly shifted my eyes up and along the length of his muscular body until I reached his face.

"On," I said as our eyes met.

Okay, Jackson the biker, you've got my attention, now what?

"On a scale of one to ten, how much of a turn on?" he asked.

The sound of motorcycles pulling into the parking lot diverted my attention toward the entrance. Motorcycle after motorcycle came into the lot, one after another, all ridden by men who could have doubled as Jackson's brothers. The rumbling of their exhaust echoed through the alley alongside the bar and caused goosebumps to rise along the backs of both of my arms.

"Your friends?" I asked as I tossed my head in the direction of the motorcycles.

"I asked you a question," he said as he raised his index finger in the air.

"I don't like repeating myself, Emily, remember that," he said.

His voice was stern, but not in an angry sense. My mouth went immediately dry. In anticipation of at least attempting to respond, I swallowed the lump in my throat and nodded my head.

"On a scale of one to ten, how much of a turn on," he asked again.

"Twelve," I managed to respond.

"God damn, Killer. We got tied up at the DUI checkpoint. Fucking cops made us all blow in one of those breathalyzer things. Fucking pricks," a man said as he walked up beside us.

He was big, the kind of big that made people stare. He had a shaved head and a long dark beard that was sprinkled with gray hairs. His head was covered in various tattoos, and he looked like a pretty serious criminal. As he opened his arms and laughed, I noticed his hand, fingers, and at least one wrist were all heavily tattooed.

Jackson hugged him as they shook hands.

"Ready for a drink?" the man asked.

I shifted my eyes to Jackson.

"I'll be back in a bit. This girl's friends left her here. I gotta give her a ride home," Jackson said as he nodded his head toward me.

I attempted to hide my excitement.

"Worthless bitches," I sighed.

"Hurry the fuck up, we're gonna close this fucker down, but it won't be any fun without the Killer," the man growled.

"Don't hold your breath, Sarge," Jackson chuckled as he extended his elbow toward me.

As if he'd somehow programmed me to do so, I reached for his arm and followed him to his motorcycle. I had no clue where we were going, and no idea what he had planned, but I really didn't care. Something about him told me I would always be safe in his presence.

As I stretched my leg over the back of his seat, the late evening breeze blowing into my shorts reminded me of what he'd done to me when he squeezed my neck. I really had no idea of what he meant by being dominant, but if what he had just done to me was any indication as to what would follow, I was ready to find out more.

"I live at the corner of Thirty-third and…" I whispered.

"Not going to your house. We're going somewhere to talk," he said as he started the motorcycle.

"Okay," I responded, disappointed slightly, but attempting not to show it.

"You ready?" he asked as he reached for the levers on the handlebars.

And, as strange as it seemed to respond as such, I was. I was ready for whatever he wanted to ask me, tell me, or show me.

"Yes," I responded as I leaned forward, pressing my boobs into his back, "I sure am."

JACK

June 6, 2006

"And, if you aren't able to do that, there's no sense in taking a single step in the direction of even going on the first date," I explained.

She gazed at me blankly as if she was thoroughly confused by my question. After a few seconds of silence, she blinked her eyes a few times and spoke.

"So, what exactly does 'submit to you sexually' mean? I'll need you to explain it, like I mean *really* explain it," she said.

I nodded my head as I lifted my coffee cup from the table.

"You make a conscious decision to surrender yourself to me sexually. For *my* personal taste, outside of the bedroom, you and I are equal. Well, pretty damned close to it, anyway. Not many dominant men would agree with me in this regard, but I suppose I'm different than most. So, you make a decision to give me control of you - sexually. You *submit* yourself to me. Some men prefer that control to be twenty-four hours a day, seven days a week. I prefer it to be sexually, and depending on your personality and needs outside the bedroom, I'd consider taking more control. If you were willing to consider submitting, we would discuss what each of us expected, agree on specific limits, establish boundaries, and proceed slowly," I explained.

She leaned onto the edge of the table, rested her elbows on the

15

surface, and peered upward. The excitement in her eyes was obvious as she spoke.

"So, during sex, you would call the shots? Doggy style, missionary, reverse cowgirl, stuff like that?" she asked.

I took a slow drink of coffee as I studied her, pushed my cup to the side, and shook my head. "It's not that easy. So, let's say one night we may have casual sex. On another, I decide to tie you up, and have sex with you, but not allow you to touch me or maybe even deprive you of seeing me during the encounter. On another night, I may require you withhold your orgasms for all or most of the sexual act. Blindfolded, bound, the position, length of time, everything is up to me. It's as much of a psychological surrender as a sexual surrender."

"Oh wow," she gasped as she leaned into her chair, "No orgasms, really?"

"Really," I chuckled as I reached for my cup of coffee.

I raised the cup to my mouth and sipped the warm coffee as I waited for her to consider what I had provided her as an explanation.

"Okay, fuck it, I want to give it a try," she said as she leaned forward.

I laughed so hard I choked on my coffee. After coughing and hacking as if on my death bed for five solid minutes, I finally regained my breath, took a drink of water, and wagged my finger in the air.

"It doesn't work like that," I assured her.

"If we agreed this was what we both wanted, it would be a long, and I mean *long* time before we had sex," I explained as I reached for a napkin.

She wrinkled her nose and stared.

"Why?" she asked.

I raised my hand in the air, extended my index and forefinger, and

SCOTT HILDRETH

spread them wide.

"I can count on these two fingers how many women I have had sex with. One I was in a relationship with for four years, and the other was almost five years long. I'm damned near thirty, you do the math," I said.

Her eyes widened as she continued to stare.

I maintained eye contact with her as I continued, "I'm not going to accept you without knowing, and I mean *knowing* you're a match for me. And casual sex isn't an option. Never has been, and it never will be. So if you want to give this a try, I'm game. And just so we're in agreement this means we'd get to know each other, not start fucking. You've got a good attitude, you're attractive, and you're willing as fuck. For me, it's pretty damned difficult to find someone who meets my needs, so bumping into you tonight is pretty god damned exciting."

"I'm going to ask you a few questions, okay?" I asked.

"Yeah, you don't even want to know how many guys I've…yeah… questions, fire away," she chuckled.

"First, I have a few personal things. Try not to ever interrupt me. And remember, I hate repeating myself. Understood?" I asked.

She nodded her head as she tapped her temple with her fingertip, "Got it."

Emily was an extremely attractive woman. She had dark brown hair which could pass for black in the dim light of the diner and the darkest brown eyes I had ever seen. Her complexion was clear, and her little button nose was the perfect complement to her narrow face and high cheeks. Her lips were full, but not to a point she had what I would have described as *pouty* lips. She was tall, roughly five foot six or five foot seven, and I guessed her weight at about one hundred twenty pounds. Based on the muscle tone in her arms, she seemed to be athletic, and I

17

suspected she was disciplined in that regard. Her only downfall was her age. She was in a club drinking alcohol, so I hoped she was of legal age to drink, but she sure didn't look it.

"Age?" I asked.

"Twenty-one."

"Parents? Alive or dead? And if alive, is your relationship with them good or bad?"

"Alive, and I'd say pretty good," she said as she shrugged her shoulders slightly.

"Graduate high school?" I asked.

"Yes."

"College?"

"No."

I leaned forward, rested my forearms on the edge of the table, and studied her. As she began to outwardly express signs of being uncomfortable, I continued.

"If we were in a relationship, and you did something…I don't know…say, disobeyed me…or maybe made a decision that really upset me, and I was disappointed in you - and not just disappointed - but *so* disappointed that I expressed my disappointment to you," I paused and studied her reaction.

While I spoke, her eyes widened drastically, as if she was horrified at the thought of what I asked. Satisfied her answer was going to be favorable, I continued.

"How would that make you feel? That you'd done something to disappoint me?" I asked, maintaining focus on her eyes as I spoke.

She gazed down at the table as if ashamed. After a long hesitation, she glanced upward, but didn't maintain eye contact for very long.

"I wouldn't like that. I wouldn't want to disappoint you," she said under her breath.

I realized fully that I didn't expect her to cook, clean, and wash and fold my clothes, but most naturally submissive women loved to feel as if they were providing for their Dom. Cooking and baking was truly satisfying to them; it provided a feeling of purpose, and also gave a manner for them to measure their own successes, based on their respective Dom's praise or rejection of the meals. I decided to test the waters.

"Would it satisfy you to cook for me? Say, cook me a meal and have me enjoy eating it?" I asked.

"Oh, yeah. I'd love that," she responded with a huge grin.

I glanced at my watch, studied it for a few seconds, and shifted my eyes across the table. "It's still pretty early, want to go somewhere and grab something to eat?"

She grinned and nodded her head eagerly.

"Sure," she responded.

"Where do you want to go?" I asked.

She shrugged her shoulders. "I don't care. Where do you want to go?"

"Pizza, sound good?" I asked as I leaned back in the booth.

"Sure," she grinned.

I gazed down at the table for a moment, glanced up, and acted as if I'd had a revelation. "How about Mexican?"

"Sounds good to me," she responded.

"Chinese?" I asked.

"Sure."

"Fuck it. You decide. Where do you want to go?" I asked.

"Oh, I don't know. Wherever you want to go," she responded.

Everything she had done, said, and expressed indicated she was naturally submissive, even if she didn't realize it. I had never taken the time to actually search for a woman; I fully realized my relationship needs prevented me from being in a relationship with anyone but a true submissive. In my opinion, converting an independent woman into a submissive was nothing short of impossible; so I had always believed sifting through the throngs of women in search of a perfect submissive was wasting my time. In the unlikely event that I encountering a submissive, however, deciding if she was an acceptable match for me was something I felt I must do...

If presented the opportunity.

And Emily, in her entirety, was presenting all the opportunity I needed.

As I watched her admiringly, I decided our having met each other was not by chance. I intended to make every effort to see if she was exactly the woman I had been hoping to find since the loss of my former lover, and my quest for answers was going to begin immediately.

"Do you prefer Em, or Emily?" I asked.

"Em," she responded, "But, I mean, you can call me Emily if you want to."

"Em, do you have to work tomorrow night?" I asked.

She shook her head, "Nope. It's Saturday, I'm always off on the weekends."

"I'm going to pick you up tomorrow night. If you've got plans, I'll need you to cancel them. Wear something you're comfortable riding with," I said as I reached for my wallet.

She grinned and nodded her head. "Okay, what time?"

"I'll pick you up at seven. Plan on being out late, real late," I said as I tossed a twenty dollar bill on the table.

"Okay. What are we doing now?" she asked.

"We're headed back to the bar, but you're going to get in your car and go home," I said as I pushed myself away from the booth.

"You're the boss," she responded as she stood from her seat.

I wish it was that easy, Em.

I really do.

EMILY

June 7, 2006

As a girl, or young lady as I liked to refer to myself, I longed for attention, affection, and ultimately...

Sex.

The attention I received at the beginning of a relationship was much more satisfying than what followed after the new had worn off. I didn't seem to desire a relationship per se, but the sex, physical attention, and the focus a newcomer provided caused me to bounce from one person to another; never taking the time to develop anything more than a long list of sexual partners.

At one point, I wondered if I was addicted to the attention, praise, and remarks men made during the onset of a relationship, because the relationship in itself didn't particularly satisfy me. I decided I was, and switched to alcohol, followed by coffee, and eventually sweets.

I soon viewed myself as an addict of everything that provided me mental stimulation, and even reached a point I considered seeking treatment. I eventually dismissed my thoughts, however, convincing myself I was not an addict, but someone who simply needed to focus on my cravings until my passion changed.

There was no doubt desire was the spice of my life, but I couldn't help but wonder. What if my deepest desire was not for the object of my affection, but for the longing itself?

I now longed for Jackson's approval. He was a very intriguing man, and the thought of being his sexual interest consumed me. Considering what he shared with me regarding his sexual prowess, my desire to be included in his short list of sexual partners weighed on me quite heavily.

"So what exactly is this?" I asked as I stirred the noodle dish with my chopsticks.

"Malaysian rice noodles," Jackson responded.

The noodles were thin, orange in color, and were mixed with various vegetables, chicken, and an unidentifiable spice which all but took my breath away with each bite. In short, it was repulsive.

He paused. With his elbow resting on the table, noodles dangled from the tips of his chopsticks. "Do you like it?" he asked.

I nodded my head and forced another bite into my mouth.

"It's good," I lied.

I wasn't certain, but I suspected everything he was doing with me was a test of some sort. As I forced myself to consume the fiery noodles of Malaysian origin, I imagined him sitting at a computer, Googling 'ten most repulsive dishes of all time' - only to find Malaysian rice noodles at the top of the list. Upon determining the food was impossible to enjoy, he searched for a restaurant that was willing to risk their reputation, the lives of customers, and a few million respective taste buds by serving the dish to the unknowing - or the occasional innocent woman who desperately desired to be accepted - all the while hoping the acceptance would allow her to submit sexually to a handsome biker with quick fists, a soothing voice, and an iron stomach.

I continued to force the food into my mouth, doing my best to wash away the taste every three or four bites with a drink of water. Soon,

I was in a rhythm, shoveling the food down my unwilling throat no differently than a fat kid at an all-you-can-eat cupcake buffet.

"So, you like curry?" Jackson asked.

"Huh?" I shrugged as I reached for my glass of water.

"Curry. The spice. I'm guessing you like it," he said as he nodded his head toward my almost empty plate.

I swallowed the water, pressed my tongue against the top of my mouth, and attempted to rid it of the spicy film that covered it.

Curry?

Actually, I hate it.

"Is that what this is? The spice? Curry?" I asked as I dragged my tongue across my teeth.

He nodded his head.

"That's it. It's common in India, Indonesia, Vietnam, Thailand, China, Japan, Malaysia, Jamaica...I even think the Japanese use it in a few dishes," he said.

"It's okay," I shrugged as I picked up my chopsticks and prepared to force myself to eat the remaining noodles.

He glanced at his plate and plucked a piece of chicken from his noodles. I sat with the chopsticks dangling from my fingers and stared at him admiringly. He seemed too good to be true. He was articulate, intelligent, had a very attractive body, was handsome, and although he had proven his toughness, explained he would never harm me. The entire biker thing he had going on was enough of a bonus to place him on a pedestal clearly out of reach by all of the other men I expected I would ever encounter.

I gazed at him while he ate, waiting for horns to pop from his forehead or his wife to storm into the restaurant screaming, but neither happened.

I studied his hands, his face, and his pattern of eating. Thrilled to be in his presence, and eager to make long strides toward my ultimate goal of finding out if the entire submissive thing was for me, I eventually shifted my focus to what little of my meal remained. After a few well-placed Kung Fu chopstick grips on my noodles, I dropped the orange stained utensils onto my plate.

Finito.

What do I win?

Jackson took a few more slow bites and laid his chopsticks on the side of his plate. After taking a drink of water and wiping his mouth with a napkin, he pushed himself away from the table and studied me.

"I want you to know something," he said after a long but not-so-awkward silence.

"Okay."

I sat nervously as he continued to study me, his eyes shifting from my face to my hands, and then along what portions of my body were exposed from the structure of the table in front of me. I wanted to ask if something was wrong, but I believed with Jackson the less I said the better off I would remain. As I began to squirm in my seat, he took a shallow breath and grinned slightly.

Just slightly.

"You're a beautiful woman, Em," he said.

My heart rose into my throat. I didn't know how to respond, so I simply sat and basked in his compliment until I began to believe him.

"Thank you," I responded.

"You ready?" he asked.

I wasn't. As much as I enjoyed being on his motorcycle, I wanted to sit for the remaining portion of the night, admiring him, and having him admire me.

"Sure," I responded, even though it was on the threshold of being a lie.

As he reached for his wallet, I objected.

"Not really," I blurted.

He paused, crossed his arms, and widened his eyes slightly.

"I really don't know what I'm doing with all of this, you know, the submissive thing. But I've always been a straightforward person, so I'm just going to say it," I hesitated and bit my lower lip as I collected my thoughts.

"I like it when you look at me like you were a minute ago. It makes me feel good. And when you said what you said, the *beautiful* thing? Yeah, that really made me happy. You intimidate me, like a lot. I feel comfortable with you, and protected - but you scare me. I'm afraid I'm going to do something and you're going to just snap and say something like 'okay, Em, that's it. Sorry, but you failed', and I don't want that to happen," I said, my voice beginning to show the emotion I felt as I spoke.

He raised his index finger in the air, "The first woman I was with?"

I nodded my head as I fought back tears that were unnecessarily filling my eyes. I wanted him to want me so desperately, but I feared I would undoubtedly fuck something up. In no way was I in love with him, nor was I even close, but for some reason I wanted his acceptance, and it bothered me that I didn't feel I was obtaining it.

I nodded my head, "Yeah."

"She was killed in a car accident," he said flatly.

"Oh, I'm so sorry," I said.

He wagged his finger in the air as he shook his head. "And the second was in the Air Force. She got deployed to Iraq, and while she was there, had a reaction to a shot they gave her - some vaccination or something. She died a few days later."

"I believe in God, and I believe God provides me with challenges and rewards. I'm not a religious man, but I'm what many refer to as spiritual. I don't believe I have to sit amongst the masses within the walls of a church to be accepted as being one of his children, I believe we all are, regardless. I have my own set of rules I live by, and most don't agree with me. I'm an Outlaw, Em. I've always been one, and I always will be, but I believe God accepts me regardless. Now, the reason I told you about the two former loves of my life was to try to assure you of something," he leaned forward and exhaled sharply.

"We didn't break up. There wasn't a disagreement. They both died. Why? I have no idea. But I haven't attempted to be with another woman since, and I really haven't had a desire. It's been almost two years since, and I've done nothing but wait for God to provide. Now, I am of the opinion you and me didn't meet by accident, I really am. Does that mean I'm going to go back to your house and fuck you? It sure doesn't. Does it mean this is destiny or some ridiculous shit? No, it sure as fuck doesn't. But, does it mean I'm interested enough in you to give this a try? Yes, Em, it does. And, if it appears you're someone who can put up with me and my faults, and I'm willing to accept yours..." he leaned back into his seat and reached for his wallet.

As he placed a fifty dollar bill under his glass of water, he continued.

"Well, I suppose this might last a lifetime, or until you're sick of me, whichever comes first. But I can promise you this far in advance," he said as he stood and extended his hand.

I felt better about our situation, but I felt sorry for him. I wanted to hug him, hold him, explain my beliefs in God, religion, fate, love, lust and acceptance…but I remained silent and reached for his hand instead.

"Along the way, I'm going to do things that'll make you second guess whether or not you made the right choice," he said as he positioned my hand on the inside of his bicep.

"When will you know if we're going to give it a try?" I asked.

He shrugged his shoulders, "I'll just know."

As I gripped his arm lightly, I didn't care what he might do to make me second guess myself or when he would know if I was capable of pleasing him. At that time I *really* didn't care. During that moment, as we walked out of the restaurant and to his motorcycle, I was with him.

And that was all that mattered.

JACK

June 13, 2006

There seemed to be something about everyone that eventually came to the surface and bothered me. With Em, I had yet to have anything she said or did get under my skin. I suspected in time there would be *something*, but to date she had revealed nothing that caused me to take a step back and wonder. As a result of the perfection she portrayed, I made every effort to expose a part of her that I would find unacceptable.

"Hand me the ratchet," I said as I nodded my head toward the pile of tools on the garage floor.

After a short study of the items in front of her, she handed me the ratchet. I didn't *need* the ratchet, I needed the allen wrench set, but I had asked for the ratchet with the hope of frustrating her. To be honest, inviting her to my home while I worked on my bike was done solely to frustrate her. I placed the unneeded ratchet beside the chrome air cleaner cover and gazed in her direction.

"Allen wrenches, please," I said under my breath.

She reached for the allen wrenches, picked them up, and studied them intently for a short time.

"It doesn't say if they're standard or metric, which do you want?" she asked as she handed me the set of wrenches.

31

"Well, damn near everything on a Harley is standard, so this is the right set," I responded.

I had purchased a small rolling stool to relieve my knees while working on my motorcycle. It was twelve inches tall, rectangular shaped, and designed for mechanics to use while working on cars. As I worked on various areas on the bike, the stool allowed me to roll from one end to the other without repeated standing or kneeling. In a short time I purchased another, because it seemed there was always someone showing up and crouching beside me as I worked.

As I sat on one stool and stared blankly at the carburetor, Em began to slowly twirl in circles on the other stool. Watching her made me feel young and happy - something I felt from time to time, but never as frequently as I liked.

"You seem to know your way around a set of tools, where'd you learn about them?" I asked as her face twirled past me.

She stopped on her next rotation and grinned as she responded. "My dad. I used to help him work on his cars when I was little. Well, I didn't help him do the work, but I'd hand him the tools. It made me feel good to be helping him. This kind of reminds me of it."

I nodded my head, "Well, you're a great help."

She grinned and began to spin in circles again.

"Thank you," she said as she began to twirl faster and faster.

"You're cute," I said as she continued to pick up speed.

She planted her feet on the floor, stopped spinning, and slowly inched her way around until she faced me.

"Thank you," she said with a grin.

I removed the allen wrench from the set and tightened the air cleaner backing plate to the carburetor bracket. After checking the bracket for stability, I glanced in her direction. Still spinning in circles, she seemed to truly be enjoying herself.

"Come here for a minute," I chuckled as I shook my head in more of an envious manner than anything.

I often wished I had fond memories of being a child and doing childish things. Forced to immediately grow up after the death of my parents, I felt the need to be a man much earlier than most boys my age. By the time I was ten years old I was taking care of my younger sister no differently than if I was her father. We lived in a foster home at the time, but the family didn't provide any nurturing or love to either of us. Now, as a grown man, I felt as if I had missed out on being a child.

She stopped the stool from spinning and scooted it from the rear of the bike to the side where I was working.

"Yes?" she asked.

I pointed toward the air cleaner backing plate and glanced in her direction.

"See this?" I asked.

She stood from the stool, pressed her hands against her bare thighs, and stared intently at the bracket almost as if she were trying to decide if it needed to be reengineered. Dressed in her jean shorts, sneakers, and a loose fitting tee shirt, she looked absolutely adorable. As she continued to gaze at the bracket, she reached for the strands of her hair which hung down into her line of sight. As she brushed them behind her ears, she grinned.

"Yep" she said as she continued to study the bracket.

I tore my eyes from her and turned toward the motorcycle. It was becoming increasingly difficult not to stare at her. As time passed, I found her to be more attractive, and in ways and manners other than her appearance. As difficult as it was becoming, I forced myself to maintain a level of discipline and not outwardly express my attraction.

"This gets loose from all the vibration. Then, the air cleaner rattles, and it drives me fucking insane. So, you've got to tighten this up from time to time. Now, when I bolt the air cleaner back on, it won't rattle," I explained as I tapped my finger against the bracket.

"Good, because it drove me nuts too," she responded.

"Oh really?" I said with a note of sarcasm in my voice.

"Yep. When we were at a stoplight, and at about, oh I don't know, maybe thirty miles an hour or so. Didn't notice it much any time other than that. But it was annoying," she said with a nod of her head.

At an idle and thirty miles an hour was exactly when the air cleaner rattled. Surprised that she noticed the noise, I narrowed my eyes slightly and gazed blankly at the air cleaner.

"Alright, go back to doing what you were doing," I said under my breath.

She flopped onto the stool, gazed in my direction, and grinned.

"I like watching you," she said as she twisted her knees back and forth, swiveling the stool from left to right.

"I'm growing pretty fond of watching you too," I responded.

"What's the big guys name again? The one that came by the bar last night for a minute?" she asked.

"Sarge, why?" I responded as I tightened the bolts in the air breather cover.

"Well, that's what I was thinking, and his little patch says that, but you called him something else," she said.

"I call him a lot of things. But his name's Sarge," I said as I gathered up the tools.

"I like him, he's nice. He scared me the first night, I didn't know what to think. He's huge. I mean you're huge, but he's like *huge*," she said as she spread her arms wide.

I nodded my head as I stood from my stool. "He's a good man. And you're right, he's pretty damned big," I agreed.

She nodded her head and grinned.

"Alright, we're done with the bike," I said, "You ready?"

"Yep," she responded as she stood.

I laid the tools on the bench beside where she stood and turned to face her. No differently than any other man, I wanted a female companion. Knowing me, I realized simply having a female in my life didn't solve any problems, and in fact, it created them. Having the right woman in my life, however, filled a desire within me completely; leaving me with very little need in life. In many respects, the motorcycle club acted as my means of satisfaction in the absence of a woman.

After spending the last ten days with Em, I was slowly beginning to believe she was potentially the answer to my life's hope to feel complete. As I gazed at her blankly, satisfied with who she was and what she seemed to offer me, I decided to press a little further and see how she reacted.

"If you did something that really pissed me off, and I reacted physically, how would that make you feel?" I asked.

She narrowed her eyes slightly and scrunched her nose.

"What do you mean, physically?" she asked.

I did my utmost to remain straight-faced and show no emotion as I spoke.

"Physically. If say you did something and I hit you or slapped the shit out of you in response?" I asked stone-faced.

"Seriously? Is this one of your little tests? I'm not a doormat, Jackson. I may want to be your significant other, and I might show signs of being submissive or whatever, but that doesn't mean I'm a punching bag. If you hit me or slapped me, I'd leave you," she said in a matter-of-fact tone.

I nodded my head as I studied her posture. Now standing with her arms crossed and leaning away from me, it was apparent she took exception to my question. Satisfied with her response, and knowing I would never physically harm her no matter what she did, I believed I should clarify myself before she became even more angry thinking about it.

I raised my hand in the air and extended my index finger. "I'll never hit you or do anything for that matter to hurt you physically. I just wanted to know how you'd react to the thought of it," I said.

She gazed down at the floor and shook her head. "The thought of it makes me sick. One thing I liked about you from the beginning is that you said you'd never hurt me."

She glanced up and grinned. "Well, that and the entire take charge of me sexually thing," she said.

I nodded my head, satisfied she was proving to be the woman I so desired. As I considered reminding her we were leaving, she slowly walked in front of me and toward the bike. She turned her head to the side, her eyes locked on mine as she walked by.

I wanted to pull her close, wrap my hand around her neck, and kiss her until she melted into a puddle on the floor. As I felt my cock rising against the fabric of my jeans, I pushed my hand into my pocket and resituated myself. I pointed toward the motorcycle as I turned away.

"Get on the bike and wait for me. I'm going to go wash my hands,"

I said as I turned away from her.

"Okay," she responded as she carefully positioned herself on the back of the bike.

I walked into the kitchen and washed my hands. To my satisfaction, my swollen cock relaxed and became much less of an eyesore. As I gazed out the kitchen window and into the yard, my mind slowly drifted to thoughts of Em, and eventually migrated to tying her to my bed and teasing her. Within a few seconds, I felt myself becoming aroused again. I turned the faucet on again, and splashed my face with cold water. After a moment of attempting to regain control of my wandering mind, I dried my hands and face and turned toward the garage.

Typically, once my mind was made up, it was difficult for me to change my way of thinking, and it appeared my mind was made up. Em was a woman I was interested in attempting a relationship with. As I stepped into the garage she was still sitting on the back of the bike with her hands on her thighs, waiting patiently for me to return.

"Ready?" she asked, grinning as she spoke.

"I think so," I responded.

I felt myself begin to become aroused again. As my stiffening dick rose to attention, I pressed against it with the palm of my hand. I threw my leg over the seat and positioned my feet on the controls as I started the engine. As the engine warmed up to speed, I glanced down at my steadily rising jeans.

And, in all honesty, I *was* ready.

EMILY

June 13, 2006

We had ridden for some time, and the air cleaner never rattled. After a long period of wondering when we might stop, Jackson pulled over for a cup of coffee. We relaxed outside Starbucks in the early evening's blazing sun, watching people walk in and out and talking about everything under the sun.

Everything except whether or not we were making progress toward a relationship.

As I baked in the sun and sipped my glass of mango tea, he sat in his chair and quietly watched people pass. I watched him intently as he studied the people coming and going, but I couldn't tell what he was looking at unless he made a comment about it. Knowing what he was thinking was another thing altogether, he was impossible to read. As I sat and waited for the next word to spring from his lips, it became very apparent I wanted more from him.

Much more.

"I don't like not seeing your eyes," I said under my breath without looking up from my glass of tea.

"Too fucking sunny to take 'em off," he said as he waved his hand toward the western sun.

I nodded and gazed down at my glass.

He tilted his head in my direction.

"You ready?" he asked.

I nodded my head reluctantly, leaned forward, and sucked the remaining iced tea through my straw. Still slightly disappointed at our lack of progress, I stood from my seat, grabbed my empty glass, and turned toward the trash can. As I walked toward the corner of the building, the sound of motorcycles caught my attention, and I shifted my eyes toward the noise and out into the street. Two men wearing leather vests similar to Jackson's were slowing down in traffic to enter the parking lot. I tossed my empty cup into the trash and quickly turned around.

Although I hadn't realized it, Jackson somehow had positioned himself immediately behind me. As I turned to face him, he reached up, gripped my neck lightly, and pushed me into the wall of windows which separated the patio area from the inside of the coffee shop. With my back pressed firmly to the glass and his hand gripping my neck, he pushed his sun glasses on top of his head and leaned in for a kiss.

I opened my mouth slightly and waited, feeling like a complete novice and hoping my knees would continue to hold me up. This was at least one of the moments I had been waiting desperately to arrive, but for some reason I had no idea what to do, and time seemed to be standing still.

Our lips finally met, and as they did I closed my eyes. He kissed me aggressively, pressing himself against me fully as his tongue explored my mouth. He kissed me deeply and passionately, biting my upper lip each time he pulled away for another breath. The waiting for this moment and the weeks of longing for his embrace all came rushing from me in an instant, and as all of the uncertainty of the first kiss escaped me, my pussy began to throb.

His free hand gripped my butt cheek and his fingertips sank deep into the skin of my inner thigh. My entire body started to tingle as I fought to stay on my feet. My head started to spin, my stomach went into a mild frenzy, and he continued to kiss me as passionately as I had always expected women in some corner of the world were being kissed by someone who loved them.

But that person had never been me.

As the passage of time slowed to a point that seconds seemed like a lifetime, our mouths parted. He bit my upper lip lightly and released it. I opened my eyes and glanced upward. As our eyes met, he narrowed his slightly, and the corner of his mouth curled into a smirk. His hand still gripping my neck, he squeezed with a little more force as if to remind me he was the one in charge.

He leaned back and studied me.

"God damn, Killer, get a fuckin' room," a voice behind me growled.

Still gazing into my eyes, he lifted his free hand in the air as if to silence his friend. As they stood at our side staring, his eyes never shifted away from mine. His intensity was apparent, and it was ten-fold of what I had previously witnessed. He tightened his grip on my neck and tilted his head to the side ever so slightly.

He released my neck and slid his hand upward slowly. As the web of his hand met my chin, he squeezed ever so slightly, resting his thumb along my jaw and his index finger on my cheek. As he lightly tapped the tip of his finger against my face, his eyes widened a little.

"You're mine," he breathed.

The moment I waited for was upon me. I had considered all of the possibilities of when and where it might happen, and rehearsed what I would say and do when the time arrived that he realized we were going to take the next step. At that moment, as I gazed into his eyes, my mind was blank and I was an emotional disaster. Incapable of speaking, I swallowed heavily and simply nodded my head.

"Mine," he repeated as his finger tapped lightly against my cheek.

My eyes fell closed and I nodded my head in agreement, satisfied I was nothing less than his. As I felt the tip of his finger tracing along my jaw, I wondered what was next. Where I was and who I was surrounded by mattered not one bit. As the anticipation of what was to come built inside of me, his hand gripped my neck once again and he pushed me into the glass.

As he pressed his lips against mine, my mind drifted away. At that moment, as he kissed me, I knew very little, but I knew one thing for certain.

He was absolutely right.

And as odd as it might have seemed to a conventional woman, Jackson had somehow taken ownership of a very large portion of my heart.

And nothing else mattered.

JACK

June 20, 2006

In the two weeks since I had met Em, my thoughts regarding attempting a relationship with her had changed from considering it to doing it. I had never moved so fast making a decision about anything in the past, but I always believed with matters of the heart, when the time comes it comes. To resist what feelings naturally developed between two responsible adults seemed foolish and slightly selfish. Acting on my desires was beyond satisfying, and Em was quickly proving herself to be exactly what I had so deeply desired.

What little time I had spent with my club brothers since meeting Em was littered with thoughts of her and uneducated guesses at what the future might hold for us. I hoped for the best, prepared for the worst, and felt guilty for the time I was spending with her - but found no way to reduce or set aside my need for her companionship.

I had ridden with Hell's Fury Motorcycle Club for roughly ten years. The club provided me a family - something I had never known as a child. Although there were men in the club I didn't care for as much as others, I accepted them all as my brothers. Some men were better than others - at least in my eyes - and Sarge was one of those men. He was an intense man of much greater than average size, and the sound of his voice alone intimidated almost all who didn't know him. The remaining few were terrorized by his menacing appearance.

Covered from head to toe in tattoos, his long brown and gray beard stood in complete contrast to his cleanly shaven head. A little more than six feet tall, and tipping the scales at over two hundred and fifty pounds, he wasn't a man many would attempt to argue with. His position as President of the club was not only where *he* believed he belonged, but where the club needed him the most. Considering the savagery of a typical member of Hell's Fury, knowing Sarge had clawed his way through every single one of them to make it to the top made his position on the presidential pedestal an honorable one. His only life was the club, and the decisions he made regarding the club, club business, and his many brothers were all made with the best of intentions.

"So, what's the deal with the skinny little bitch, Killer?" he growled.

"Just feeling her out and seeing if she's capable," I responded as I raised my hand in the air and waved toward the waitress.

"Capable? Of fucking what? Being around the fellas? Shit, bring her around and see how she acts. You'll know in a quick minute," he chuckled.

I felt no real need to provide Sarge with details of our quickly developing relationship, and intended to merely extract his opinion on a few matters that were beginning to bother me. I had never been one to share my sexual experiences with my brothers in the club. Many of the men, and most bikers for that matter, took great pride in sharing their sexual escapades with anyone who would listen. Some of the men held their women, and their stories, as a trophy. I, on the other hand, viewed my life with a woman as sacred, and something she and I shared together. Providing the time we spent together in the form of a story to any or all who might care to listen would cheapen the relationship, making me question if it was for all the wrong reasons. As a result, I chose to keep my experiences and feelings regarding women to myself.

"No, she'll be fine around the fellas, just seeing if I think she can put up with my shit," I responded as the waitress leaned over the table.

"Two more?" she asked.

I nodded my head, "You hungry?"

"Look at me? Do you *really* need to ask that question?" he asked.

"I'll have a burger. The biggest one you've got. Lettuce, tomato, pickles. No cheese," I said.

"Fries?" she asked.

"Fuck no, he ain't gonna eat fries. Look at him. He's afraid he'll end up looking like me. He eats like a high school girl on her first date. Bring me two burgers and his fries," Sarge said.

"I'll bring the beers right back, burgers will be a few minutes, we make 'em fresh," she explained.

"Sounds good," I said.

"So what's the problem? Why are we here again?" Sarge asked as he reached for his beer.

"Lucky. He keeps going on and on about guns. Motherfucker keeps asking everyone what they've got, and what they're going to bring to our annual shoot out at Chili's place. The other night he was asking if anyone had machine guns and shit, the motherfucker makes me nervous. Just seems a little too eager to get in everyone's business," I explained.

Lucky was a huge concern, but not my main concern. I really wanted Sarge's opinion about my previous relationships, his thoughts on karma, and whether or not he believed the deaths of my previous two love interests were a result of my having been bitten by karma. I

45

didn't, however, want to come right out and say it. A weakness regarding women, at least in Hell's Fury's eyes, was grounds for questioning a man's sincerity with the club.

"Well, Spike vouched for him," Sarge said as he raised his beer bottle. "Guess they've known each other for a bit. Been with us for what? Almost two years now? Seems he irritates some of the fellas, but others like him just fine. Just like everyone else, I suppose, he'll have his friends and his enemies."

I pursed my lips and tightened my jaw as I studied the label on my bottle of beer.

"More to it than that?" Sarge asked.

I glanced at the waitress as she slid two bottles of beer across the table and turned to walk away. As she disappeared toward the back of the bar, I shifted my focus to Sarge and shook my head.

"Guess not. If you're not worried about him, I'm not either," I shrugged.

"Now god damn it, Killer. If *you're* worried," he hesitated and leaned forward.

As he cocked one eyebrow, he continued, "*I'm* worried."

"I'll just say this. If the cock sucker keeps asking to come over to my place and look at my guns, I'm going to knock his ass out," I said as I reached for my beer.

"Fucker might just be a gun nut," he said as he slowly raised the other eyebrow.

"And he might be some nosy prick who's looking to come rob me some night when I'm not home. Fucker makes me nervous, and not many motherfuckers do. That's all I'm saying," I said as I lifted my bottle of beer to my lips.

Sarge relaxed into the back of the booth and crossed his arms in front of his massive chest. After glaring at me for a short moment, he cocked his head to the side. "So you wanted to meet for a beer to tell me Lucky's a nosey fucker? What the fuck else is going on?" he asked.

I shrugged my shoulders as I slid my empty beer bottle toward the end of the table. "Fuck I don't know."

He sat and stared in apparent disbelief.

"You believe in karma?" I asked.

"Now we're headed for the rest of the story," he chuckled as he slid to the center of the booth.

He nodded his head as he reached for his beard. As he stroked the long strands of hair in his hands, he grinned.

"Sure do, why?" he asked.

"You know, my two Ol' Ladies, they both passed away. Hell, neither of them was thirty years old, just seems kind of weird when you stop and think about it. You know, for a man to go through losing two Ol' Ladies in five or six years. Whatever it's been," I said as I reached for my bottle of beer.

"No disrespect, Killer, but you thinking they both had it coming? Or are ya thinking your fate is sealed, based on what you've done in the past?" he asked.

I shrugged my shoulders.

"Well, you asked, so gimme your opinion. I know you got one or you wouldn't of asked in the first fucking place," he said as he took a drink of beer.

"The girl I gave a ride home from the bar the other night, when we met at Joe's. She and I been fucking around and spending some time together, and I just got to thinking. What if my future with anything or anyone is sealed from what I've done in the past. You know, what if God's position on how I've lived my life is way different than mine? Hell, I think I've been pretty damned good at making sure I don't cross those lines. Doesn't mean the man upstairs agrees," I paused and shrugged my shoulders.

He nodded his head and continued to massage his beard in his fingers as the waitress walked up with our food.

"Here we go, One half pound burger," the waitress said as she placed a plate in front of me.

"And two half pound burgers and fries," she said as she handed Sarge his plate.

"Condiments are right there," she said as she pointed to the wire basket at the end of the table, "Anything else?"

I shook my head, "Appreciate it."

She grinned and walked away.

I pushed my plate to the side and continued, "So we've either got two really strange circumstances, or one undeniable case of being bit by karma."

Sarge picked up one of his burgers, held it in front of his face, and after a long pause, sighed.

"You're a good solid motherfucker. A lot of the fellas ain't. Hell, some of them are just plain shitty assed dudes, but you ain't one of 'em. And you ain't one of 'em because you think before you make a move. Sometimes you make a decision pretty fucking quick, but you always think before you act. So," he paused and took a bite.

After chewing and swallowing the mouthful of food, he continued, "What it gets down to is this: is your head full of what's good or what's bad. I think we both know the answer to that, Killer."

Sarge was the type of man to say exactly what he thought. I had always believed I stood for what was right - at least in my mind - but often wondered what others thought of me. Being known as a man who was quick to stand up for what I believed in didn't necessarily make my beliefs just or morally acceptable to all.

"So you think their deaths are coincidental?" I asked as I slid my plate in front of me.

He shook his head as he took another bite. "Nope," he said as he chewed.

After he swallowed, he took a drink of beer, "Fuck, nothing's coincidental. Shit happened for some kinda reason. Don't mean the reason's something that has to do with you and the way you've lived your life in the past. So you're worried if you make that little gal your Ol' Lady something's gonna happen? Karma's gonna get ya?"

I shrugged my shoulders as I reached for my burger, "Something like that."

Sarge shoved the last bite into his mouth and shook his head.

I bit into my mine wondering if I could mentally accept the loss of another woman in my life. As I focused on my food and attempted to clear my mind, Sarge pushed his plate to the side and continued.

"I'm sure losing them two gals hurt ya. You know it's the pain that's making you second guess yourself, right?" he asked.

I nodded my head as I continued to eat.

"If you ask me, it gets down to acceptance. If you'd accepted their deaths, you wouldn't still be feeling the pain. And if you weren't still hurting, you and I wouldn't be having this talk," he paused and reached toward his plate.

He raised his second burger to his mouth and held it in front of his face as he continued, "Accept the fact that what happened just happened. Stop trying to figure out why the fuck it happened, and just accept that there was a reason; and the reason *wasn't* karma."

He took a bite and immediately shook his head as if something came to mind. Before swallowing, he spoke over his mouth full of food.

"Wait a minute, you're talking about the little gal from the night we all got stuck in that fucking DUI checkpoint deal?" he asked as his eyes narrowed slightly.

I nodded my head.

"Hell, fucking her is breaking the law, ain't it?" he asked.

I shrugged my shoulders as I took the last bite of my burger, "How so?"

"She looks like she's fucking fifteen, Killer, God damn. How old is she?" he asked.

"Twenty-one," I responded.

"Shit. She ain't twenty-one. You better check that fucking ID or you'll end up doing time for fucking a youngster," he chuckled.

"Well, she's old enough to drink, so she's at least twenty-one. She said she was when I asked, and believe me, I asked," I responded.

Emily did look young, but she sure didn't look fifteen. She looked her age, but to Sarge, who was used to seeing the leathery-skinned women our MC Brothers typically fucked, making the comparison was a difficult stretch.

"Yeah, I've never known a gal to bullshit one of the fellas," he said as he tilted his bottle of beer toward me.

I flipped him my middle finger with my left hand as I grabbed my beer with my right. As I took a long drink from the bottle, I recalled Emily's facial features and smooth wrinkle-free skin. If she spent much time on the back of my bike in the sun, things would change and change fast.

"Alright," Sarge said as he wiped his hands free of a wad of mustard, "So Lucky gets on your last nerve, and you're gonna start fucking a cute little high school girl. That about sum it up?"

I shook my head and grinned, "Suppose so."

And, as simple as it sounded, it did sum it up. Lucky was a man I didn't trust and never would, and I felt the need to make my position clear. I certainly didn't need Sarge's approval to proceed with Emily, but hearing his opinion on karma helped matters slightly. As he waved his hand toward the waitress, I considered what he said about acceptance.

He was right. If I could accept my loss as being nothing more than life running it's course, I didn't need to understand it. I simply needed to accept it and move on.

And I was eager to do both.

EMILY

June 21, 2006

Two weeks. Two weeks wasn't enough time to wage a war, prepare for a marathon, end the hockey playoffs, or even grow tomatoes in my makeshift garden - but it was more than enough time for me to understand Jackson was the man I had spent my lifetime searching for. He was a very unique person, and not at all what I expected an outlaw biker to be. Although I was quite certain he wasn't the *typical* biker, and I was extremely grateful he *was* different, I stood in wait for him to become someone else. It seemed eventually all men changed into who they really were and I expected in time he would do the same.

His statements regarding what was acceptable to him were easy for me to understand and follow. In my opinion, knowing in advance what he found tolerable and what he believed to be disrespectful was priceless. In general, it seemed men made an assumption regarding a woman's understanding of them, and when their respective other did something contrary to their belief of what was acceptable; they would come apart at the seams. Having Jackson explain himself beforehand left little doubt in my mind. Because of my willingness to eagerly accept his relationship requirements, it was easy for me to hope that I was naturally the woman Jackson had been waiting for.

For me, it wasn't a matter of making adjustments to how I behaved or what I believed in; I was simply able to be myself. And for once in my life, being me didn't raise eyebrows or turn heads. If nothing else, it appeared being me was able to satisfy someone greatly. And satisfying Jackson, for whatever reason, satisfied me.

According to Jackson, the time had come for us to *have a talk*. Since the night we met, we had spent almost every night together - and as many days and evenings as I was able. Although I was prepared for my little world to come crashing down around me, I reserved hope our talk was going to be a productive one and only reveal how happy he was with who he had found me to be. As odd as it seemed to be spending so much time with someone and still not having sex, it was a pleasant feeling to know a man could actually enjoy being with a woman and *not* be fucking her. Truthfully, kissing Jackson satisfied me much more than any sex I had experienced in the past, so I wasn't about to complain.

"Here's what I'd like to do," he explained.

I sat on his couch, staring into my lap, waiting anxiously for him to continue.

"Are you paying attention?" he asked.

I glanced up and nodded my head.

"Yes," I responded.

"Are you alright, Em? You look like something's bothering you," he said as he stood from the chair he was sitting in.

As he walked in my direction, I forced a smile. I figured it was my best effort to convince him everything was fine. And, for the most part, everything *was* fine. I'd never really lacked self-esteem, nor was I a woman who was constantly worried or depressed, but with Jackson, I found myself wanting what it was he offered so deeply, that the thought of *not* having him all but seemed to consume me.

And I was left waiting for the proverbial axe to fall.

"Look at me, Em," he said as he placed the tip of his finger under my chin and lifted it slightly, "We're only having a talk. You need to understand, I'm always here to listen just as much as I'm here to talk. Not just now, but always. Understand?" he said in a soothing tone.

I nodded my head as I glanced upward. It was almost as if he had read my mind.

"Okay," I responded.

He released my chin and sat down beside me. As he situated himself, he placed his hand on my thigh and turned to face me.

"I'm ready to begin a sexual relationship with you. Sitting here talking about it may seem insensitive, but I can assure you it is not. In fact, it's absolutely necessary," he said.

I repeated his every word in my mind. As his mouth continued to move, I heard very little. Containing my excitement was impossible, but somehow I managed to do so, at least for a while.

I'm ready to begin a sexual relationship with you.

I'm ready to begin a sexual relationship with you.

I'm ready to begin a sexual relationship with you.

"...and it's important that you always remember that," he paused and waited for me to respond.

Shit.

I hadn't heard a single word he had said.

Considering one thing he had drilled into my head was how much he hated repeating himself, I contemplated my options to get him to repeat himself without making it seem like he was repeating himself.

"Do you have a pen and some paper? Or maybe a notepad?" I asked.

He appeared confused, at least for a moment. After standing, he turned toward the back bedroom and walked away. When he returned to the living room he carried a pad of paper and a pen in his hand.

"Here," he said with a slight laugh as he held the pad and pen at arm's length.

His normal attire was jeans, a white tank top, and boots. Although the jeans changed daily in their style and the color of the denim or their wash, the shirt was always the same - as were his boots. It was something I expected he was comfortable with, and seeing him wear the same thing for a few weeks straight didn't bother me at all.

Until now.

Seeing him now, knowing I was going to be in a sexual relationship with him allowed me to see him in more of a sexual manner than simply an attractive one. With his arm extended, holding the pad and pen, he waited for me to accept his offer of office supplies. I was no longer interested. The muscles on the back of his arm flexed slightly as he held his arm in place. A large portion of his chest was now bare, stretched beyond the limits of his small shirt. The praying hands tattooed to his chest were slightly exposed, and for some strange reason were becoming a huge turn-on. As he shook the paper in front of me, his bicep flexed again, causing my focus to shift once again.

I blinked my eyes as I realized I was drifting away.

"Thank you," I said as I reluctantly accepted the pad and pen.

As he sat down, I leaned into the corner of the couch and turned to face him. After placing the pad in my lap and drawing a few circles in the corner of the page, I glanced up and grinned.

"Okay, I know you hate repeating yourself, but I think it's important I get everything down in notes - I'm an avid note taker. So, can you start at the beginning?" I asked.

He grinned and shook his head. "Okay."

"I'm ready to start a sexual relationship with you. Although sitting here talking about it may seem insensitive, I can assure you it isn't. It's absolutely necessary, so we both have an understanding what it is we want, expect, and won't accept. This relationship will always hinge on open communication between us both, and you need to remember it's important to me that you always act like yourself, and you need to know that will please me more than anything. I don't want you to try and become or be something you're not," he paused and gazed down at the empty pad.

Shit.

I scribbled my best recollection of what he had said onto the pad.

Sexual relationship.

Understand what we want.

Open communication.

Be yourself.

As I finished writing, he continued.

"What it gets down to is this, Em. You need to fall in love with yourself before you can fall in love with someone else. Are you comfortable being you?" he asked.

I raised my index finger in the air as I scribbled.

You need to fall in love with yourself before you can fall in love with someone else.

I glanced upward and tried to keep from smiling. It didn't work for long.

"Yes. I think so. Well, at least now that you said that, I am. Can I ask a question?" I asked, my mouth still curled into a full-on grin.

57

"Absolutely," he responded.

"So you just want me to act like I'd act if you weren't around? Like be myself? The way I've acted my whole life, and you won't get mad at me?" I asked.

"I'll never get mad at you for being you, no," he responded.

I pressed the tip of the pen into the pad.

Never gets mad.

I glanced up from the pad as I tapped the pen on my cheek.

"Okay that's it for now, continue," I said.

"I'll be committed to you, and I'll need you to be committed to me. I'll never cheat on you in any way, and I expect the same from you. I'm not controlling, and I won't limit who you can see, when you can see them, or tell you what you can or can't do. Just be comfortable with what you're doing, and always do it with our best interest in mind. Is that understood?" he asked.

I nodded my head as I scribbled.

Committed relationship.

No cheating.

He's not controlling.

"Got it," I said as I tapped the pen against my temple.

"I've said it before and I will remind you again. The MC is my family. The men are my brothers, and they may not always come first, but they're pretty damned close. No matter what becomes of us, club business will always be club business, and it will *never* be open for discussion. That'll never change. It has nothing to do with you, or my trust in you. And, just so you know, I won't discuss our relationship with the club. Is this understood?" he asked.

"Yes," I responded as I nodded my head.

Club business is club business, and not MY business. I scribbled as he sat and studied me.

"Now, the sex," he paused and leaned forward.

Saved the best for last…

He rested his forearms on his knees and sighed. After inhaling a shallow breath and exhaling slowly, he turned to face me again.

"We need to decide what our limitations are. What we're willing to do, and not willing to do. Nothing is worse than not knowing what a partner's limits are, hopefully anticipating something, and finding out she's not willing to proceed with your desire. Knowing in advance will prevent disappointment and confusion for both of us. So, we'll need to spend some time discussing these matters," he said.

I sat, waiting for him to continue. After a long silent pause, I explained myself.

"I've been reading about this type of relationship on the internet. My limitations are pretty easy to remember. I'll agree to nothing that includes piss, shit, or cutting me. My thoughts on cutting may change in the future, but the piss and shit will never change. I'm really excited to give everything that pleases you a try. I just really hope piss and shit aren't included on your list of wants," I blurted.

He shook his head and sighed. "What if I want to tie you up and spank you?" he asked.

"Spank away," I responded.

"Nipple clamps. Ever heard of nipple clamps?" he asked.

"Not until last week, but yes, I have. And yes, I'm ready," I responded.

"Butt plugs, anal play, piercing, fisting, electrocution, bondage…" he paused and raised one eyebrow.

"If it turns you on, let's give it a try," I responded. "I want to be the woman you've always dreamed of. And not because I think that's what you want to hear, but because it's what *I* want. I really want this to work, and I want it to work without many limitations at all."

"Very well," he said as he stood from the couch, "Want a drink?"

"Sure," I responded, "Water."

As he walked past, I gaze down at the pad. After a few seconds of staring blankly at my notes, I scribbled a few more.

Fisting??

He wants to electrocute me.

Google BDSM piercings. WTF?

"You sure you're ready for this?" he asked as he handed me a glass of water.

"Very much so," I responded.

"Alright," he said as he sat down, "As of right now, you're committed to me, and I'm committed to you. Our current limitations are no watersports, no feces, and no bloodletting. We need to decide on a safe word, and it'll need to be something you'll always remember, even when you're under duress and possibly confused," he paused and inhaled a deep breath.

"You do know what a safe word is, don't you?" he asked.

I nodded my head, "A word we use if for some reason I want to stop or if things get out of hand."

"Any ideas?" he asked.

I gazed down at the pad and thought. After a few minutes, I scribbled my safe word.

Caterpillar.

"Okay," I said.

"Okay, what?" he asked.

"Caterpillar," I said.

"What?" he asked as he began to laugh.

"Caterpillar. You know, they change into a butterfly - a metamorphosis - changing from one thing to another. That's what's going to be happening with me, so caterpillar is the best I can think of," I shrugged.

"Well, caterpillar it is. So, do you have any questions?" he asked.

I nodded my head. "When can we start?" I asked.

He shook his head, "We already have. And you'll be screaming caterpillar before you know it."

"Wanna bet?" I snapped back.

For a long time, he studied me. After what seemed like an eternity, he shook his head.

"No, something tells me you'd damn near die before you gave up," he said.

He was right.

And I was more than ready to prove it.

JACK

June 26, 2006

My having only had two previous sexual partners set me apart from almost every thirty year old man on the planet, and was definitely in clear contrast to the sexual escapades of every one of my brothers in the MC. My sexual partners, adventures, and who I was committed to never came into discussions with the Fury, and most of the men realized even asking was going to piss me off, so they didn't bother.

Being in a 1% club wasn't for everyone, and for the select few who chose it as a way of life, nothing would ever compare to the feelings of family, brotherhood, or excitement associated with being a patched in member. Riding into a town twenty deep and being stared at by every civilian that passed by - out of either disgust or envy - was a thrill in itself.

Rolling through a small town or a major city, and being followed by the cops - knowing they were either wondering what brought an MC into their town or pondering just what may be boiling behind the scenes - was a satisfying and exciting feeling unlike many others.

Protecting my brothers, and in turn protecting the club that the assembled brotherhood formed was something I didn't have to think about. For me, a natural protector of what I loved, it was as easy as allowing my heart to beat.

The men who knew me often described me as intense. I spoke very little, glared much more than I probably should, and always stood ready to react to any and all adverse situations which may present themselves. Protecting what I loved and what I believed to be mine was the only way of assuring myself that my life would continue to be tomorrow everything it was for me today.

And so far, every 'today' I had lived was pretty damned close to perfect.

Sarge glanced around the crowd of men. He reached toward his beard, gripped it with his tattooed fingers, and stroked it slowly as he gazed out into the shop. The tugging of his beard was reserved for intimidation purposes or when he was thinking, and he sure wasn't trying to intimidate his brothers.

"Well, we knew this day was coming. Fat Bart and Woody were rolling into town and one of the Shovelheads was flying a lower rocker claiming our territory after refusing to pay us their tax. I'm sure most of you already heard, but Fat Bart forced him off the road and before he got his bike picked up, Woody stomped the shit out of him and took his cut. I've got his colors locked in the safe," he paused, released his beard, and clenched his fists.

As the men began to talk amongst themselves and grumble their opinions of what may be next, Sarge held his left hand in the air to quiet them.

"Let's just say, right now, you can figure we're about one step from being at war with Shovelheads MC. That one lone member of their MC rolling through the outskirts of the city wasn't the only one of them fuckers with a rocker on their cut. These cock suckers are asking us if we're prepared to protect what's rightfully ours, and I'm standing here asking you. Are you fucking prepared?" he shouted.

The group erupted into cheers, thrusting their fists into the air and explaining to the man at their side what they'd do if they encountered a member of the Shovelheads claiming our territory as theirs.

In the civilian world, what they had done was the equivalent of a home invasion. And, if said civilian woke from his sleep only to find a burglar sitting on his couch drinking one of his beers, there would be hell to pay. After questioning the thief produced a response of 'this is going to be my house from here on out, you'll need to leave,' the civilian would certainly react in a manner which would be protective of what he believed was rightfully his.

And we were no different; we simply reacted in a manner indicative of the world we lived in.

One with very few rules, and almost no laws.

"Alright, alright, settle the fuck down. Jesus H. Christ, men, that wasn't all we came here to discuss. Let's see," Sarge paused and glanced down at the notepad he was now holding in his hand.

"So keep your eyes peeled for Shovelheads wearing a lower rocker. And keep me fucking posted on anything and everything you see. Now, Ride for the Red is next Saturday. This thing started last year, and it supports the American Red Cross. This is one of a few organizations that aren't affiliated with the government, and they rely solely on volunteers and donations. One hundred percent of what they raise in the poker run goes to the Red Cross. Last year they raised about ten grand, and this year they're hoping to double that number. I'm not making this a mandatory ride, but if you don't show up, you can bet I'll be paying you a personal visit when the ride is over. I want every one of you to plan on being there, and I want you to dig deep in those pockets of yours for a little extra money. Costs twenty-five bucks to ride, and that'll get you a shirt, lunch, and a chance to win six hundred bucks if you've got the best poker hand. I'll tell you right fucking now, if one of you wins that pot, you're giving the money right back to 'em. These fuckers just might save the life of one of your family members when a disaster hits. Show of hands, who's gonna attend?" he looked up from the pad and gazed around the room.

Every arm was high in the air.

Sarge gazed down at the pad, "Alright. Shovelheads, Red Cross, and now for the closer. Chili is having a kegger at his house next Saturday night, after the poker run. It ain't mandatory, but it'll sure be a lot of fun. If you come, feel free to bring your Ol' Ladies. Fat Bart's donating a couple of hogs, and he's also volunteered to cook 'em, so they'll sure as fuck be worth eatin'. Damned sure be better than what Woody tried to cook last year that made every one of us sick. Guess that's it. Any new business needs discussed?"

"So what if we run into a Shovelhead, it's just on?" Woody asked.

Sarge shook his head as he tossed his notepad onto the bench beside where he stood.

"No, it ain't just *on*. If they ain't flying a bottom rocker, leave 'em alone. If for some reason you run into one of 'em and they are, well, I ain't gonna give you a list of what to do and not to do, but if you respect your colors and the club, you'll know what to do. Anything else?" Sarge asked.

Short of a few men talking amongst themselves, the shop fell silent.

"Meeting adjourned," Sarge growled.

I walked toward Sarge and stood a few feet away while a few of the men talked to him on their way out. As I began to speak, Lucky stepped to Sarge's side and began yapping like a little Chihuahua.

"That's really something about the 'heads. Hard to believe them fuckers are tryin' to fly a bottom rocker in our territory, huh, Killer?" Lucky asked openly as he glanced back and forth between Sarge and me.

I crossed my arms in front of my chest, rocked back on my heels, and gazed down my nose as his irritating little ass.

"You wanna know what's even harder to believe?" I asked flatly.

He gazed at me with wide eyes, waiting for me to continue.

"That you'd step in the middle of my conversation with Sarge without an invite. It ain't a fucking secret that you irritate the shit out of me, so why don't you go find some rocks to kick on your way out to that little Sporty you're riding?" I said through my teeth.

"Damn, didn't mean to irritate you, Killer. I was just…" he began.

"You were just leaving, that's what you were just doing. Fucking leaving. Now kick rocks," I said as I uncrossed my arms and narrowed my gaze.

"Yeah, I better get. I'll leave you two to it. See ya at the kegger," he said as he turned away.

After watching him walk out of the shop and into the parking lot, I turned to face Sarge.

"Irritating little prick," I hissed as I turned around.

"Still a brother," Sarge shrugged.

"Red-headed fucking step-brother," I chuckled.

Sarge shook his head and laughed.

"You fucking hard ass," he said as he turned toward the fridge.

"Want one?" he asked as he opened the refrigerator door.

"One. I'll have one, then I gotta get," I responded.

Sarge handed me a beer and tipped the neck of his bottle toward me before taking a drink. I returned the toast, and drank half the beer in one long gulp.

Truthfully, I was eager to get home to Em, who was cooking dinner. Each day that passed gave me a new reason to be pleased with my decision to invite her into my life. I was quite confident many men would be pleased with her good looks alone, but for me there was far more to it than that. Em was a simple woman capable of pleasing me to no end by merely being herself, and it was the little things about her that pleased me the most.

Her ability to sit quietly and enjoy life as it passed by was comforting. Her apparent admiration of me was almost humbling, and although I didn't necessarily need it, massaged my ego slightly. The eager attitude she expressed at each and every obstacle that presented itself to her suggested she was a person who wouldn't easily give up on anything she desired or held sacred. And it was that attitude and that attitude alone which convinced me I was going to have a tough time breaking her spirit.

As I had in the beginning, I continued to stand back and wait, knowing eventually there would be something about her that rubbed me the wrong way or irritated me. Contrary to my expectations and certainly contradictory to my experiences with women - and people in general - she had yet to do, say, or suggest anything that I took exception to.

My life was beginning to once again feel like it was complete - something I had felt in the past, but doubted I would ever feel again.

"So, what do you see coming of this mess with the Shovelheads?"

I asked.

He shrugged his shoulders, "They paid tax for a while then they stopped. When I talked to their president about it, he told me they were done paying for the right to wear the rocker. I told him without paying their dues they were done wearing the rocker. He agreed. Hell, you and I both know they haven't worn it for years. Well, now it looks like they're considering fighting us for the territory. Territory we claim and rightfully so, I might add. Suppose it coulda been one lone wolf out riding in his old cut, but we both know that's wishful thinking."

I swallowed the rest of my beer and nodded my head as I reached for the trash.

"Another?" he asked.

I shook my head. "Not tonight. I'm going to get home."

"You alright?" he asked.

"I'm good," I nodded, "That little girl from the bar's cooking me some dinner."

"My Ol' Lady's cooking me some, too. As soon as all of these motherfuckers are outta here, I'm headed home to see if it's worth eatin'. Hard saying with her. She's hit and miss," he said.

"This is her first attempt, so we'll see," I said, knowing she had actually all but expertly prepared all of our meals for the last five days.

"If I see a Shovelhead flying that rocker I'll do a little more than kick him in the face," I said as I turned away.

"Fear the act of no man..." Sarge said.

"For the fury of hell is yours," I said as I walked toward the door.

The club motto was an easy one for the majority of the men to adopt. As most of them believed they were individually strong, they further believed they were invincible with the strength of the club and their brothers at their side.

I didn't disagree, but I felt confident I could take care of most all of my problems alone. As I got on my bike and started the engine, I considered what may happen if I encountered a Shovelhead flying a rocker claiming territory.

I shook my head as I swept the kickstand into the frame with my boot. I pulled in the clutch and gazed out past the parking lot and into the street. I didn't want to accept the possibilities of what might happen. Instead, I said a short prayer asking that the rival club have enough common sense not to consider an act so blatantly disrespectful.

And I thanked the man upstairs for allowing Em to enter my life.

EMILY

June 26, 2006

I had no more than pulled our dinner from the oven, and I heard Jackson's motorcycle in the driveway. As the sound of the garage door going closed caught my attention, I ran from the kitchen cupboards and into the dining room, tossing plates and silverware onto the table as I rushed past.

Although he hadn't formally invited me to do so, I had all but lived with him since the Saturday night we had *the talk* and officially began our committed relationship together. So far, everything I had cooked he enjoyed, and he even took the time to compliment me each night as soon as he finished eating. The feeling of having him truly appreciate me was beyond my expectations of what I had always believed to be satisfying.

What little time I had spent with Jackson was redefining so many things in my life. He now filled my every thought. While I worked, I thought of what I was going to cook for him - frantically searching for a better or newer recipe on the internet. While I cooked, I thought of how he may react when he tasted it, and I filled with anticipation of what he might say when he was done. His courteous behavior was still difficult for me to believe, and I wondered just how much he would change in the presence of his club brothers.

Overall, and considering everything, I was in heaven. Although we

71

still hadn't had sex, I had a taste of what Jackson was going to be like in the bedroom, and I was beyond excited. I had been tickled with feathers, teased, tied up, deprived of hearing him, seeing him, and touching him. I had never in my life been as turned on as I had with him, and if it was any indication as to what sex might bring, I was worried that I may just burst into flames when the time came.

I realized the decision making process regarding sex was his and his alone, and I respected him for not rushing into anything. I suspected in his mind he was slowly building my trust, but to be honest, I trusted him already. I had developed a new level of respect for him, and I guessed if nothing else, he had accomplished that much in the six days since our agreement.

"Smells good," he said as he walked into the kitchen.

"Thank you," I responded with a smile.

Anticipation of the inevitable was always something I enjoyed. Reaching the apex on a rollercoaster, the assured surprise of the Jack-in-the-box immediately before it sprung from the confines of the box, and waiting for Christmas morning to arrive were things I truly enjoyed growing up. Now, as an adult, waiting on Jackson provided the same satisfaction. Knowing his routine was to kiss me before removing his boots caused my stomach to swirl with butterflies until he did so.

As he sauntered past, he reached out, grasped my neck lightly, and spun me half way around. Surprised by his sudden movement, but not surprised as much by the kiss, I gasped as our lips melted together. After a passionate kiss, he released me without speaking. I sighed as he turned toward the bedroom, wanting more, but having enough discipline not to ask or complain. I had no idea if the entire neck thing was going to always act as the precursor to a kiss, but I sure hoped it was his intention.

While he removed his boots washed his hands, the buzzer on the oven went off. I removed the chicken and set it aside. After removing the salad from the refrigerator, I prepared our plates and carried them to the table. I no more than placed the plates in front of our seats, and he walked into the room.

"Perfect timing," I said as he walked up to the table and gazed down at his plate.

"Well, I've never been one who's fond of being late," he said as he sat down.

"Damn that smells good, what is it?" he asked.

"Chicken," I responded.

"What kind of chicken," he asked over his shoulder as I walked into the kitchen.

"The kind with feathers. Beer or water?" I asked.

"Water, you little smart ass," he responded.

I carried two glasses of water into the dining area and handed him one.

"It's special chicken. See if you like it. There's spinach salad, and I cooked new potatoes in olive oil. They had some really little guys at the farmer's market on Saturday. I think the little ones taste better, see what you think," I said as I sat down.

He watched me as I sat, obviously eager to start eating. After I picked up my fork and pierced a potato, he began to eat. I watched out of my peripheral as I chewed a potato, hoping the chicken I hadn't taken time to taste was satisfactory. After slicing one of the breasts on his plate into half a dozen slices, he finally lifted his fork to his mouth. He no more than closed his mouth and started to chew and his eyes widened drastically.

Please be good.

I held my left hand under the edge of the table and crossed my fingers.

"Holy shit, that's the best fucking chicken I've ever tasted. What is it?" he asked.

"Boneless chicken breast," I shrugged.

Although I never told him where I got the recipes, most of them came from the internet. Men seemed to think - my father included - that women were some type of walking computer when it came to cooking, plucking recipes from the backs of their minds and working some type of voodoo magic with their preparation of a meal. Most men perceived cooking as something akin to nuclear science or biochemical engineering - they found it interesting, but impossible to comprehend.

"God damn it, Em. What did you do to it? Shit, that's fucking incredible. You could open a restaurant and just sell this shit right here. Fuck, you'd be rich," he said as he pointed his fork toward the chicken.

He poked another slice of chicken into his mouth and as he chewed it, immediately stabbed another with the tines of his fork.

"Seriously, what is it?" he asked as he chewed the piece of chicken.

"Well, its Dijon mustard, maple syrup, salt, pepper, and rosemary. Not a big deal," I said without looking up from my plate.

No differently than if I'd eaten the chicken a thousand times, I nonchalantly lifted a piece from my plate, shrugged my shoulders, and poked it past my lips.

Oh. My. God. That's fucking incredible.

I had typed 'best chicken ever' in the search engine and searched for recipes. The recipe I used was one of the first ones to pop up, and the pictures were pretty, so I tried it. I had no idea it would taste as good as it did.

"Jesus, woman. These potatoes are…" he paused as he turned toward me.

A potato teetered on the end of his fork, a second away from gravity pulling it down to his plate. With his eyes locked on mine, he guided the fork to his mouth, only to lose the potato half way there. As the empty tines contacted his lips, his eyes shifted downward.

"Should have been paying attention to my food," he said as he reached for the elusive potato.

"Say you got these little fuckers at the farmer's market?" he asked as he tossed the grape sized spud into his mouth.

I nodded my head.

"Last Saturday," I said.

"Go back this weekend and buy a hundred pounds of these little bastards. Jesus. Woman, you can cook a meal. I'm telling you, I've never eaten so good in my fucking life. You know what we're going to do?" he asked as he began to slice the other chicken breast.

"What's that?" I asked.

"Open a restaurant. I'm not shittin'. One of these days, you're going to open a restaurant. We should all focus on what we're good at. Me? I'm a natural outlaw, good at riding a bike, mean muggin' assholes, and being devoted to my lady. You? You're a natural at cooking. Shit, working at that office as a receptionist? One of these days that's gonna have to change," he said with a nod.

The thought lingered with me as he continued to eat. Having a restaurant would be a dream of mine, but I was no better of a cook than any other woman. I may have taken more time in my preparation, or had slightly more pride in the finished product than some women, but to think I could cook well enough to serve it to the public was almost laughable.

Hearing Jackson praise me was one of the greatest things to ever happen, and I hoped it would never change. I ate my food quietly as I watched him finish his plate, eating his salad last, as always.

"Let me get you some more, there's plenty," I said.

He shook his head as he wagged his index finger in the air.

"Hold up a minute. You'll need to excuse me for a second, I'm gonna grab my phone out of my cut. I gotta send Sarge a picture of this meal. His Ol' Lady can't cook a lick, and I want him to see this shit I'm eatin'. How much is left?" he asked as he pushed his chair away from the table.

"Well, I cooked six breasts. I've had one, and you've had two, so there's three left," I responded.

"I might save one for him to try. Be back in a second," he said as he stood from his seat.

Little things about Jackson not only surprised me, but provided support to his claim of being different than any of the men he rode with. He never carried his phone with him in the house, and rarely used it when we were together. Other men I had been with were constantly texting on their phones. Jackson didn't even have a Myspace account, and had no interest of ever setting one up. Although he had sent me a few text messages, it wasn't common for him to do so. He typically called me before he left the shop, just to let me know he was on his way.

His home was filled with pictures of Sarge, Chili, Woody, Fat Bart, and his sister. According to him, they were his family. Accepting him as being an orphan and not having family was easy, but understanding what he had been through as a child was impossible.

His manners, excusing himself from the table, and saying 'thank you', 'please', and 'you're welcome' on every occasion he felt necessary was a result - according to him - of being raised by a preacher who demanded the foster children adhere to his policies regarding behavior in the home.

He walked into the kitchen, flipped open his phone and held it over the chicken. After taking a few pics of the potatoes and salad, he sat down and tapped his fingers against keys and texted the pictures to Sarge.

Upon satisfying himself the photos had been sent, he stood, walked to the bedroom, and promptly returned.

"Sarge's Ol' Lady can't cook to save her ass. He eats it anyway, but he always bitches," he said as he carried his plate to the kitchen.

He returned with two more chicken breasts, half a plate of salad, and several of the potatoes. As he sat down, he clutched the plate in his hands, turned toward me, and smiled.

"I'm grateful for you, Em. I really am. Not for the things you provide me, but for how you make me feel. As far as I'm concerned, you're proof the man upstairs hasn't given up on me yet. You're never going to regret taking this step with me."

He sat there for a moment, blankly gazing beyond me. He was as handsome of a man as I had ever seen in person, and believing he was satisfied with me was difficult, but I forced myself to accept it. Each time I studied him, I became more aware of just how handsome he really was, and a strange pride developed within me as I realized of all available women, he was committed to me.

Eventually, he gazed down at his plate and shook his head. After a short hesitation, he glanced upward. A smirk washed over his face and he chuckled lightly.

He didn't laugh very often, but he did smile much more than when we met. The dimples I had thought were almost non-existent had become rather common, but I knew better than to point them out. I simply looked forward to him producing them, knowing they were reserved for when he was happier than any time at all.

His dimples were my little secret.

"What?" I asked.

"I was just thinking of the hog we ate last year that made everyone sicker than absolute fuck. Woody had the entire club sick because he had no idea how to cook it. Meat temperature was probably way too low. Anyway, on Saturday we've got a poker run and a keg party at Chili's place afterward. I want you to plan on going," he said.

Eating raw pork, food poisoning, and barfing were on my list of things *not* to do. I had no real idea what a poker run was, but I'd heard Jackson talk about them, and suspected it was some type of a biker rally. Although none of those things were something I would have done six weeks prior, and I would never do them alone, in Jackson's presence I would try almost anything.

"Okay," I said as I chewed my chicken.

"And when we're done eating, I want you to go take a warm bath. I'll clean up the dishes," he said.

I knew better than to even attempt to argue with him or make any effort to try and change his mind. A warm bath sounded good. As I finished my meal and watched him finish his, I realized the thing I wanted the most had become the least of my worries. Jackson's warm heart, simple way of living life, and constant praise provided me with more than enough satisfaction.

The sex would come eventually, I was sure of it. But for the time being, I was quickly becoming the happiest woman on earth.

One stolen internet recipe at a time.

EMILY

June 27, 2006

Being deprived of my eyesight wasn't something I had ever dreamed of happening to me, nor was it something I ever thought could or would be sensual. What little I knew of being blind was that the remaining senses, according to my understanding at least, were heightened or more refined.

I now had first-hand information to support my previous beliefs.

Long after he walked out of the room - and he had done so several times already - the smell of his cologne lingered. When he returned, his footsteps echoed throughout the house until he reached the carpeting in the bedroom. His breathing sounded as if he were a bull preparing to charge the matador in some third world country - even though I realized it was no different than any other breathing that had gone unnoticed on previous nights we had spent together. I had no idea of how long I had been deprived of my sight, but I suspected it had been at least a few hours.

I knew one thing and one thing only.

The size of the wet spot my overly aroused pussy had deposited on the comforter was large enough I could feel it against my hips.

With my hands and feet secured to each corner of the bed, I was face down, naked, blindfolded, and whatever the polar opposite of exhausted would be. I felt the way I suspected a meth-head would feel after smoking a paycheck's worth of rock over the course of a weekend. As my heart continued to beat out of my chest in anticipation of what may or may not be happening next, Jackson startled me as he dragged something along the skin of my inner thigh.

My every muscle tensed and my pussy ached as if it were going to pop.

I bit my lower lip and pressed my face into the comforter. Enveloped in complete darkness, I could hear the springs in the mattress creaking as he shifted his weight from side-to-side on the bed.

The tickling of my inner thigh ceased. Short of the ceiling fan and his breathing, the room was now silent. In the distance, I heard the refrigerator humming. The sound of the ceiling fan whirring above me became the center of my focus, the dull drone comforting me, slowly bringing me back down to earth with each rotation.

I flinched as I felt something pressing against my aching pussy. Whatever it was slid inside of me without much effort what so ever. As I moaned into the surface of the cool comforter, I wondered if his decision to not gag my mouth was by mistake or part of a careful plan he had devised.

As I became lost in what I now believed was his finger inside of me, I decided nothing Jackson did would be without thought.

Having him not speak to me the entire time was something that took a little getting used to, but looking back on the entire experience, his initial demand of 'unless I speak to you, do not say a word' answered my question of whether or not the lack of a gag was intentional.

He was testing my ability to follow his demands.

Or something of that nature.

As his finger slowly worked my pussy into a lathered up little mess, I decided I really didn't give a fuck if he planned it or not. Whatever he was doing was working and working well. I had never been so sexually aroused in my life, and I felt as if each minute would certainly be my last, my death a result of some profound reaction of my brain's inability to process my aching twat's signals into meaningful feelings. His finger continued to torture me, the tip tickling my g-spot with each stroke. An odd tingling sensation began deep inside my pussy and rang throughout my body, eventually making my overly sensitive nipples feel as if they were being mildly electrocuted. I had officially reached the point of climax, a heightened feeling of sexual bliss I had never known to exist. All as the result of a little light tickling, slapping my ass with a paddle, and his finger inside of me.

I bit into the down comforter and prepared for an earth shattering orgasm which was slowly building within my soul.

He pulled his finger from my pussy and wiped it on my cheek.

Fuck.

His breathing came closer and closer until I felt it against my neck. As the warmth of his breath against my ear caused me to wince in anticipation, he spoke the first words I had heard in hours.

"If you have an orgasm, I'm going to deprive you of sex for six months. Is that understood?" he asked.

I nodded my head, "Uh huh."

His weight shifted from the bed. I heard light footsteps across the room, some shifting of objects, and slight weight on the edge of the bed again.

Whack!

I felt the pain a fraction of a second after the sound of the paddle slapping my ass filled the room. I yelped out in pain against the comforter.

The stinging was like fire against my skin. I tensed my muscles and pulled against my fur lined restraints, preparing for another slap of the paddle against my overly sensitive skin. The cool flat surface of the paddle pressing against my left cheek startled me as his breath filled my right ear.

"If you have an orgasm, I'm going to deprive you of sex for six months. Is that understood? A *Yes, Sir*, or a *No, Sir* will suffice as a response," he breathed into my ear.

I swallowed heavily, licked my lips, and responded.

"Yes, Sir," I murmured.

I heard the paddle fall to the floor beside the bed. The unmistakable metallic clank of his belt unbuckling followed. Then, I grinned as I recognized the sound of his zipper being unzipped. As my ass continued to burn from the previous swat of the wooden paddle, I heard a noise similar to opening the mints the usher gave away at the movie theatre.

A condom?

The left edge of the bed shifted downward as it absorbed his weight, and almost immediately I felt his massive chest press against my side. As the forearm of his right arm pressed into the middle of my back, his hand gathered my hair and gripped it tightly. He pulled against it, lifting my head from the bed as he breathed into my right ear.

"Not a word," he exhaled into my ear.

Fearing the paddle if I responded, and further fearing the paddle if I didn't say 'Yes, Sir,' I opted to keep my mouth shut. As close as I was able to discern, I only needed to respond if he asked me a question.

And, he had not.

With my muscles tensed in anticipation of the swat, he crawled on top of me. I felt his cock against my inner thigh as he situated himself, and realized as much as I wanted him to be inside of me, his instructions were clear.

No orgasms.

As I felt him begin to guide himself into my throbbing mound, I realized I had never seen him naked. I had never seen his cock. I had no idea if he was massive, sufficient, or small. Although it didn't really matter at this point in time, I for some reason found it odd. While my mind soared into the possibilities of someday seeing him naked, his lack of continued penetration left me wondering just what he was packing between his legs.

And, as soon as the wonder filled my mind, the feeling of being impaled removed all speculation.

Oh dear lord.

I arched my back the best I was able and attempted unsuccessfully to lift my ass in the air. The angle at which he was now fucking me was determined primarily by the fact I was tied to the bed and stretched to my limits. My arms extended straight out toward each corner of the bed, and my legs stretched in the same manner, he was forcing himself inside of me at an odd angle.

Odd, but beyond pleasurable.

With each stroke, the tip of his apparently massive cock was grinding against my g-spot. At this rate, I knew I'd be lucky to last thirty seconds. I had no idea what the punishment would be for not following his instructions, but granting his request of not reaching climax was going to be impossible.

As he rhythmically worked himself in and out of my ever-so-willing pussy, instead of fully enjoying the experience, I worried. After what was probably only a few seconds, but seemed like thirty minutes, I decided to count my accounts receivable list as I could best recall them.

In alphabetical order.

When I reached the letter 'D', he was roughly thirty strokes into the torturous affair. I could feel every millimeter of his length as it slid past my wet pussy lips. Within a matter of seconds, I was certain I would explode.

His tight scrotum pounding against my swollen clit didn't help matters.

As I felt him tugging against my hair, I was reminded there was a lot more going on than I was even capable of comprehending. His warm breath against my right ear warned me he was going to say something, undoubtedly causing me to make a decision I would inevitably screw up.

"If you pleasure yourself with an orgasm, Em, there'll be hell to pay," he breathed into my ear.

Fuck...

I bit my lower lip and began my effort to recall all of my clients in reverse, starting with 'Z'.

He continued to pull against my hair, pound his hips against my ass, and force every inch of himself inside my aching pussy, all the while breathing into my ear with each stroke.

After a few more minutes, my level of arousal had risen to a point of no return. The absence of my sight, his warm breath against my ear, the sound of his skin slapping against mine, and the lingering smell of sex proved to be more than I was able to dismiss. I felt myself begin to contract making each stroke of his cock that much more pleasurable.

"If you come, I'll paddle your ass so hard you'll wish for the next year you hadn't," he growled, "Do you understand me?"

"Yes," I whimpered.

As I felt his weight begin to shift, I corrected myself, "Yes, Sir!"

His torture continued. Now fucking me as if I were his last potential piece of ass on earth, he pulled my hair taught, arching my back, and thrust himself into my twat as if possessed by the devil himself. Although the entire event had previously been without speaking for the most part, his methods changed within an instant of his newfound energetic pattern of providing me pleasure.

"Fuck yes, Em, that little pussy of yours is a tight little fucker," he bellowed.

"You like that big cock?' he asked.

"Yes, Sir!" I shouted.

His free hand slapped against my ass. As I whimpered to myself from the pain, I was grateful, if even for a short moment, it took my focus away from him fucking me.

He leaned forward, smashing me into the comforter. As his chest pressed into my back, he bit my earlobe and exhaled into my ear.

"I'm going to pull this cock out of you and come all over that cute little face of yours, you submissive little shit. Do you understand me?" he growled.

"Yes…Yes, Sir," I cried.

His scrotum pummeled my overly sensitive clit, causing the little love button to send a tingling sensation throughout my entire body. As he lifted his weight from my back and pulled against my hair sharply, I arched my back for a little relief.

"Don't do it," he demanded.

"No, Sir!" I wailed in response.

The weight of his body shifted as he fumbled around on the bed. After a few seconds of awkward feeling sex, his hands fumbled with my nipples, and then a pinching sensation…

Holy fucking…

Oh…my…god…

They felt as if they were on fire. I didn't need to see them to understand what he had done. My nipples were in clamps, and ached like hell.

The feeling soon became a strangely satisfying one, and as he thrust himself in and out of my soaked and seemingly never-going-to-dry-up pussy, the ends of the devices he had clamped to my nipples scraped against the comforter with every few strokes of his cock. I could feel the sensation shooting through my body, all the way to my pussy.

He pounded away, and each time, my body tingled from nipple to crotch. The sensation was so pleasurable it was more than I was capable of enjoying without reaching climax.

Note to self: I love nipple clamps.

As I fought to forget what was happening and tried to force myself to hate it, I eventually embraced the feelings and allowed myself to enjoy them fully and totally, escaping into a blissful part of heaven only I knew to exist.

His screaming cast me from my safe place and brought me back into the reality of being fucked to death by a biker on a squeaking bed.

"You may…" he grunted.

He pressed himself against my back. "Reach…"

"Climax…" he breathed into my ear.

Confused, excited, and somewhat scared, I tossed my thoughts aside and focused on my throbbing clit and cock-filled pussy. As he continued to pound himself into me, the only noise in the room was the flesh-on-flesh sound of my wet pussy being owned by the most intriguing man in the world.

I arched my back, lifting my nipple clamps from the comforter slightly. As the tips of them brushed against the fabric, almost bringing me to climax, my entire body began to tingle. He continued to slide in and out, filling me with his manhood, and all of a sudden, my ears began to ring…

And my body began to shudder.

And something happened that had never before happened.

I bellowed out onto the room as my body convulsed into an orgasm unlike anything I had ever experienced. My body convulsed, my pussy clenched his cock, and my butthole puckered to the size of a grain of sand.

Although the dull thud of him continuing to fuck me continued long after I reached climax, I didn't necessarily *feel* it. Everything became distant and foggy, like a dream. After what I expected was a few minutes time, I felt him folding my arms in front of me, and rolling me onto my back.

The lights of the bedroom seemed blindingly bright as he rolled beside me and softly spoke into my ear.

"Em…Em…are you alright?" he asked.

It was as if he was somewhere else, but I knew he wasn't. Incapable of responding, but feeling the need to do so, I said 'Yes, Sir' in my mind, but the words never escaped my lips.

"Em…come on back, Em…come on, Baby…" he said softly.

I felt him caress my face, and rake his fingers through my hair. After a few minutes time of him whispering into my ear, and softly touching me, I returned from wherever I was, and into an state of something close to reality.

He lifted me from the bed and carried me into the master bathroom. I blinked my eyes and attempted to focus as he lowered himself into the tub, holding me in his arms. The warm water felt fabulous against my skin.

I glanced around the bathroom, still slightly confused, almost as if I had never seen one before. On the wire shelves beside the tub, were towels, washcloths, and fruit…

Fruit?

"Is that fruit?" I asked as I blinked my eyes and tilted my head toward the rack.

"Yes, you'll need the nourishment," he responded.

"What happened?" I asked.

"You went into what's called subspace. It's a rush of endorphins that literally send you somewhere your mind has never experienced. The intensity of the orgasm from a session like that is ten-fold of what you're used to. Then, you crash back down to earth. It's called Sub Drop. If that's not where you are now, you'll probably be there pretty damned soon. Don't worry, I'll take care of you," he said assured me.

He stood from the tub and grabbed a banana. As he turned around, I gazed at his body. His chiseled torso had three words tattooed below his waist. As he peeled the banana, I studied the tattoo, and realized it was written in Latin.

"What does that mean?" I asked as he handed me half of the banana.

"I came, I saw, I conquered," he responded.

I bit into the banana as I nodded my head.

"When did you run the bath water?" I asked as I glanced around the spacious bathroom.

"When I left the room earlier. When I left the room a few minutes ago, I turned it off," he said as he reached for the switch on the wall.

"I'm going to turn on the jets. Ready?" he asked as he held his hand over the switch.

I nodded my head, still pretty oblivious to my surroundings. "Yep," I responded.

I felt like it was the morning after a bad drunk. Mentally, I was completely lost. As he stepped into the tub, I focused on the half of a banana he held in his hand.

"You gonna eat that?" I asked as I pointed at the banana.

"No," he chuckled.

"It's for you," he said as he handed me the remaining banana.

"So, what did you think of that?" he asked as he reached for the soap.

"The banana?" I asked, knowing he meant the sex, but making at least an effort to be cute.

"Yeah, Em, the banana," he responded sarcastically.

"The banana was kinda squishy, but the sex was some insane shit. What did you think?" I asked.

"Me?" he said as he squirted some soap onto a Loofah, "I couldn't be any happier."

Truth be told, I couldn't have been any happier either. But what mattered more than anything was that he was happy, and knowing the answer made me even happier yet. As he wiggled his way past me in the tub and began to wash my back, I remembered the night we met, and how he beat the absolute shit out of the guy who was grabbing my boobs. I never would have guessed the man in the bar that night would be carrying me into the Jacuzzi tub and washing my back as I ate fruit.

But again, I expected Jackson Shephard was unlike any other man on this earth.

And he was slowly proving me to be right.

JACK

June 28, 2006

Hearing, smelling, and tasting had always been senses that brought back memories - some good and some not-so-good.

The odor of Pine-Sol wasn't something I ever cared to smell again, but sooner or later, it seemed to happen. Each time my nostrils flared from the scent, memories of the foster home filled my mind. The wife of the preacher cleaned everything with the solution at full strength, filling the house with a permanent stench of the cleaner. My memories of my slightly abusive and extremely controlling preacher who was our foster father were not fond, and in fact, I fought with myself not to return as an adult and beat him within an inch of his life.

The taste or smell of bananas, however, was comforting to me. The small grocery store at the corner on our way to school always had ripe bananas, and often on our walks to and from school, the grocer would step out onto the sidewalk - his white apron tied tight around his waist - and give Sydney and me a banana as a treat. It wasn't free, or provided out of sorrow; I cleaned his storage room on weekends - but I never told Sydney about my having worked to obtain the fruit. I allowed her to believe then, and continue to believe throughout our time in the foster home that there were people on this earth who were filled with love, willing to graciously provide gifts to children who were kind, polite, and eager to return the love with a gentle grin or the wave of an appreciative hand.

As a teen, the earthshaking roar of a group of motorcycles was one that not only caused the hair on the back of my neck to stand, but something that I perceived as being a resemblance of power.

When I was a thirteen, a motorcycle club moved into town, opening a new chapter. Members wearing their cuts from Colorado Springs came into the city, and stayed for some time. After a matter of months of admiring them on every opportunity I was provided, a local chapter developed. As the number of members grew from six to over twenty, I watched in admiration of the power, the brotherhood, and the elegance of the club as they rode together side-by-side, ten motorcycles deep in a long thunderous line.

I told myself one day I would join them, and counted the days until I was eighteen and able to escape the rules and regulations of my foster home. I knew as soon as I was able to buy a motorcycle, pay my dues to the club, and become a vest-wearing member of their club that no harm would come to me or those I loved, because as far as I was concerned, the men in the leather vests were untouchable.

Em gripped my waist lightly as we pulled out of the fourth stop on the poker run. The day couldn't have been nicer even if it had been chosen solely for our enjoyment. For late June in Kansas it was unseasonably cool, but at eighty-two degrees and sunny, it was perfect for riding, enjoying the scenery, and spending time with the woman I had come to believe was placed on this earth for one reason and one reason only.

"There's a river down at the bottom of the hill. Close your eyes and see if you can tell when we pass it," I said over my shoulder as I rolled on the throttle.

Two motorcycles were in front of us, riding side-by-side. The side-by-side pattern continued for approximately fifty bikes behind us. A large group of us left the American Red Cross building together, and had ridden as a group throughout the day. The rumble of the exhaust from the motorcycles could be heard and felt for miles prior to our arrival in the small cities we were riding into.

The streets in the small town of 691 people we had just ridden out of were lined with children and their parents, gathered on their respective lawns, waving as we passed by on our way to the fire station. If being an outlaw, riding a Harley-Davidson, and being admired by the children of a small town in the Midwest wasn't my calling in life, it sure was something I enjoyed.

As I passed the spring-fed river, Em tapped me on the shoulder. A combination of the shade from the trees, the cool water, and the lower elevation caused the temperature to drop ten degrees as we rode over the bridge.

"I love it," she whispered into my ear, "Smell the flowers?"

I turned my head to the side slightly and nodded once. I had ridden by the river countless times, more often alone than with a group. The all but deserted county roads in the state were perfect for late evening rides as I attempted to accept the deaths of my two previous lovers, and I enjoyed the road we were riding along more than many of the others in the state.

Riding with Em was similar to riding alone in some regards. Many women who had ridden on the back of my motorcycle looked at it as an opportunity to twist, turn, shift their weight, and test the resistance of the rear shock absorbers by bouncing in the seat.

Each movement on the rear of a motorcycle not only had an effect on the path the motorcycle would take, but the stability of it while doing so. To have someone ride on the back of the seat and actually sit still was priceless. Em was a natural at riding, and she allowed me to enjoy having her with me as much as she was appreciated being there.

As we pulled into the next town, lining the street in front of the bar, I couldn't help but grin. The 'town' of a claimed 138 people had a bar, a post office, and a handful of houses. Our presence wasn't as welcome - or at least not as appreciated - as it was in the much larger town of 691 we had just left.

"Is this the last stop?" Em asked as we rolled to the stop.

"This is it," I said as I shut off the engine, "Latham, Kansas. Big fucker, ain't it?"

"I didn't realize there were still towns this small. Did you see the sign when we pulled in?" she asked as she stepped off the back of the bike.

"Which one?" I asked.

"It said Latham, population 138," she responded.

"Yeah," I chuckled, "I've had the pleasure of being here before. Quite a few times, actually."

"Can I get the card punched?" she asked as she pulled it from the front pocket of her shorts.

"Yeah, it's across the street," I said as I tossed my head toward the bar.

"Fu...fu...fu...fucking...tah...tah...town gives me the wuh... willies," Chili said as he stepped off his bike.

"Afraid one of these farmers is going to shoot your ass, Chili?" Sarge chuckled as he walked alongside our bikes.

Chili gazed up and down the two blocks that made up the small

96

town. After a short study of the dozen or so homes, he removed his sunglasses, narrowed his eyes, and ran his hand through his short salt-and-pepper hair as he shook his head.

"Luh…Luh…like a fucking go…go…ghost town," he said.

"I'm hungrier than a motherfucker, they got food in that shit-hole bar?" Sarge asked as he rubbed the sweat from his bald head.

"Hamburgers and hot dogs from what I can remember," I shrugged.

Chili tossed his hands in the air as if frustrated. "Cuh…cuh…come on. I'm creeped the fuh…fuh…fuck out."

Chili was as solid of a man as I had ever met, and would do for his brothers in the club much more than he would do for himself. He was a man of average height with an above average build who stuttered terribly unless he was drunk. When he was drunk, his speech was soft, clear, and concise. When sober, he had a difficult time saying almost anything at all; therefore he chose short simple sentences. His stuttering and stammering earned him the name Chili, a modified version of *chilly*, a description the club decided fit him well, as it initially appeared he was always stuttering as a result of the chilly and wet winter weather when he began prospecting for the club.

"Well, let's get this over with, Chili. A forty minute ride and we'll be home," I said as I stepped around him.

"You ready?" I asked Em.

She nodded her head as she studied the envelope she held. The card hidden inside was marked along the outer edge with each of the fifty-two cards from a deck. On the outside of the envelope were fifty-two numbers. At each stop, a random number was drawn from a sack of chips, and the respective number on the card was punched with a hole punch. As each of the cards hidden inside the envelopes had playing cards in different orders, and no one was able to see into the sealed envelope, no one knew until the ride was over who had which cards punched on the card inside their envelope.

After the completion of the ride, the envelopes - each marked with a rider's name and telephone number - were provided to a proctor who opened the envelope and ranked the hand as if it were a poker hand. The three best poker hands of the ride won prizes, the best hand of the ride receiving six hundred dollars.

Over the years, I had won with five of a kind, and had a hand as bad as ace, deuce, three, five, six. It was anyone's guess what you'd receive, and there was certainly no skill whatsoever required to win.

"It creeps me out a little bit, too, Chili," Em said as she stepped between us.

Chili nodded his head and patted her on the shoulder as we walked across the street toward the bar. A line of thirty or so people still filtered out the door into the street, all waiting on getting their card punched.

As we waited in line, Sarge stuck his head inside the door and screamed toward one of the many waitresses working the bar.

"Gimme five cheeseburgers and another one without cheese. Just holler at me when they're done. I'll be standing out here in the sun withering away," he chuckled.

"You skinny little fucker, you need to eat something," he said with a laugh as he slapped his hand against Em's back, almost knocking her off balance.

"I had eggs, a bagel, and some sausage for breakfast," she said as she spread her feet shoulder width apart, undoubtedly preparing for the next playful slap of Sarge's hand.

"Stuh...stuh...stop picking on my guh...guh...girl, you big fuh...

98

fuh…fucker," Chili said as he put his arm around Em.

I glanced over my right shoulder as she playfully nestled her head into Chili's chest. As our eyes met, she winked. I winked back, not really caring if either of the two fellas saw me or not.

Contrary to the belief of most, one-percenters were not all lady sharing, womanizing, male chauvinists. Over the years, I had been around a few dozen one percent clubs, thousands of various members of clubs, and countless parties, clubhouses, and bike rallies. One thing shared by all members of one percent clubs that many civilian 'riding clubs' didn't practice was respect of a member's Ol' Lady. If a patched member had an Ol' Lady, no one messed with her. Sometimes the men accepted an Ol' Lady easier than others, and often they simply put up with them because they had to, but they never treated another brother's Ol' Lady with anything but respect. The receipt of an Ol' Lady with open arms generally meant she was perceived as being as solid as her Ol' Man.

Club whores, stripper poles in the clubhouse, and orgies amongst the ranks of the club weren't something that ever happened in my presence with Hell's Fury, nor in the presence of any of the other clubs I had exposed myself to. The stories of such things were often told by the liars, wannabes, and bullshitters.

There was no doubt life in a one percent club was full of fights, shootings, felonious activities, murder, and an occasional alleged rape, but often the allegations of rape were not true and sprouted as a result of a barfly who got fucked in an alley, only to find out the man she had just fucked was married or had an Ol' Lady waiting in the bar.

It satisfied me greatly to see Sarge, Chili, and the other men accept Em as being an extension of me. Although I didn't share my sexual experiences with the men, they all knew I was far from promiscuous. They more than likely perceived Em as being no different than the two women who had been in my presence in the past - a permanent fixture in my life - and therefore an eternal extension of one of their brothers in the club.

"Fifteen dollars," the waitress said as she raised a brown paper bag dripping with grease in front of Sarge.

"Fifteen bucks?" he shrugged, "For six fucking burgers?"

"Two fifty each," she nodded.

Sarge reached for his wallet, pulled out a ten and a twenty and handed her both bills.

"There's thirty, keep it," he said as he stuffed his wallet into his pocket.

"Thank you," she said cheerily as she shoved the money into the back pocket of her jeans.

"Here," Sarge said as he slapped a burger against Em's back.

She shook her head and chuckled as she reached over her shoulder and grabbed the burger.

"Whu...whu...what did I...tuh...tuh...tell ya?" Chili said as he raised his fists in front of his chest.

"He doesn't scare me, Chili," Em said as she waved her hand toward Sarge.

"Here," Sarge said as he handed Chili and me each a burger.

The line slowly progressed as we stood eating our burgers. As I suspected, Sarge ate two, we each ate one, and there was one left. As Sarge shoved the remaining burger into the front pocket of his cut, Em challenged him.

"What's that for?" she asked as she wadded the wax paper from her burger into a ball and nodded her head toward Sarge's cut.

"What the fuck you think it's for? It's for fucking later," he responded.

"Just wait, he'll pull it out and eat it on the way home while we're riding down the highway eighty fucking miles an hour," I assured her.

As a group of four men stepped through the door and past where we stood, I realized we were next in line for having our cards punched.

"Next," the man sitting behind the table bellowed as we stepped into the bar.

The previous four stops had three or four people working at each table. The lack of progress in our line was now apparent as I realized one lone man was working the line which would eventually produce over six hundred cards.

"Ladies fuh...fuh...first," Chili said as he released Em and patted her on the back.

"I need a winner," she said as she reached into the bag of chips.

She removed her hand, looked at the chip, and screeched as she held it in the air for me to see.

"Twenty-one," she wailed.

"What the fuck's that got to do with anything?" Sarge complained as he reached for his ears.

The man took Em's card, punched the number twenty-one, and handed it back to her. She turned to face me, raised herself onto her tip-toes, and leaned into my shoulder.

"Our anniversary," she whispered.

I nodded my head, slightly shocked she remembered the day I made our relationship official, and equally surprised she labeled the day as such.

"We're gonna win," she announced as she waved the card toward

Sarge and Chili.

The sound of the long line of bikes riding out of town reminded me we had a forty mile before we would have our envelopes opened and judged. I turned toward the street, fully hoping Em was right. She seemed to get tremendous satisfaction out of small things, and seeing the look on her face if she won the grand prize would be a joy in itself.

As we sat on our bikes in the sun and waited on the rest of the fellas to make their way through the line, Em tapped me lightly on the shoulder. I glanced over my shoulder, well aware her chin was resting against my upper back. As our eyes met, her mouth curled into a genuine grin.

"Best day ever," she whispered.

I reached over my shoulder with my right hand, gripped the back of her neck, and pulled her face forward, pressing it against mine. As I positioned my mouth against her ear, she closed her eyes.

"I'm going to fuck your sexy little ass ragged at Chili's party later. When we're done it'll be the best day ever," I growled into her ear.

"Oh god," she cooed.

"Oh god is right," I said as I released her neck and started the motorcycle.

"Let's get this show on the road, huh Sarge?" I said over the rumble of the exhaust.

"Just as well," he shrugged as he nodded his head toward the bar, "This could take all fucking day."

Em turned her head toward Chili.

"When's your party start?" she asked.

"Soon as wuh…wuh…we…get buh…buh…back," Chili responded as he started his bike.

"I'm ready," Em announced cheerily.

"I doubt that," I chuckled as I released the clutch.

But, deep down in my heart of hearts, I was pretty damned sure she was ready for anything I had to offer.

EMILY

July 26, 2006

Although it had only been two months since Jackson and I had met, we really hadn't been separated at all during that period of time. And, if a person had the means and methods to measure the quality of time we had spent together, they would without a doubt agree our life together had been nothing short of a living dream.

As a young girl, I often guessed what my life would become, and when I would reach a point that I was satisfied with what I had either obtained or achieved. I suspected I would be fifty or maybe even slightly younger, but certainly not twenty-one. If given an opportunity as a high school girl to paint a perfect picture of what I expected my dream man to be, I never would have painted a picture of Jackson, but maybe that's why so many relationships when we are young and foolish just don't seem to last beyond a matter of weeks.

In my opinion, when we're young, we don't really know what we need, and it seems we settle for what we desire. Our desires are based on the thoughts and feelings of our inexperienced youth, and therefore aren't in line with what we truly need, leaving us in the not-so-distant future in a position to choose either settling for what it is we have, or moving on in an attempt to find what we have come to believe we actually need.

And most women I knew seemed to settle for what they had, choosing not to seek what it was they truly needed.

I was fortunate. Jackson found *me*. And, be it by blind luck or fate, he had proven to be exactly what I needed.

"Put the fuckers wherever you want them," he said as he wiped the sweat from his brow.

The July sun bore down on us like a heavy weight, the humidity from the previous night's rain making the air so thick it was difficult to breathe. As if the temperature and my exposure to the sun over the course of the morning had caused mild brain damage, I continued to stare like an idiot at the ground.

"Okay," I said as I gazed blankly at the pots of flowers we had brought home.

Jackson stood, studying the hole he had dug, and eventually turned away and walked into the garage. In a few minutes he returned with a small green box and carefully placed it into the hole. After tossing some dirt on top of the box, he lowered the rose bush into the hole and began adding some of the bagged soil we had purchased.

In the previous month I had backed out of the lease on my apartment and moved all of my belongings into Jackson's home. Although he continued to call it *our* home, I really felt like it was his, and that I was invading his space. The addition of the flowers we had purchased together was a great help in convincing me it was a home we shared, and not one I was simply a guest in. As I continued to stare at them, I wondered if he realized in suggesting we plant flowers together that it would make me feel more comfortable.

"You realize those impatiens are annuals, and they won't come back next year, don't you?" he asked as he finished planting his rose bush.

"Huh?" I responded as I gazed down at the pots of flowers, confused on where to put each one of them.

"Annuals will last for this season and die. Perennials will come back year after year. The rose bush is a perennial; we'll have it for as long as we live here. It'll be ours forever…well…as long as it lives, but they say they live thirty years or longer…" he explained as he shoveled the extra soil into the wheelbarrow.

"So these guys are gonna die?" I asked as I peered down at my flowers.

"That's why they were on sale. We can enjoy 'em for the rest of the summer, though," he said as he pulled his shirt over his head and tossed it aside.

"Put it back on," I said jokingly as I covered my eyes.

Seeing him shirtless was sheer torture. His body was as perfect as I suspected anyone's could ever be, and seeing it covered by a tight white tank tormented me enough. When he removed his shirt, I was forced to accept him as being a shirtless gorgeous tattooed biker until he chose to make sexual advancements toward me.

I had learned a lot about Jackson since we met, and although I initially tried dressing scantily, acting horny, and making idle sexual suggestions, I learned he was a far too disciplined to allow me to coerce him into sex. I simply had to enjoy watching him and wait until he decided he was ready.

As he pushed the wheelbarrow toward where I was standing, the muscles on his biceps flared. His washboard abs appeared to be chiseled out of stone, a product of his daily workouts, eating properly, and rarely enjoying sweets. The closer he got to me, the more I wanted to look away, but doing so was as impossible as any other time he was close enough for me to admire. As the sweat covering his torso glistened in the hot afternoon sun, I forced myself to tear my eyes from him and once again gaze down at my poor choice in flowers.

"Staring at 'em isn't going to do a lot of good," he said as he shoved the end of the wheelbarrow into my thigh.

"Hey, watch where you're going," I said as I shoved against it.

He released the wooden handles, walked around me as if I wasn't there, and slapped my ass as he passed by. After turning on the garden hose, he dragged it toward the rose bush he had planted, placed it on top of the new soil, and returned to my withering one-time-only and soon to be dead choice of flowers. As he placed his hands on his hips and gazed down at the flowers, he exhaled a sigh and shook his head lightly.

"What did you bury with the rose bush?" I asked.

He shifted his eyes upward, met my gaze, and grinned.

"Something we'll dig up together on a rainy day," he responded.

"What are we going to do with these guys?" I asked as I kicked my toe against one of the pots.

"Don't get mad because they're going to die, Em. Everything dies. Everything has a beginning and an ending. Just be glad you're allowed to enjoy them while you're able," he said as he picked up two of the pots and placed them into the wheelbarrow.

"Where are we taking them?" I asked.

"Well, they're best in low sunlight, so maybe if we take them to the north side of the house and plant them over there…"

"Which way's north," I asked.

He shook his head, "Where the front door is."

"Oh," I said with a nod.

"There's a planter over there under the window outside the kitchen, we can put them in the planter, it'll look nice," he said.

"A what?" I asked as he picked up two more of the pots.

"A wooden fucking box affixed to the side of the house, Em. You probably didn't notice it because it's empty. Grab those two and come on," he said as he began to push the wheelbarrow toward the gate.

"You can't go out front with your shirt off," I said as I bent over to pick up the flowers.

He stopped the wheelbarrow and turned to face me. "Oh no?"

I shook my head. "Neighbors will complain."

He cocked one eyebrow and stared. "About?"

"Uhhm. Half-naked bikers?" I shrugged.

The thought of another woman walking by, driving by, or peering out her window at him made me angry. I would have never described myself as a possessive person, nor had I ever been the jealous type, but with Jackson, things were much different. As comfortable as I was in his presence, and as pleased as he made me with his treatment of me, I lived in constant fear of losing him. I really had no reason to believe my fears were warranted, and in fact, they weren't, but I harbored them nonetheless.

"Well, can I take off my shirt?" I asked.

"Sure," he shrugged as he pushed the wheelbarrow through the gate.

"Don't think I won't," I said.

He stopped, turned to face me, and stared for a moment. Standing with a flower pot in each hand, I wondered what I might have gotten myself into. As I stood knowing he was going to do or say something to make me regret my smart assed remark, he grinned and lifted his chin slightly.

"Take it off," he said.

I gazed around the yard. The back yard was protected slightly by a privacy fence, but it in no way prevented everyone from seeing in the back yard. The neighboring homes were two story houses, and anyone from a second story could see right into the yard if the wished.

"Come on, let's get these planted," I said as I took a few steps in his direction.

"Take off your shirt, Em," he demanded.

I lowered the flower pots to the ground, glanced around the yard, and lifted my shirt up and over my braless boobs. Now standing shirtless in the blazing sun, I felt slightly embarrassed, but the embarrassment only lasted for a few seconds.

As the sun warmed my bare skin, I began to feel sexy and increasingly horny with each passing second. With the shirt dangling loosely from my fingertips, I waited for further instructions. I had learned over the last few months I wasn't only acting as a submissive to fulfill Jackson's desire, but I was doing so for myself. From what he had explained, and it made perfect sense, I desired pleasing him as much as he desired being pleased.

In short, I yearned to make him happy with me, and knowing he was pleased with my actions, decisions, or thoughts pleased me to my core.

After a few minutes of admiring me, he waved his arm toward my shirt-filled hand.

"Put it back on," he said flatly.

I pulled the shirt over my head and down along my sweaty torso. Surprised my hardened nipples hadn't shredded the fabric as I pulled it past them, I situating it along the waist of my shorts and waited for his next demand.

He pointed toward me and wagged his finger up and down.

"Take 'em off," he said.

"My shorts?" I asked.

"No, your fucking Chuck's, Em. I want you to take off your shoes. Jesus H. Christ, yes, your god damned shorts. And if you've got on any fucking panties, I'm going to drag you in by your heels and paddle that ass of yours until you can't walk for a week," he said.

I had found out he preferred I not wear panties, but it certainly wasn't natural - at least initially - for me to do so. I had worn panties with every outfit I had ever chosen to wear, and the thought of not wearing them had never really crossed my mind - pre-Jackson, that is. Although I had acquired quite the collection of panties over the years, I now found not wearing them a guilty little newfound pleasure. As I unbuttoned my shorts and pushed them down my hips, I twisted my mouth to the side and acted as if I didn't want to take them any further.

"Off," he demanded.

I kicked my ragged shoes to the side and continued to play the hesitation game as I watched him become more anxious. Eventually I pushed my shorts down my thighs and dropped them to my ankles. As they came to rest at my feet, I stepped through the leg with my left foot and kicked my right foot upward. My shorts flew in a perfect arc toward where Jackson stood. Without expression or changing his stance, he reached up and plucked them from the air as if it were a daily occurrence.

Now standing in the back yard with my cleanly shaved pussy out in the open for all to see, I waited eagerly to see what his next instruction was going to be. I suppose I should have felt embarrassed, or maybe even slightly guilty, but I didn't. My only concern was what Jackson expected of me. As I stood twenty feet in front of him naked from the waist down, my pussy began to tingle as I thought of the possibility of him fucking me in the grass.

As he stood and gazed at me, I focused on the crotch of his jeans. The shape of his zippered area changed from flat to full, and then slowly began to rise.

Score!

"Get your little ass in the kitchen," he demanded as he pointed toward the door leading into the garage.

"Yes, Sir," I responded as I slowly walked toward the garage in my best sexy runway model impersonation.

As I stepped over the threshold of the door, I feigned stubbing my toe, and bent over as if to grab my damaged digit. With my ass in the air and my pussy pointed directly at him, I winced in non-existent pain and waited for him to scream.

"In the kitchen, you little shit," he bellowed.

I stood, hobbled through the garage as if damaged, and ran into the kitchen as soon as I was out of his eyesight. Once in the kitchen I waited eagerly for what was sure to be some insanely satisfying sex for us both. As I leaned against the kitchen counter waiting for him, I did my very best to arch my back and thrust my non-existent ass in the air.

Although I initially expected all of our sex would include some version of me being bound, gagged, or mildly tortured, I was proven wrong. I learned the BDSM acronym stood for Bondage, Discipline, Dominance, Submission, Sadism, and Masochism. With Jackson, his satisfaction wasn't so much about any one of the aspects of the acronym, it was about control.

He enjoyed variety, and in fact, we had sex on many occasions that was pretty conventional. Regardless of the flavor or intensity of the sex we both enjoyed it very much; but he was always in control, even if it was something as simple as telling me to get my ass in the kitchen. The control satisfied him, and me relinquishing control, and my living in the unknowing world of what was next satisfied me.

He told me in the beginning he was different that anyone else I could ever encounter in life, and he was sure right.

"Stand on your fucking tip-toes," he barked as he entered the room.

The sound of his voice startled me.

"Yes, Sir," I gasped as I stood on my tip-toes and peered over my shoulder.

"You didn't stub your fucking toe, you little shit. You think sticking your little pussy in the air is enough to fluster me?' he asked as he walked toward the sink.

As he washed his hands, I responded.

"No, Sir," I said over my shoulder.

It wasn't necessarily the truth, but it was without a doubt what he wanted to hear, and therefore what I needed to say.

"Face the other direction," he demanded, "and don't turn around again."

I turned away, wondering if he was really upset over the toe thing or if it was just a show. Most of the time, I never knew for sure. I guessed it was probably best that way, and although it often caused me slight grief, I realized it was exactly what he wanted.

I rested my elbows on the kitchen counter and anxiously waited for him to call the next shot. After a few seconds, he leaned forward, pushing his massive chest against my back. His forearm slid against my right elbow, and his mouth moved alongside my cheek, resting at my right ear. His warm breath against my ear sent chills down my spine.

"Put these in your mouth," he whispered as he held three ice cubes in front of my face.

What the fuck?

As I reached for the ice cubes, he placed a small glass bowl of ice on the countertop in front of me. The ice wasn't the square or rectangular cubes, but the half-moon style the ice machines on refrigerators typically make.

I slid the three cubes into my mouth and began juggling them with my tongue. About the time I realized my mouth was much fuller than I was really comfortable with, and as I hoped the ice would quickly melt away, his freezing cold finger pressed into the folds of my pussy and caused me to jump.

With my mind focused on the mouthful of ice, I was beyond startled by his half-frozen fingertip being shoved into my twat. I immediately jumped, banging my hips on the edge of the countertop. I then gasped from the pain, choked on my mouth full of water, and immediately coughed. Water shot out of my mouth and all over the counter. As I wailed in pain from my soon to be bruised hips, a piece of the melted ice escaped my mouth and slid along the length of the kitchen counter.

"Did I tell you to suck on that shit for a minute, and then spit it across the fucking kitchen?" he asked as he continued to finger fuck me.

"No, thir," I said over the pieces of remaining ice I was shuffling with my tongue.

He reached for the bowl and plucked two more pieces of ice from it.

"Here," he said as he held them in front of my face.

Oh, fuck.

Luckily, the previous pieces were almost melted away. I poked the other two in my mouth and sucked on them like a mad woman, hoping my desire alone would melt them instantly. After an amount of time I'd be incapable of guessing, I realized once again he was fingering me and had probably never stopped. My sole focus had become getting rid of the ice he was making me suck on, which left little room for me to enjoy the sex.

As the small pieces finally dissolved, I opened my mouth and sighed. *Finally.*

"Here," he said as he handed me two more.

Son-of-a-bitch.

I poked the two pieces of ice into my mouth with much reluctance. I considered chewing them and allowing him to spank me as punishment until his arm was too tired to swing the paddle, but opted to at least attempt to entertain him.

As I sucked on the cubes and became all but hypnotized with his fingering of me, the sound of his belt unbuckling caused my eyes to widen slightly. I bit my lower lip in anticipation and pressed the ice against the roof of my mouth with my tongue.

He pushed his finger downward, stretching my pussy open from the force. While I leaned forward, pressing my chest into the countertop and wondering just what the fuck he was doing, his cock slowly slid inside and joined his finger as an instrument of my pleasure.

Now finger fucking me and shoving me full of cock at the same time, but on alternating cycles, his cock slid out as his finger slid in, and vice versa. With my mouth full of ice, and my mind trying to decide what in the hell was going on, I felt as if I was being fucked by at least two people at the same time.

After several strokes of preparation, he was now fucking me with full force, sliding his cock all the way out and slowly pushing it in until his hips pressed against my ass. His finger had been swapped with what I was pretty certain was his thumb, and the web of his hand was wreaking sexual havoc on my swollen clit. I swallowed the little remaining ice, and closed my eyes as I rested my head on the countertop, doing my best to focus on the fabulous feeling of having him fuck me.

He leaned forward, pressing his chest against my back and forcing my boobs into the countertop. As I opened my eyes his hand gripped my jaw and turned my head to the side.

"When you reach climax, I want you to scream. Is that understood?" he breathed into my ear.

"Yes, Sir," I responded through my tightening throat.

He released my jaw, pressed his hand against my back, and slowly but rhythmically began to steadily fuck me into the edge of the countertop. Feeling his cock inside of me was so much different than anything I was used to, and although I wasn't sure of the difference was purely from his increased girth, or if it was a result of me being more in tune with my feelings, I felt no real need to determine the answer.

I simply enjoyed every minute that Jackson was fucking me.

As every one of my muscles slowly tensed and my clit began to develop the itchy feeling, the sound of his hand in the bowl of ice shifted my focus for a split-second. After a second or so of no demand on his part for me to eat another piece of ice, I assumed he must have eaten it himself. I sighed lightly and attempted to focus on my quickly approaching climax.

His cold fingers in between my butt cheeks startled me slightly, but the piece of ice he slid in my anus caused me to immediately inhale a choppy breath.

Without any other indication of his action, he continued to fuck me while his thumb worked immediately below his throbbing shaft, and the web of his hand pounded against my clit. All things considered, it was just too much.

The ice cube in my ass was an oddly satisfying sensation, but was one more thing demanding my focus, and prevented me from allowing myself to relax. I desperately wanted to concentrate on him fucking me, and, ultimately, reach climax.

While he continued to slap his hips against my ass and force himself completely inside of me, the freezing sensation in my ass eventually subsided. Now completely focused on being fucked, I once again clenched my eyes closed and relaxed onto the countertop.

I opened my eyes slightly as his finger fumbled between my butt cheeks again. The freezing cold water dripping along my inner thigh was all the proof I needed that he was going to do it again.

And he did.

One ice cube in my ass, and another in my already full pussy…

My freezing cold ass was soon forgotten as my pussy became my only focus. Everything he had done before continued, but the water from the melting ice worked against my natural lubricants, causing the act of fucking to become much more brutal, create far more friction, and in turn, arouse me even more.

Incapable of even understanding all of what was happening, my mouth was agape and my mind was reeling. The sound of his hips slapping my ass echoed throughout the small kitchen, filling it with the sounds of nothing but sex. My eyes widened and I stared into the dining area searching for answers to my question of what was happening to me.

His hand gripped my neck, forcing my head to the side. As his mouth pressed to mine, his hand grasped my neck tighter. Our tongues tangled together became yet one more thing my mind had to dissect, and it was beyond full of sensations, feelings, and his previous shallow demands.

Kissing Jackson was beyond pleasurable, and almost incapable of putting into words. As he continued to kiss me deeply and squeeze my neck, my pussy began to throb from deep inside.

It was coming.

He clenched my neck a little tighter as he bit my upper lip.

And that was it. I began to shudder from head to toe. I raised myself onto my tip-toes and moaned into his mouth. He released my lip from his teeth, turned my head to face forward, and growled into my ear.

"Scream, you sexy little bitch. Let it out," he growled into my ear as he thrust himself into me.

"Whaaaaat…"

"The…"

"Fuck…" I bellowed into the room as the equivalent of small electric shocks pulsated throughout my body.

His hand still gripping my neck, he turned my head to the side and kissed me deeply. As I continued to have more slight mini-orgasms with almost each slowly decreasing stroke of his cock, he proceeded to kiss me.

After a few more strokes, I was done. It was obvious he realized it, as he stopped fucking me at the exact time my pussy went into some hyper-sensitive state. As he flopped free of my throbbing muff, he leaned to the side and gazed into my eyes. As I did my utter best to force myself to smile, he picked me off of my feet and plopped me onto the countertop.

And it was at that moment, while he stood directly in front of me gazing into my eyes, his body covered in sweat, muscles tensed, chest flaring from his heavy breathing, and his biceps still littered in the soil from our having planted flowers together, that I realized I wasn't only being fucked by Jackson Shephard.

I was deeply in love with him.

JACK

August 7ᵗʰ, 2006

The time during the middle of the week that I typically spent riding alone or with whichever of the fellas was available quickly changed. If someone had asked me one year prior if my schedule would ever change, I would have laughed, knowing I would never make an adjustment to my daily pattern of living life. Now, spending time with Em was more important to me than spending time with anyone, my brothers in the club included.

I didn't think less of them, nor did my value or perception of the club change, but my way of living life clearly had. For the first time in my life, the club and my woman had equal shares of my attention, heart, and plans for the future.

As we rode down the highway toward town, my mind was where it often went after a late evening ride on a beautiful summer night. The sun hadn't set just yet, and it wasn't quite dusk, but it was the few minutes of time immediately prior to it. Low western clouds shaded the last remaining rays of sun, and the sky off to our left side was glowing with pinks, purples, reds, and oranges. Gazing off in the distance, I didn't pray, but I did *something*.

I filled so full with gratitude for what my life had become that something inside of me clicked, like a switch had been flipped, leaving me appreciative of simply being allowed to live life. As Em's hands rested lightly against my thighs, I twisted the throttle and got one last run at freedom before slowing down to come into town.

"It's like being an angel," Em said as we rode into the edge of town.

"What?" I chuckled over my shoulder.

"Riding. It's like we're angels," she said.

I nodded my head, "Something like that."

I felt her shift her weight as she leaned back and faced the sky.

"I love it," she screamed.

Em had quickly become the perfect companion, lover, and friend. She possessed all of the qualities in a woman that I seemed to possess, short of the alpha male bravado bullshit. Her desire to be on the bike, sit quietly at home, and simply enjoy watching the world around her was equal to mine, something I had yet to find in any man or a woman other than myself.

I glanced at the gas station on the side of the road, and tilted my head to the side.

"Gas," I said as I pointed off in the distance.

I released the throttle, downshifted, and coasted until our speed had slowed considerably, the exhaust popping as the engine slowed the bike down to almost 30 miles per hour. As I leaned to the side and changed lanes, I noticed a lone bike at the gas pump. An older Harley Shovelhead which seemed to be in pretty damned good condition, the bike immediately caught my eye because it wasn't something I would normally see on a daily basis. As we pulled in behind the bike at the adjacent pump, a man walked out of the gas station and into the parking lot.

Immediately, he froze.

Fuck.

"Em, get off the bike and stand on the other side of the pump," I said through my teeth.

"What's wrong?" she asked.

"Em…"

"Yes, Sir," she said as she climbed off the bike.

I reached down and lowered the kickstand as I maintained eye contact with the man. After a long pause, he began to slowly walk our direction. He had a little swagger to his step, expressing either confidence or stupidity, I couldn't decide which. In his mid-thirties and muscular, but not as big as me, he seemed to be sizing me up as he walked toward his bike.

I needed to see the back of his cut.

His eyes locked on mine, and still taking the last few steps before he got on his bike, he turned his body to the right, but craned his neck over his shoulder to maintain eye contact. As he turned to the side I noticed his Shovelhead colors, but no lower rocker.

Thank God.

I exhaled, stepped over the seat, and reached for the pump. As I shifted my eyes toward his bike, he turned and spit in my direction.

"Got something you need to say?" I asked.

He spit toward me again, turned around, and reached for his ignition switch.

The last thing I wanted to do was start a war with anyone. If the Shovelheads were going to stitch a lower rocker on their cut it was one thing, but they had every right to have their MC as long as they weren't going to try and claim what was rightfully ours.

Allowing a man to disrespect me, my Ol' Lady, and my colors was another thing altogether.

I relaxed my grip, dropped the gas pump, and glared at him.

"Show respect, get respect, motherfucker," I said as I took a step toward him.

"Turn around and get back on that little softy of yours, Fury boy, or I'll make your Ol' Lady watch me whip your ass," he said over his shoulder.

When it comes to fighting on the street, not many men have morals, rules, or a conscience. I had always prided myself in being the exact opposite, and never hit a man who didn't have the ability to at least see it coming.

"Don't move," I said over my shoulder, making certain Em didn't get hurt in what was sure to be one hell of a fight.

"Get off the bike," I seethed as I turned around.

He released the ignition, stepped off the side of the bike, and turned to face me. He was a little bigger than I had originally thought, and appeared to be wearing nothing under his cut. His muscular arms were covered in tattoos, and his hands were now raised and ready to fight, giving me the go-ahead to do the same.

As he glared at me, he reached down, gripped the bottom of his cut, and pulled it off. I stood and stared in absolute shock as he hung it on the grip of his handlebars. A man's cut is to be protected at all times, never fall into the hands of an outsider, and never hit the ground. For him to have placed it where he did, in my opinion, was a huge mistake and nothing short of an invitation.

I stepped to him and all but lifted my chin, inviting him to take the first punch. He immediately fulfilled my request with an uppercut-cross combo.

I leaned rearward and both punches swung past me, throwing him slightly off balance.

This isn't my first fight, you dip-shit.

As he stumbled and attempted to regain his balance, I leaned in.

"Get him, Jackson," I heard Em holler.

Don't worry, babe, I'm going to.

I swung a left uppercut, connecting with the right side of his jaw. As he stumbled rearward I swung a right hook into his ribs, causing him to lean forward and at least attempt to grab his stomach. As his hands lowered, I pummeled his face with a series of straight right and left punches.

As he fell against his bike, he extended his arms to the rear, attempting to break his fall. One of his hands became tangled in the handlebars and he - and the bike - fell to the concrete. I'd never received any formal medical training in my days on earth, but I didn't have to be a doctor to see that he was unconscious. I reached down, picked up his cut, and gazed down at his face.

Not a single scar.

Well, here's your first, you disrespectful prick.

I raised my boot, swung my leg to the rear, and kicked him in the cheek as hard as I could with the toe of my boot. Before my boot was back on the ground, a cut on his face opened up and began to bleed.

"That'll take a dozen stitches," I said as I turned away.

"He didn't even hit you," Em said as I stepped around the pump.

"Most of 'em don't," I responded.

"What are you going to do with that?" she asked as she nodded her head toward the cut.

"Hang it in the garage," I said as I got on the bike.

"Get on, we're gonna get the fuck out of here before we get shot," I said.

I wasn't so stupid that I believed all fights ended when a man hit the ground. I had enough gas to get home, and that was all that mattered.

I folded the cut, placed it under my thigh, and started the bike.

The ride home was a quiet one, and after we pulled into the garage and parked, I pulled the cut from beneath my leg.

As I held it in the air and studied it, I was once again relieved there was no bottom rocker claiming territory. I proudly walked to my workbench, grabbed the hammer and four nails, and tacked the cut to the wall. After studying it for a moment, I walked to my cabinet, rifled through the cans of paint, and removed a half-full can of red paint. I shook the can in my hand, glanced at Em, and grinned.

As I raised the can in the air and painted a big red "X" on the back of the cut, she gave her voice of approval.

"I like it better now," she said.

"Me too," I nodded.

I stood admiring the cut, knowing I wouldn't tell anyone of the altercation if no one asked. I didn't need the recognition, sure didn't need to start a poll of opinions, and was never one to brag about fighting. What I had done had nothing to do with him being a Shovelhead, but it had everything to do with him being disrespectful.

He'd have a nice scar to remember me by, and he'd have hell to pay for losing his cut.

Me?

I still had my pride and Em was unharmed.

And that was all that mattered.

EMILY

August 9th, 2006

In high school, Laura Mora was the envy of every other girl. In middle school she had been the recipient of all of the taunting, hatred, and pranks of her classmates, primarily because of her name. Children can be so insensitive, and because her name rhymed, she was an easy target.

Laura Mora is a whore-a.

If I had a nickel for every time I heard that chant, I would be a rich woman. I suspected the teasing and taunting caused her to be a little more cautious with her choice of boyfriends, and as a result, by the time we were in high school, she was far from the whore everyone claimed she was.

Her boyfriend was the football quarterback, who was the stereotypical high school football quarterback. Vince Pegalli had dark hair, dark skin, and a lightly cleft chin. He was, by everyone's admission, perfect.

And he was Laura's.

I never teased her during middle school, and actually admired her for never losing her temper. When we moved on to high school, I experienced my first real envy, and it was directed at her.

And Vince.

They were the perfect couple. He was popular, attractive, lettered in every sport, and his letter jacket was covered with medals. She was the captain of the cheerleading squad and the envy of every girl in school.

During our senior year, someone put chicken guts in my locker as a joke. Although everyone told me it was Laura, I had a difficult time believing them, because I could not think of one thing that would cause her to want to do something so hateful. I carried a slight chip on my shoulder toward her for the rest of the year, and hoped one day I would be able to proudly walk past her with a Vince Pagalli of my own by my side.

I rolled onto my side, gazed at Jackson, and grinned. I had no idea what ever happened to Laura, but I really didn't care. If anyone had the ability to see through Jackson's tough exterior and into his true being, they'd be jealous of me for sure.

He shifted his eyes from the television, pushed the button on the remote, and placed it on the nightstand beside the bed. As he rolled onto his side and faced me, he grinned deep enough to produce his dimples. I smiled in return, and when I did, he pulled me onto his bare chest.

A few light kisses turned into an all-out make out session, which left my head spinning and my pussy wet. Jackson didn't disappoint me, in fact, he never did.

He rolled me onto my back, pulled the comforter to the side, and began kissing my shoulders and neck. Kisses on my neck had always driven me crazy, and Jackson kissing me on the neck caused my sexual desire to peak at an all-time high. Hoping he'd continue, and having no real reason to believe he wouldn't, I didn't dare oppose him or complain.

He moved his mouth along my neck, down to my shoulders, and along my upper chest, finally coming to a rest at my left nipple. As he playfully licked and kissed my nipple, I admired his muscular shoulders, arms, and chest.

"Relax," he breathed as he shifted his eyes to meet mine.

I did my best. It wasn't easy, but I fought not to squirm. He kissed and sucked each nipple, alternating back and forth, until I was an absolute mess. Moaning and chewing my bottom lip as I wondered where his next place of focus would be, I watched him as he glanced around my body, kissing various spots, including my hips.

Having reached a level of arousal that was difficult to hide, I continued to moan as his mouth cupped the top of my wet mound. His tongue immediately found my clit, and he began to tickle it with the tip of his tongue while he slowly slid his finger in and out of me.

Lost in the sexual satisfaction Jackson provided me, I continued to bite my lip in an effort to remain quiet. He had not instructed me to do so, nor had he advised me of anything for that matter, but in the absence of his command to do otherwise, I always chose silence.

As he continued to carefully and quietly lick my pussy, I raised my ass from the bed and arched my back. His hands cupped the bottom of my butt, holding me against his soft mouth. Being able to actually see him in the well-lit room was as much of a turn-on as anything, and seeing him do what he was doing was driving me insane.

A few more seconds of his sucking and licking my clit, I released my lower lip and groaned into the open room. The orgasm continued for as long as he licked me, which was a period of time long enough for me to exhaust myself fully.

As I collapsed onto the bed and sucked the air for my next breath, he glanced up and smiled. Still fighting against my heaving lungs, I looked down at him and wanted to say something, but realized doing so was going to be impossible. As I waited for my mind to return to the present, and my breathing to allow me to say what it was I wanted to say, he pulled himself upward and guided himself into me.

Holding my shoulders in his hands, and without speaking, his every movement and continued gentle touch said everything his mouth did not. Slowly working his hips back and forth, he moved his thickness in and out with precision, kissing me on the lips and neck the entire time.

Although having Jackson tie me up and fuck me gave me an all new level of excitement to look forward to, having him do what he was now doing elevated me to a different sexual platform altogether.

One that wasn't in the moment, but one that told me long after the sex was over, I would cling to the memories of the event, knowing it was not only special for some reason to him, but special in an equal manner to me. Dirty talk and the paddle were some of my favorite things on the rough side of sex, but this was something I had never really experienced.

He continued to kiss my neck and shoulders, holding my butt in the air and grinding against me slowly and passionately the entire time. As the sound of my wetness provided the music for his sexual dance to continue, he kissed and worked his hips in tune with my soul.

In a matter of minutes, I sank my fingertips into his back, opened my mouth, and bit into the muscle on his shoulder. As I moaned into his flesh he proceeded to push me over the edge and into a place only he could push me.

And I erupted into a heavenly state of being at the same time he erupted into me.

When all of the moaning stopped, he collapsed onto my chest and kissed my neck lightly. As our presence in the bedroom somehow changed from two people making love to become one loving sexual being, I must have fallen asleep.

And that night, in my dreams, I was the envy of every woman on earth.

JACK

August 23, 2006

Although I had never been one to allow people I didn't know or respect to have an influence my life, seeing what outsiders did or hearing their thoughts, and later considering them as an option wasn't unheard of. More often than not, I dismissed the actions, thoughts, or opinions of others, and did whatever it was I thought was best or appropriate.

"Some in the lifestyle look at it as an equivalent of marriage. Others see it as another level of commitment, a step higher on the ladder of commitment. I can't be any more committed to you, Em, and I'm pretty fucking sure you can't be any more committed to me, can you?" I asked.

"No, I sure can't," she responded from behind me as she gazed down at the table in front of the bench where I was seated.

"This isn't a conventional collar. I don't buy into all of that 'owned by' or 'property of' shit. You're a woman, an individual, and you'll never be property of mine. You and I have agreed to take this journey together, and I'm just as much yours as you are mine. Fuck, I don't know, I just want something we can share," I paused and glanced down at the two pieces of flat silver I had purchased.

"You know, people get married and share rings as a gesture in commitment, right?" I asked as I glanced upward.

She nodded her head, "Uh huh."

"Well, this will be kind of like that," I explained, "And for as long as we are together, we're never going to take 'em off, understood?"

"Yes, Sir," she responded.

"You make me happy, Em," I said as I shifted my eyes toward the bench.

"Thank you. You make me pretty fucking happy, too," she chuckled.

I slid the longer piece of silver in front of me, taped it to the steel table, and picked up the hammer. After selecting the appropriate letters from the uppercase steel stamps, I hammered the words and Roman numerals into the silver strap. I admired the craftsmanship for a moment, lifted the piece of freshly stamped metal from the bench, and stood from my seat.

In the center, our anniversary and our names were clearly marked. There would be no doubt to anyone who had an opportunity to see it what it represented. I held the soon to be necklace in front of her and allowed her to accept it as hers. As she took it from my hands, she smiled.

"I can't wait to wear it," she said softly, "How are you going to bend it?"

"I'll form it with a rubber hammer over that piece of scrap pipe I bought," I said as I tilted my head toward the table.

She glanced up and smiled. "I can't wait."

"Let me make mine," I said as I sat down on the bench.

I hammered the same inscription on a one inch wide sterling silver strap I had purchased for me to wear as a cuff.

I stood from the bench and stared down at the cuff admiringly.

JACKSON XI-XXI-MMVI EMILY

I extended my hand, took the piece of steel from her, and laid both straps on the bench beside the pieces of pipe. After a few swings from the rubber mallet, the silver was bent perfectly to form the necklace and the bracelet they were intended to be.

"Until our love for each other ends, and I pray it never does, don't remove this for any reason," I said as I opened the formed circle and stretched it around her neck.

"I won't," she said under her breath as I bent the strap into place.

I had purchased a half inch thick piece of sterling silver for her necklace and a one inch wide piece for my bracelet. The thickness of the metal made bending it by hand difficult, even for me. The quality of the jewelry was such that it would without a doubt last a lifetime

"Here," I said as I handed her the bracelet.

"What?" she murmured.

"Slide it onto my wrist, and just turn it to the side…" I said as I held my left arm in front of her.

She slid the bracelet over my wrist, twisted it into place, and gazed down at it for a long moment.

"You won't remove this, either?" she asked.

"I don't intend to," I said as I admired it.

"Promise?" she asked.

"I can't promise it won't come off, Em," I paused and cleared my throat.

"Listen, I don't *ever* make a promise I can't keep. So I can only promise you I don't *intend* to take it off or allow it to be removed, understand?" I said in a soft tone.

Still gazing down at my wrist, she responded, "Yes, Sir."

As she glanced upward and her eyes met mine, a tear rolled down her cheek. It had been three months that we had been together, but I wasn't counting. All I knew was how she made me feel, and as far as I was concerned, Em was the only woman on earth, and the only thing in my life that truly mattered.

My brothers in the club remained close, but the bond, the love, and the relationship was much different with Em. Having my MC Brothers in my life allowed me to exist and feel as if I had the family I never had a kid.

Having Em in my life allowed me to begin, for the first time, truly living life.

"I love you, Emily," I said as I wiped the tear from her cheek.

It was the first time I had told her I loved her. She inhaled a choppy breath, exhaled, and began to softly cry.

"Well, you're late," she sobbed as she reached to wipe the tears from her face.

I wrapped my arms around her and pulled her into my chest, rubbing my hands along the small of her back as I held her in my arms.

"What's that?" I whispered, confused by her response.

"You're late," she sobbed, "I've been loving you for a while now."

I held her in my arms for some time, almost afraid to let her go, and equally afraid to speak. As we rocked back and forth in each other's arms, I realized even more clearly that living life without Em would be impossible. The gesture of the bracelet and necklace were more for her than they were for me.

I knew how I felt, and leaving her would kill me.

She allowed me to see for the first time that not only is love blind, but luck is even more so, and it was by mere luck that we happened upon each other.

As we rocked back and forth in the center of the garage, our teetering soon turned into a slow dance step. And, as we danced to a song that wasn't playing, on a dance floor that didn't exist, I fell a little more in love with the woman I was certain I would spend every day of my life loving no less than I loved at that exact moment.

I closed my eyes, pressed her head to my chest, and continued to dance as if it were my last day on earth.

Yet, I felt as if it were my first.

EMILY

September 13, 2006

I finally came to the realization I didn't need to do anything but exist to keep Jackson happy with me. I really don't recall if it came as an epiphany one day, or if it was something that happened over the course of our time together, but one day things in my mind changed. I'm sure Jackson didn't see any changes, but at least in my mind, I saw significant changes in my perception of life, myself, and our relationship's ability to go the distance without effort.

Now simply doing what made me feel complete and whole left me believing satisfying Jackson required nothing more than allowing nature to take its course. As long as the world kept spinning, we were both extremely happy.

But as happy as I was, I wanted just a little bit more.

"Jesus, Em. I'm telling you. One of these days," he said as he wagged his fork toward me.

"You likey?" I grinned.

"You know, I've heard of this stuff, but I've never eaten it," he said as he shoved a forkful of the eggs into his mouth.

Seeing him so genuinely happy over something as simple as a meal satisfied me to no end. Cooking, in itself, satisfied me, and cooking for him satisfied me even more so. It wasn't a rare occurrence for him to eat what I had prepared and dislike it, it actually had *never* happened. Some meals he seemed to like much more than others, and without a doubt, this was one of them.

"So what's in this sauce?" he asked.

"You don't want to know, you'll probably never want them again," I responded as I pressed my fork through the bottom of the English muffin.

I felt no need to tell him making the hollandaise sauce was something that took several evenings of practice, ruining multiple batches before I figured out the perfect temperature, how to add the butter, and the need to stir in a few teaspoons of hot water when it got too thick. It was a time consuming process, and patience was key in the preparation.

The repeated evenings of practice allowed me on this particular Saturday morning to make the perfect sauce for our eggs Benedict and look like a true professional.

"Seriously, I want to know," he said as he shook his egg filled fork over his plate.

"Egg yolks, butter, Worchester sauce, lemon juice, white pepper, a little water, and a lot of time," I responded.

It really did taste good, and although I realized it wasn't necessarily good for Jackson and his healthy diet, it was something we could enjoy together from time to time.

"Add it to the list," he said as he shoveled the last bite into his mouth.

"Is there more?" he asked.

I nodded my head as I stood from my seat.

"Let me get it for you," I said.

"I'll get it," he said as he stood.

"Just let me do it," I sighed as I reached for his plate, "And what list?"

"For your restaurant, I'm telling you, this stuff would make a puppy pull a freight train. The fellas would kill someone for a plate of this shit," he said as he followed me to the stove.

"I don't want anyone to get hurt," I chuckled as I placed the English muffins in the toaster.

After preparing his plate, I handed it to him and followed him into the dining room. Walking in front of me, he picked up one of the English muffins and stuffed the entire thing into his mouth, egg and all. As he licked the hollandaise sauce from his fingers, I shook my head in what I wanted him to see as disbelief, but was actually pride.

Jackson made me feel good about myself. I had never been a woman who lacked self-esteem, and actually prided myself in being just the opposite, but how Jackson made me feel as a result of what he did, what he said, and how he treated me in and out of the bedroom made me feel like I was truly the most important person in his life.

And I knew from knowing him that he wasn't a man who was easily impressed.

He continuously praised me, be it verbally or from something as ridiculous as shoving an entire English muffin, Canadian bacon slice, and a baked egg into his mouth all at once. His constant praise allowed me to understand just what I meant to him, and being *that* woman was all I ever wanted in life.

Being that woman to *him*…

Explaining how it made me feel was impossible. It was something that had to be experienced. I often felt sorry for the women I saw with men when I went shopping, or as we rode together in the poker runs, wondering just how they felt, knowing there was no way their man was as good as Jackson was. I felt blessed to have him in the capacity I had him, and thanked God each day for the place he had taken in my life.

"We've talked about this a while back," I said as I poked the last piece of my muffin with my fork.

"What's that?" he asked as he shoveled the breakfast into his mouth.

"Well, summer's leaving, and it's almost October…" I said, pausing to allow him to pay attention to my request.

He glanced up from his plate and grinned.

"Your parents?" he asked.

I nodded my head, giddy that he remembered. My mother's birthday was on October 8th, and I had planned on driving to Montana to see her and my father. Having Jackson go with me, meet my parents, and see where I grew up would mean the world to me. I mentioned it once, and feared bringing it up again, but felt if I didn't he sure wasn't going to.

No differently than any other girl, I wanted all of my concerns and problems to simply take care of themselves, and never actually have to address them. In my mind, mentioning it once to Jackson was the same as begging him to go, and his not remembering the date, location of the city, or why we were going would indicate he had no desire to go, and his lack of mentioning it as the date approached would do nothing but prove it.

But that wasn't the case.

He remembered.

"October 8th, isn't that when you said her birthday was?" he asked as he wiped the little remaining hollandaise sauce from his plate with his finger.

"Holy crap, you remembered the date?" I gasped.

"Well, you fucking told me. Jesus, Em, I'm not a fucking dumb ass," he chuckled.

"Well, I didn't think you'd remember," I said.

"Thanks, you little shit. Maybe after this breakfast settles, I'll teach you a little lesson," he said as he stood from his seat.

"You done?" he asked.

"I'll get it," I said as I pointed toward his chair.

"I'll get it. Hand me your plate," he said.

I handed him my plate, grinned, and did my best to relax. I was a little more excited than I expected I would be. The thought of him meeting my parents made me nervous, happy, and extremely content all at the same time. I had told my parents about him, and was completely truthful regarding who he was, and what he was like.

Having parents who were not judgmental, open-minded, and ultimately sought only what was in my best interest was a true blessing. As Jackson walked into the dining room, he stared down at his hand as he extended his fingers and counted.

"8ᵗʰ is a Wednesday. We can leave on the Friday, Saturday, whatever you want," he said as he sat down.

"I love you," I said.

"Well, I fucking love you too. Just let me know when we're going," he said with a nod as he reached for his cup of coffee.

"I work the Friday before. Maybe if I pack Saturday we could leave Sunday, there'll be like no traffic at all," I shrugged.

"Sunday sounds good, Em," he responded.

I stood from my seat, walked to where he sat, and wrapped my arms around his neck as I stood behind him. Nothing could make me happier than spending the rest of my life with him and I looked forward to what each day brought us. I now looked forward to the arrival of Thanksgiving and Christmas, and making a huge meal for him, his friends, and possibly even his sister.

Although he spoke of his sister often, and went to see her from time to time, he was very protective of her. I hadn't met her yet, but he assured me I would soon. I realized as she was the only family he ever had that he held her in a different place in his heart than most men held their sisters. In time, I was sure his sister and I would be the best of friends.

"Now, I remembered about your mother's birthday, did you remember about today?" he asked.

I remembered nothing.

I gazed into the kitchen, rocked back and forth on the balls of my feet, and held him in my arms. As I searched through my mind for any recollection of anything he had told me, he laughed and cleared his throat.

"Got a club meeting about the Shovelheads, remember? Told ya I'd be gone most all afternoon, if not maybe into tonight," he explained.

"Oh, *that*. Yeah, I remembered," I lied as I rested my chin against his shoulder

He reached around, grabbed the back of my neck in his hand, pulled me forward, and almost flipping me onto the table.

He pressed his mouth against my ear and exhaled a long sigh.

"You didn't remember shit," he whispered.

"You're right," I admitted, finding slight humor in the irony of it all.

"Well, I'm going to go change the oil in my sled. See if you can remember to be here when I get home tonight," he said as he stood.

I narrowed my gaze and pushed my hands against his chest.

"I'll always be here when you get home," I said as I shoved him.

"And eventually, I'll always come home," he said as he leaned forward and puckered his lips.

Jackson wasn't a man I had simply fallen in love with, he had become a part of my inner being. No differently than my lungs, heart, kidneys, and liver were all needed to keep me alive, Jackson was now a necessary part of my existence. Without him, I was certain to wither and die.

With him in my life, I continued to grow, no differently than the rose bush we had planted; becoming slightly closer to heaven with each passing day.

"Promise?" I asked.

He nodded his head, "Promise."

And if there was one thing that I could always count on with Jackson, it was that he kept his promises.

No matter what.

JACK

I rarely reached a point that I got drunk, and generally stopped drinking long before I had to worry about it. Not unlike anything else, there always seemed to be a time that whatever I held in my 'yet bag' eventually escaped, and the typical day turned into a not-so-typical one. This particular night was one of those nights.

"Well, it's pretty fuckin' sad if you ask me. I ain't liking it that we're gonna have to make a stand against these pricks," Sarge said as he pushed himself away from the bar.

"We gotta do what we gotta do, Sarge," I said under my breath.

"I'm gonna piss and get the fuck out of here," he muttered as he walked toward the bathroom.

"Fuh…fuh…fuckers ain't goh…goh…got no fuh…fucking respect, kah…kah…Killer," Chili said as he finished his drink.

"Sure don't," I agreed.

The entire MC had met at a bar to discuss the problems with the Shovelheads MC, who had been caught on three separate occasions flying a bottom rocker claiming our territory as theirs. It was undisputed that the territory was ours, and every other club in existence recognized it as such, and chose to set up shop somewhere else. Their blatant

147

disrespect toward our club, my brothers, and our repeated requests to stand down had done the damage, and now it was time they pay the price.

We voted to provide a final warning, and if they were seen again wearing a lower rocker on their cut, it was agreed we would be in an all-out war.

When rival clubs declared war, and I hoped we didn't reach that point, there were no rules. Upon being in each other's presence, guns, knives, clubs, and chains took the place of fists, and generally a meeting by chance ended up in several deaths.

I took an oath when I joined the club, and as the club had held up their end of the bargain, I felt I needed to hold up mine. As far as I was concerned, the oath was a promise, and I didn't intend to ever break a promise. I would do whatever it took to keep my brothers in the club from harm, and to protect and preserve the colors I proudly wore as a fully patched in member of the MC.

"I'm gonna guh...guh...get the fuh...fuh...fuck outta here," Chili said as he stood from his seat.

"Ain't drunk yet for the night?" I asked, realizing after I had spoken it made very little sense.

"Not yuh...yuh...yet," he grinned as he slapped me on the back, "wuh...wuh...wouldn't be stuh...stuh...stutterin' if...I wuh...wuh...was."

I nodded my head and waved.

As I gazed blankly at my beer, Sarge slapped his hands on the bar beside me, startling me slightly. As I spun around, he chuckled and slapped his hand against my back.

"I'm rolling out. There's a few of the fellas still here playin' pool, you alright to ride?" he asked.

I shook my head. "Not even close," I said over my shoulder.

"Well, sober up before you get outta here. If you need, there's a hotel next door," he said as he pointed toward the door.

"I'll sober up," I said, "Gotta get home to for Em. Waiting…"

"What can I get you two?" the bartender asked.

"I'm headin' out, get him a coffee and a burger, no cheese," Sarge said as he slapped his hand against my back.

"Fear the act of no man…" he said as he walked toward the door.

I raised my finger in the air as I swiveled my stool in his direction, "For the fury of hell is yours…"

I sat at the bar for some time, and eventually, my coffee and burger arrived. As I reached for the burger, Lucky sat down beside me.

I glanced over my left shoulder, recognized him, and exhaled a sigh of disgust as I lifted the burger from my plate.

"So, Killer, what about them 'heads? Fuckers gonna get what they deserve, huh?" he asked.

I bit into my burger and shrugged my shoulders. He was part of the reason I was as drunk as I was. Over the course of the afternoon, someone continued to buy me shots of whiskey, and, upon realizing I was inebriated, I asked the bartender who my generous friend was. His response was to point at Lucky, which caused me to stop accepting the shots.

The effects of the alcohol, however, continued to creep up on me.

As did their provider.

He had asked me no less than half a dozen times what I would do if I encountered one of the Shovelheads wearing a lower rocker claiming our territory. My response was the same each time; a shrug of my shoulders and a short stare.

I figured if he had to ask, he sure didn't need to know.

"Lemme get a Budweiser for me and my buddy," he said as he raised his hand in the air.

"Ain't drinking any more. I got to sober up and ride," I said as I wiped my hands on my napkin.

"Damn, I drank one to one with you on those shots, Killer. You tellin; me I can out drink ya?" he asked.

"Gimme that beer," I said as I waved my hand at the bartender.

"That's what I'm talking about," he said as he slapped the edge of the bar with his open hand.

"Fine, I'll drink your beer," I said, knowing there was no way I'd let him out drink me.

I finished my burger with hope of it providing a little bit of a buffer between me and the drunkenness developing within me.

As soon as the beer arrived, I tilted it toward him and drank half the bottle in one swallow. Lucky followed close behind, his mouth running every second it wasn't swallowing beer.

"So those fuckers wearing that rocker on their cut, it's fucking on if we see 'em, huh?' he asked.

I nodded my head and finished my beer.

I glanced over my shoulder toward the pool table. A few of the members and one of the prospects stood by the table shooting a game of pool.

"See them fuckers behind ya?" I asked.

He turned around, gazed toward the pool table for a minute, and turned around.

"Yeah," he responded.

"I'd take a bullet for any of 'em, and I can't even tell ya their names right now. That's how I feel about it," I said as I turned toward the bar.

"But what about those fuckin' Shovelheads?" he asked, "They're askin' for it by flyin' that rocker, huh?"

"Sure are," I nodded.

"Two more," he barked at the bartender.

"I need to quit," I said, realizing the beer I had just finished was doing me no good whatsoever.

He cocked one eyebrow and chuckled, "Don't let me outdrink ya, Killer."

"Fuck it, bring it on," I said as I waved my hand toward the bar.

"So, why they call ya Killer?" he asked.

"Why not?" I shrugged.

"There's got to be a story," he said, "I wanna hear it."

"Well, I ain't lookin' to tell it, so you'll just have to leave here mad," I chuckled.

"Well, when you're ready to tell it, I'm ready to hear it," he responded.

"Duly fuckin' noted," I nodded.

The bartender placed two more beers in front of us. Disgusted at the thought of another drink, I stared at the bottle beside me as if it were poison.

"So, what if we're pulling out of here and we see one of them fuckers?" he asked.

I shrugged my shoulders.

"Shit, I'm gonna out drink the Killer," Lucky said as he reached for his beer.

I shook my head, reached for the beer and downed it in one gulp. After spinning my stool half way around, I slid off the edge and stumbled toward the bathroom. As I pissed and realized I was too drunk to even stand, I called Em and told her she could come join me in the hotel for the night, but riding home wasn't an option.

I stumbled back to the bar, sat down beside Lucky, and stared at the wall. Relieved my drunken night was coming to a close, and knowing a good night's sleep would be enough to bring me back to my senses, I gazed down at my boots and hoped the Shovelheads had enough common sense to take Sarge's final warning as what it was intended to be.

The last straw.

"So, seriously, what if one of them fuckers…" Lucky began.

"Listen you little fucker," I said as I spun around in my stool, "It's no fucking secret I don't like you. But if one of them fuckers came in here with a lower rocker claiming my MC's territory on it, I'd take a bullet for you. And, if I had to, I'd kill one of 'em, or all of 'em for that matter. You know why?"

His Adam's apple raised and lowered as he swallowed.

"Why's that?" he asked.

"Because by wearing that rocker, they're saying they're willing to kill us. I don't like it, and yeah, just like kids on the school yard, I wish we could all get along. But some people just don't play well with others. And I got a few dozen brothers, a sister, and a good god damned Ol' Lady who expect me to protect 'em, and if that means taking out one of them cock suckers before they try to kill the ones I love, well so fuckin' be it," I growled.

"Now kick fuckin' rocks," I said as I pointed to the door.

He nodded his head as if he was satisfied my explanation was sufficient. After damned near falling off his barstool, he sauntered to the door, turned, waved, and gave me shitty little grin.

After Em showed up, we rented a hotel room and shoved my bike in beside the bed.

As I gazed at my bike and slowly fell off into a drunken sleep, I wondered just what the future for the club might hold, and prayed that the Shovelheads had enough common sense to do what they had to do to prevent any bloodshed.

Wars are never won, they're only fought.

And personally, I preferred to only fight the fights I felt I could win.

EMILY

October 4ᵗʰ, 2006

I stood at the stove cooking half a pound of sausage for what I had learned to be Jackson's second favorite breakfast: a baked egg casserole. A combination of eggs, potatoes, cheese, sausage, mushrooms, onions, bell peppers, flour, and milk, the concoction after cooked was quite satisfying, and easy to eat. As far as he was concerned, it was a meal in itself, and he loved eating the leftovers.

Only one day stood between us and hitting the road to see my parents. I hadn't seen them in six months, and although it seemed like a short time, it was in that amount of time Jackson and I had become inseparable.

I drained the grease from the skillet, added the sausage to the mixture, and poured it into the casserole dish. After placing it into the oven, I leaned over the kitchen sink to clean up what little mess I had made. Cleaning up as I cooked was a habit I more than likely inherited from my mother, who was always cooking and cleaning. As a little girl, regardless of what point I ever encountered her in the process of cooking, the kitchen was always clean. She made it a point to pick up after herself and clean as she cooked, never leaving a mess for anyone to see.

As I tidied up the kitchen, I wondered just how much of my mother was within me. She was more than likely an older submissive version of me. Cooking, cleaning, sewing, and waiting on my father hand and foot were common traits of hers, and far from typical of what I had seen of other mothers. As I gazed out the kitchen window at the rose bush we had planted, I laughed to myself at the thought of my mother and me being so much alike.

Gazing blankly at the bush and sinking into a sense of love, family, and complete bliss, I thanked God for Jackson and everything he provided me. While I relished in my thoughts, a dozen men wearing military type gear and carrying rifles stormed into the back yard. Scared beyond belief, I opened my mouth and tried to scream.

Petrified, and more than likely in complete shock, my tongue didn't follow my brain's instructions. I swallowed heavily as they continued to surround our home.

"Jackson, people are in the yard!" I eventually screamed.

"What?' he yelled from the back room.

I turned and ran toward the hallway. They looked like men in the military, and there were dozens of them, all armed with guns. I didn't know what else to do, so I began screaming at the top of my lungs.

"Help!" I screamed as I ran toward the back bedroom.

Jackson met me in the middle of the hallway wide eyed and wondering what had happened. As I attempted to catch my breath and explain, the windows began to break, the doors were kicked in, and everyone began screaming at once.

"Get down, get down, get the fuck on the floor!" a man screamed at Jackson as he pointed a gun directly at his head.

They were everywhere, screaming, pointing guns in front of them, and running in every direction.

"Jackson," I cried, "What's happening?"

"Get on the fucking floor!" a man demanded as he pointed a gun in my face.

"You fucking touch her, and I'll god damned kill you," I heard Jackson scream.

"Jackson!" I blubbered as I waved my hands at my sides.

I was scared, confused, and had no idea what to do.

Jackson was on the floor beside me, down on his knees with a gun at the back of his head. The man pushed his knee between Jackson's shoulders and pulled his hands behind his back while another pointed a gun at his chest.

"Stop it, you're hurting him," I cried.

"Keep your fucking hands where I can see them," another man screamed as he pointed a gun in my face.

"Are there any weapons in the house?" A man asked Jackson.

"Ma'am, get on the ground…"

"Clear…"

"Are there any weapons in the house?"

"Ma'am, you need to get down on the ground. Do you have a weapon?"

"Leave her alone, I'll kill the entire lot of you if she's even fucking touched," Jackson bellowed.

"Are there any weapons in the house?"

"Clear…"

"Ma'am, get on the god damned ground."

I watched as two men grabbed Jackson's arms and lifted him from the floor.

"Come on, Shephard."

"All clear…"

"I want to exercise my right to remain silent, and I want an attorney," Jackson said as they hoisted him to his feet.

"Same goes for her," he hollered as they dragged him toward the door.

"Don't answer their questions, Em," he yelled as another man pushed his way past Jackson and entered the house.

"You little cock sucker, I knew it," Jackson said as he kicked his foot toward the man.

"If any one of you cock suckers touches a hair on her head, I'll fucking kill you," Jackson shouted as they dragged him through the door.

"Ma'am, get down on the floor," a man in front of me demanded.

"I want to exercise my right to…uhhm…to remain silent. And I want to speak to an attorney," I said, surprised at how calm I seemed to be.

In hindsight, I was probably in shock.

"Ma'am, I'm not going to tell you again, get down on the floor. Do you have any weapons in the home?" he asked.

The tears began to roll down my cheeks. Everything I had dreamed of, everything I wanted, and the only man I had ever loved were all beginning to spin in my head, and I had no idea of what was truly happening. The sounds surrounding me became dull, distant, and impossible to comprehend.

And, for some reason, I remembered nothing until two men were screaming questions in my face while I was handcuffed to a table in what I was told were the ATF offices.

And I began to cry.

JACK

October 4th, 2006

My entire world came crashing down in front of me as the ATF, US Marshalls, and the local SWAT team stormed into our home. Now, being questioned by a man I never liked, had a difficult time trusting, and rarely even spoke to was becoming harder and harder to accept as reality.

"Mr. Shephard, I'm Special Agent Blackburn with the Bureau of Alcohol, Tobacco, Firearms, and Explosives. For a few years, you've known me as Lucky. You, Sir, are in a world of shit," he said as he paced back and forth in the small interrogation room.

"I suggest you cooperate," the other agent sighed as he stood from his seat.

"Where's Emily?" I asked.

"She's in the other interrogation room," Blackburn responded.

"They're pounding on her right now. She's going to give you, the club, and every one of your brothers up, women always do," Blackburn chuckled.

"Meant what I said earlier, if any one of you pricks touches her, I'll fucking kill you," I hissed.

"See that?" Blackburn said as he pointed up toward the center of the

159

upper wall opposite of where I was seated.

"That's a camera. And it records sound. And you just threatened to kill and ATF agent. You're double fucked, Shephard," he said.

I shook my head and pulled against the handcuffs.

"Where's my attorney?" I asked.

"Must be stuck in traffic," Blackburn shrugged.

"Now, I'm going to ask questions, and you're going to answer them, understand?" he asked.

I didn't respond.

Blackburn rested his hand on the leather badge holder that was clipped to his belt. With his free hand, he rubbed the stubble of a few days growth of beard as he paced back and forth.

"You've been indicted for conspiring to commit murder, using a firearm in furtherance of a crime, making a terroristic threat, dealing firearms without a license, money laundering, and failure to file federal tax returns for the last five years. In short, *Killer*, you're fucked. Now, you're best bet will be to admit to your crimes, and Pratt and I will have a talk with the US Attorney and see if we can get a departure on your sentence. Right now, with the RICO Act, you're looking at life," he paused and fixed his eyes on mine.

"I know it's a difficult thing to grasp right now, but you need to think of how you want to proceed. You haven't got much time, and our capacity to modify your sentence ends when this case is filed, right Pratt?" he said as he turned to face the other agent.

Pratt nodded his head, "Right."

"So…" Blackburn paused, turned to face me, and cocked one eyebrow, "What are you thinking?"

I did my best to shrug my shoulders, pulling against the handcuffs as I did so.

"Me? I'm thinking if you get Pratt here to uncuff me, I'll beat your little ass. That's what I'm thinking," I said flatly.

"We'll give you some time to think," Pratt said, "You need a drink or anything?"

I shook my head, "No. I'm done letting ATF agents buy me drinks. It never ends well. Next time you two pricks come in here, an attorney better be with you. I'm done talking."

As they walked out of the room, everything began to make sense. Blackburn - aka Lucky - was an ATF agent, and he had spent the last two years trying to make a case against the MC. As I sat and gazed down at the table, I wondered how many of my brothers were handcuffed in various rooms in the building, and hoped no matter how many there were, that they had the ability to be as resistant as me to answer any questions.

I closed my eyes, pulled against the handcuffs, and eventually relaxed, resting my forearms on the steel table in front of me. I prayed that Em was holding up well under the pressure they were sure to be putting on her, and that she would be able to understand what had truly happened and not hold it against me. Regardless of the long list of bullshit charges that Blackburn had blurted out, all I had done was express my willingness to protect the people in my life who were important to me.

The men and two woman who I loved enough to sacrifice myself to protect. I sighed heavily, glanced up at the camera, and extended my middle finger. As I raised my hand in the air as high as the handcuffs would allow, flying the universal sign of 'fuck you', I grinned.

NWA said it best.

Fuck the police.

EMILY

October 28ᵗʰ, 2006

It had been two weeks since they arrested Jackson. Although they didn't charge me with any crimes, they claimed they could have. At first I was terrified, but after talking to an attorney I was pretty confident they couldn't charge me with any crimes whatsoever. It was now Sunday, the only day they allowed me to see Jackson.

Seeing him in the Federal Holding Facility wasn't an easy thing for me; glass separated us, and I wasn't able to touch him. Seeing him wearing the orange suit seemed strange because he looked like a common criminal, and regardless of what they were saying about him, he was far from common, and he was not a criminal.

"Good morning, Miss Stewart," the guard said as I dropped my car keys and purse into the basket.

"Good morning," I responded, surprised that he'd remembered my name.

"Just walk though slowly," he said as he pointed to the metal detector.

I held my arms to my sides and walked through the contraption, expecting it to beep. After passing through without incident, I turned to face the guard and grinned.

"Have a nice day," he said as he handed me the basket.

163

"Thank you," I said.

The guards at the facility were far more pleasant than the ATF agents who arrested us. I had always believed law enforcement officers were hired to *serve and protect* and not harass, ridicule and lie. The level of unprofessionalism I witnessed from the agents on the day we were arrested was beyond what most US citizens would even believe, and I expected not many realized just how arrogant and rude the ATF agents really were.

As I walked down the long corridor I cringed at the thought of seeing Jackson while he was incarcerated. Although I fully realized I would wait for him as long as I had to, seeing him on the other side of the glass wall was difficult for me.

Knowing I had no other choice was easy for me to understand, but not something I naturally accepted as being what was best for either of us.

Jackson wasn't someone I could ever replace. Not having him at home left me feeling empty, alone, and without purpose. I had spent the last two weeks cooking, cleaning, and crying. I hadn't even returned to work, fearing I may have a breakdown if I even attempted to talk to anyone about what had happened.

Strangely, none of Jackson's brothers from the club came around or even asked about him, and from what little was reported in the newspaper, Jackson was the only man the ATF had arrested. Maybe it was some type of biker protocol, but if you asked me, I felt his brothers in the club were more like shitty friends or associates, and much less like the true brothers he believed them to be.

"Shephard?" the guard asked as I opened the door into the visitation room.

I nodded my head and attempted to force a smile.

"Booth "A"," the guard said as he pointed to the steel chair bolted to the floor in front of the glass partition.

I sat down in the chair and gazed through the thick glass which was reinforced with strands of wire. After a few minutes of staring blankly into the opposite room, I saw Jackson approaching out of my peripheral.

I smiled and pressed my hand against the glass. As he sat down, he did the same.

"How you holding up?" he asked.

"Rock solid," I responded, doing my best to hide the fact I was lying.

"Yeah, me too," he grinned.

His beard was thicker than normal, and his hair was slightly longer than it had been on the previous week. Normally, he trimmed his beard every two or three days, leaving nothing but short stubble on his face. Now, his beard was fuller and resembled an actual beard, which seemed odd. Seeing the changes in his appearance provided affirmation that changes were taking place in his life as well as mine.

"Is everyone leaving you alone?" I asked.

"Babe, they've still got me in solitary confinement. I'm all alone. Probably best," he said.

I fought against the growing pressure in my throat and swallowed heavily. It was very difficult seeing him in this manner, and not anything I would ever become comfortable with.

"Well, at least nobody's messing with you," I said.

"I'll be fine whenever they let me out into population, believe me," he said.

"Any of the fellas stop by?" he asked.

My throat tightened. I wanted to lie and tell him they had all stopped

165

by, worried about his well-being, and that they had been taking donations to assemble a legal team capable of crushing the charges against him, and that he'd be free in no time to speak of. Instead, the scared little girl in me surfaced, and my lower lip began to quiver.

He gazed down at the floor and shook his head.

"It ain't easy for any of us," he said as he shifted his eyes upward.

"You get my cell phone and stuff?" he asked.

Still biting my lower lip, I nodded my head.

"Any of 'em text or call?" he asked.

I remembered the items they provided me at the front desk after he was arrested: his cell phone, keys, wallet, and his silver cuff. As I shook my head from side-to-side, my lower lip freed itself from my teeth and I began to sob.

I shook my head and wiped my eyes.

"I'm sorry," I said as I tried desperately to keep from crying.

"Em…"

"Em…"

"Emily."

I wiped my eyes, took a shallow breath, and glanced upward.

"Yes, Sir?"

"You got the key to the safe deposit box, right?" he asked.

I nodded my head.

"There's about eighty grand in there in cash. I want you to use for whatever you need to. To survive through this," he said.

My eyes widened and my heart filled with a little more hope.

"We could get you a real attorney, one who is mean, and tough, and…" I blurted excitedly.

He slapped his hand against the glass.

"No. Listen to me, Em. That money isn't going to some fucking attorney. Do you understand me?" he said.

"Yes, Sir," I responded, "But…"

"But nothing, Em. But fucking nothing. I've got a court appointed attorney. I'll be fine. I set that money aside for whenever I might need it. And now, I need it for you. Keep paying the rent, keep your spirits up, and this'll be over before you know it, okay?" he said as he raised his hand to the glass.

I raised my hand to the glass and situated it to meet the outline of his.

"Okay," I said.

"Over before you know it," he said.

"Promise?" I asked.

He nodded his head, "Promise."

JACK

November 20th, 2006

After filing a motion for a right to a speedy trial, the court date was set for the end of November. According to my attorney, it was a case of circumstantial evidence, primarily testimony, and a few recorded conversations. Strangely, the recording of the night I stated I was willing to kill a member of the Shovelheads wasn't legible, and therefore wasn't included in evidence.

The remaining charges were dropped, and according to my attorney, were simply bullshit used to persuade me to plead guilty to the only offense they intended to charge me with.

Conspiracy to commit murder.

My attorney seemed confident without the recording, and without anyone to corroborate the story of the night in question, that the trial would be short, without any surprises, and I would be a free man when it was all over.

Eager to get it all behind me, and disappointed at the US Attorney's office for filing a motion to keep Em out of the courtroom, I sat through the trial alone, short of the presence of my sister. Surprised very little by the lack of attendance on Hell's Fury's part, it still disappointed me greatly that the men I perceived as brothers were all absent when I felt

I needed them the most.

According to my attorney, the motion filed to keep Em out of the courtroom was done as a tactic to keep me agitated and therefore easier for the US Attorney to irritate on the witness stand. My irritated nature would then support their claim of my temper and state of mind as the killer they represented me as being.

Claiming they may decide to have Em testify against me, as she wasn't protected by the clause preventing wives from testifying against their husbands, she was prohibited from observing any of the testimony in the trial.

After having sat through the trial laced with lies, lost recordings, and false accusations, I was grateful she wasn't in attendance.

"And when you questioned him, specifically what was asked, Special Agent Blackburn?" the US Attorney asked.

"I made reference to the rival club, the Shovelheads, by simply mentioning there had been discussions regarding them wearing a lower rocker claiming territory," Blackburn responded.

"And the defendant turned to me and offered his resolution to the statement," Blackburn continued.

"And, according to your earlier testimony, the lower rocker as you called it, was nothing more than a piece of cloth with the Kansas embroidered on it. Is that correct?" the US Attorney asked.

"That is correct," Blackburn responded.

"Continue. The defendant's resolution to the rival club wearing a piece of cloth with the name of the state in which they resided was what?" the US Attorney asked.

"That he would kill each and every one of them," Blackburn responded.

You worthless little bastard.

"And how did you react?" the US Attorney asked.

"Contrary to my training and instructions from the main office, I was actually in fear for my life, Sir. It was no secret his road name was Killer, and he was prepared to kill anyone who opposed him," Blackburn responded.

I swear, if I ever get my hands on you...

"Road name? Can you expand, and explain to the jury what that means?" the US Attorney asked.

"Absolutely. When an individual prospects for an outlaw club, they are trying out for a spot, say, no differently than trying out for a football or baseball team, say, as a free agent. During that process, every move, reaction, personality trait, everything is observed by the club. In the end, if accepted as a member, the recruit is given his colors, or *patch* as it is referred to, and a club name. The name is called a *road name*, and it is indicative of the man who wears it," Blackburn explained.

"And his was Killer?" the US Attorney asked.

"Yes, Sir," Blackburn said with a nod.

"And were you given a name? When you were patched in, as you said," the US Attorney asked.

"Yes, Sir, I was," he responded.

"And may I ask what it might have been?"

"Lucky," Blackburn responded.

"Interesting. Would you care to share why that particular name was chosen?" the US Attorney asked.

"One night at the clubhouse, while acting in the capacity as an undercover agent, and attempting to be accepted as a prospect, we were all playing poker. I had won no less than half a dozen hands, and everyone called me lucky. The name just stuck," he responded.

You lying little prick. You got that name after you wrecked that little Sportster, and made it out alive.

I tapped my attorney on the shoulder and whispered in his ear.

"He's fucking lying," I said.

"What did you expect?" my attorney responded.

"So, based on your observation as a trained ATF agent, what would your testimony be regarding the earning of road names by a patched in member be?" the US Attorney asked.

"Without a doubt, they are indicative of the who the man is, and what the club perceives him as being," he responded.

"An accurate description?" the US Attorney asked.

"Yes, Sir," he responded.

"No further questions," the US Attorney said.

"Your witness," the judge said.

"No further questions, your honor," my attorney stated.

"You're not going to ask him about the lies?" I whispered.

"His testimony is made under oath. It is assumed everything he is saying is the truth, and I can't question him regarding your opinion that it's a lie. It's for the jury to decide," he responded.

"My opinion? It isn't a fucking opinion, he's lying," I said through my teeth.

"The United States rests, your honor," the US Attorney said flatly.

My attorney glared at me, stood from his seat, and made his statement.

"The defense rests, your honor," he said.

Feeling cheated, and incapable of saying what I felt I needed to say in the manner I needed to say it, I was frustrated by the Federal

Government's procedures, policies, and the rules of law regarding how testimony was treated, accepted, and processed.

After receiving instructions regarding decision making and the charges against me, the jury was excused to deliberate.

And I faced life in prison if convicted of the crime.

Negotiating for a lesser sentencing was not possible. Charged under the provisions of the Racketeer Influenced and Corrupt Organizations Act, or RICO, I was fucked if convicted.

But I sat stone faced, somewhat confident that the United States of America would not convict one of its own citizens for making an idle comment in a drunken stupor one night in a bar.

"They'll take you back to your cell and after the jury decides we'll assemble for the verdict," my attorney said.

"Any thoughts?" I asked.

"Hard to say anything for sure, but I'm feeling pretty damned good. Now, I've got to run," he responded as he reached for his leather bag full of files.

I stood and placed my hands behind my back, all but inviting the US Marshall to handcuff me.

After he did so, he led me to the holding facility. The walk was eerily quiet, and made me feel even less like the US citizen I had always believed was a title I was naturally able to claim.

"Not supposed to say anything about the trial or give an opinion," the Marshall said under his breath as he stopped outside the door leading into the holding facility.

"Don't expect you to," I said.

"Goes without saying, I didn't say this," he said.

I nodded my head toward him and made note of his bronze name tag.

L. R. Stone.

"Blackburn's a god damned liar," he said through his teeth.

"Appreciate it," I said in response.

"Hope the best for you, son," he said as he pressed the button on the wall, opening the door.

Another guard led me to a meeting room where I waited in my slacks, jacket, and tie for the jury to reach a verdict.

While I sat and considered what the future might hold, I prayed not for freedom, or for a favorable verdict, but for Em. I prayed she would have the strength to rise above all of this, regardless of the outcome, and proceed through life as if it never happened.

And I prayed for the ability to accept an unfavorable verdict, should it come to that, as the man I had always represented myself as being.

EMILY

November 20ᵗʰ, 2006

Waiting for the court to decide Jackson's fate wasn't an easy thing for me. I was prohibited from seeing the trial, but now that it was over, I was allowed to go into the courtroom for his verdict to be read. I prayed all night, all morning, and even in the hallway for Jackson, and for me. I prayed that regardless of the verdict, we both would be provided the strength to continue living life loving each other and cherishing what we had the opportunity to share together.

Life without Jackson was impossible for me to comprehend, and although I had made it the last two months without seeing him very often, it wasn't easy for me at all. My heart felt empty, and I felt alone. Now walking into the courtroom, I felt as if my heart was a hollow shell, dangling ten feet behind me by a string as I made my way to my seat.

"Are you Em?" a woman asked.

She was small, cute, and very soft spoken.

I nodded my head and forced a smile, something I had become quite good at in the last few months. The gathering of ATF agents, many of which I remembered from the day of the raid stood beside her, all talking and laughing as if they didn't have a worry in the world. I found it terribly wrong that if Jackson lost, he went to prison, and if the ATF lost, there was no punishment. In my opinion, if the government stood to lose the same as the citizens they tried to wrongly prosecute, they'd attempt to convict far fewer citizens.

"I'm Sydney, Jackson's sister," she said.

"Oh my God," I gasped as I raised my hands to my face and covered my mouth.

"I heard they prohibited you from seeing the trial," she said as she shifted her eyes toward the ATF agents.

I nodded my head. "They did. But I get to be here for this."

"Nice to meet you," she said as the jury walked into the room.

I stood and stared blankly into the courtroom, almost unaware of her or anyone else's presence. As the US Marshall brought Jackson into the room, I admired his nicely trimmed beard, fancy clothes, and how he held his head high as he entered the room.

"He looks good," I said as I tilted my head toward him.

"He does," Sydney responded.

"So, you were there the day they…"

"All rise," the bailiff bellowed.

The courtroom all stood. The judge entered the courtroom from the back, undoubtedly from a secret place where no one could get to him. I shook my head the thought of the secrecy of it all. After he sat down, the bailiff barked out into the room.

"You may be seated."

After shuffling some paperwork on his large wooden platform, the judge leaned toward the microphone.

"In the matter of the United States versus Jackson Shephard have you reached a verdict? The judge asked.

"Yes, your honor, we have," the juror responded.

"And how do you find the defendant?" the judge asked.

The man looked down at a sheet of paper he held as if he was uncertain of their finding. I crossed my fingers and began to pray as he read the verdict.

"In the matter of the United States of America versus Jackson Shephard, we, the jury, find the defendant, guilty of conspiracy to commit murder," the juror said.

My throat convulsed and I almost vomited. As the passageway in my throat constricted to a point making breathing difficult, I realized I was still standing. I fell to my seat and covered my face with my hands.

This can't be happening.

As Sydney sat beside me sobbing and rubbing my back, loud cheers from the ATF agents erupted into the courtroom.

"In the back!" the judge hollered.

"There will be no outbursts in my courtroom. Cease or I will find you in contempt," he demanded.

The ATF agents became quiet, now laughing and chuckling in a dull roar.

"Em…"

I glanced upward. Jackson stood in front of me with his hands handcuffed behind his back, separated by the short wooden decorative wall standing between us. Still sobbing, I stood and stumbled to the wall.

"Mr. Shephard, you need to come with us," A Marshall said as he reached for Jackson's arm.

"Get your fucking hands off of me," Jackson said through his teeth, "I need to say something to her."

"Mr. Shephard…" he repeated.

I hated seeing Jackson upset. As I began to plead with the Marshall, Jackson turned around, scanned the courtroom, and shouted.

"Marshall Stone!" he yelled.

Another US Marshall quickly walked toward where we stood and talked to the first Marshall.

"I can give you just a minute, Shephard," he said.

"Em, listen," Jackson paused and cleared his throat, "Just let me go. Get your stuff out of the house, take the money, and go. Go open a restaurant, and start a new life somewhere…"

"Stop talking like that," I cried, "I love you…we just…"

"Em, I love you, too," he said, his voice carrying all of the emotion he was feeling, "but I'm not coming back. Now, take off that necklace and go somewhere…"

"I'm never taking it off," I interrupted.

"Don't leave like this," I said as I attempted to find words to say all of the things that were running through my head.

My entire world was crashing down around me and I had nothing to pick up the pieces.

"Promise me. Promise me I'll never see you again," I blubbered between the sobbing and tears.

"Em, I gotta go," he said as the Marshall tugged against his arm.

"Love you, Syd," he said as he shifted his eyes toward his sister.

He clenched his jaw, obviously fighting against his emotions.

"And I love you, Em," he said through his clenched teeth.

"Promise me I'll never see you again," I said.

"I gotta go, babe," he said as he turned away.

"Promise me," I shouted as he walked away, peering over his shoulder as he took each step.

And, as he walked away, he never said a word.
Not a single one.

JACK

December 16, 2006

Do you have any regrets? Would you do anything differently if you could do it over? If you could turn back the clock Mr. Shephard, what, if anything...

Each time someone asked me one of those questions, they got the same response as the person before them. Regret wasn't something I had ever known. I lived life by my own set of rules, and I had never been ashamed of anything I chose to do in living it. Not always were my choices in line with the law, society's belief, or what most considered to be moral or just; but that didn't make my decisions - or me - wrong. Because of my personal opinions and my adherence to my own set of laws, I had always perceived myself as being a man of honor, and one with a purpose. It didn't necessarily provide any assurance other people understood me or agreed with me, but changing my ways wasn't an option.

I realized in living my life I had made mistakes, I was no different than any other man; but acknowledging when I made them set me apart from most men. Recognizing my errors and realizing just what series of circumstances allowed them to come into play paved the way for me to always improve, making the days in my future fractionally better than

181

the ones in my past.

Each new day in my life was always better than the one which preceded it.

Always.

He crossed his arms in what I had learned to be the standard prison Peckerwood pose, leaning to the side and studying me from head to toe as he did so. Standing six foot two and weighing roughly 220 pounds of solid muscle, Deuce would be intimidating to most men. No one, however, intimidated me. As he studied me I gazed around the cell, admiring the cleanliness. His cell was spotless and smelled like a hospital - at least what I remembered them smelling like when I was a kid.

"You can't just go knocking a motherfucker out in this joint, especially one of the blacks. You ever done federal time before?" he asked.

I shrugged my shoulders, "Been in jail a few times. Never locked up like this, no."

He lifted his chin slightly and looked down his nose at me as he narrowed his gaze. "You bother to notice there's segregation here? Cops don't put blacks and whites in the same cell. Don't mix whites and Mexicans either - or blacks and Mexicans for that matter. You notice at chow the blacks are on one side and the whites are on another? Same thing at the phones. Hell, look out on the run, they've even got their own place to post up. You notice that? Pretty hard to fucking miss."

I'd never considered myself to be a prejudiced man. As far as I was concerned, men were men, and placing one in a category of any kind prior to knowing who a man was or what he stood for was wrong. I understood prison was different, and would require adjustments on my

SCOTT HILDRETH

part, but I didn't have to agree with why it was the way it was. After a short glare for him having me redirected to his prison cell in the first place, I nodded my head once in affirmation.

"Yeah, I noticed. Just what's the fucking problem, Deuce? It's Deuce, right?" I paused and glanced over my shoulder toward the man who was slowly inching closer to where I was standing.

"The problem is this. A white bustin' the head of a black, especially the one you busted, can pop off a riot in here. You need to ask permission before you go thumpin' another black," he explained.

As Deuce spoke, I noticed the man who shadowed him everywhere had moved half the distance between the cell door and where I stood. I immediately turned to face him and raised my hands into a defensive posture.

"You wanting to fuck me or something?" I asked as I shifted my eyes along his lean muscular frame.

He was of average height, a little smaller than average size, and covered in an overabundance of prison tat's, primarily swastikas and other white pride tattoos, including a 14/88 over his left eyebrow. I later learned 14 was the 14th letter in the alphabet, N, which represented the word Nazi, and 88 was the eight letter, H, twice, and stood for Hail Hitler. Dressed in white boxer shorts, white socks, no shirt, and his shower shoes, he looked like every other Peckerwood I'd seen, but the fact he was invading my bubble set him apart from the rest.

His eyes widened as he stammered to form a response, "I was just..."

"Well, you just better back the fuck up a few feet, little man. You rolling up on me like that is making me want to add you to the list of motherfuckers I've knocked out today," I said through my teeth.

He leaned to the side and attempted to look around me - and toward

183

Deuce - for answers.

"Stand outside, Junior," Deuce chuckled from behind me.

"I'm not fucking around," I said as I turned to face Deuce.

"You're gonna have a tough life in here, Killer," Deuce sighed, "You need to figure out how to do your time and keep your time from doing you."

I shook my head from side-to-side as I gazed down at the toilet blankly. After a moment of collecting my thoughts, I shifted my eyes toward Deuce and pursed my lips. As soon as he showed outward signs of being nervous, I relaxed, realizing he was no different than anyone else.

Shot caller, my ass.

"Doing time?" I said with a laugh, "I'm not doing time. I've got life in this place. Far as I'm concerned, this is my new home. I don't let people disrespect me in my home, and I'm sure as fuck not going to let them do it here - and as far as I'm concerned the color of a man's skin doesn't protect him from shit."

He nodded his head and turned his palms upward. "In here it does."

"Got my own set of rules," I seethed.

He raised his right hand and extended his index finger. "If he disrespected you or the race, that's one thing. But you need to get permission. There's always, what do you call it? Circumstances. God damn it I can't think of it right now, but it's a kind of circumstance that lets you, you know, kind of step away from what's normally..."

"Extenuating circumstances," I interrupted.

"Yep. Extenuating. Appreciate ya," he nodded, "So I heard he called you a 'Wood, and you started beatin' on his black ass?"

I shook my head, "Don't know where you get your information,

184

but that's not even close. Here's what went down, and I'll tell you in advance, I don't like repeating myself, and I've never been one to go over things and second guess my actions. Where I'm living doesn't change that, so pay attention."

He widened his eyes as he knelt down and squatted, pressing his back to the wall as he did so. I'd seen many of the people relax like this in the five days I'd been in prison; it was almost as if they were sitting, but without the aid of a chair.

"Have a seat," he said as he tossed his head toward the toilet.

The six foot by twelve foot cell was no different than the other 1800 cells in the prison. It had two steel beds on one wall, one over the other, a steel desk anchored to the wall, a one-piece steel toilet with a sink contoured into the top of it, a steel locker anchored to the wall, and a steel cell door with a hinged slot. After excluding the space taken by the beds, toilet, and desk, there wasn't much room left. I glanced toward the toilet, shifted my eyes toward him, and shook my head.

"No disrespect, but I'll stand. So we were in the kitchen, in the dish room. He told me to work the back of the machine, grabbing the dishes as they came off the washer. I'd been working on the front of it for four hours, and I just got the hang of it, you know, I was kind of in a rhythm. So I told him to fuck off. I said 'unless you're a cop, you got no fucking business telling me what to do'. The motherfucker sized me up, pointed to the rear of the machine, and told me to 'get back there, you punk ass bitch,'" I paused and waited for his reaction.

"Those exact words? Called you a 'punk ass bitch?'" he asked as he slowly rose from his seated position.

I nodded my head. Calling someone a punk in prison, or a bitch for that matter, was about as disrespectful as one could be toward another man. Men will generally fight for honor, to protect those they love, or to support their system of beliefs. It really was no different in prison. Calling someone a punk was indicating he'd let another man fuck him - and become his *bitch*. For a heterosexual man, the thought is unthinkable. To simply allow another man to do something like that would suggest he was weak and incapable of standing up for something he held sacred.

And I was far from a weak man.

"Those exact words. So, I busted the disrespectful fucker in the gut with all I had. When he was trying to figure out what planet he was on, I got his ass in a headlock and beat him until my arm got tired," I paused and shrugged my shoulders, "That's pretty much it."

"Well, if that's what he said, he deserved everything he got. I'll go to the black shot caller and explain, so there's no need to worry. But there's one more thing," he paused and stepped within a few feet of where I stood.

"He's tellin' all the blacks he beat *your* ass. Price you pay for not markin' his ass up," he said under his breath.

Deuce had been locked up for eight years, and was the shot caller for the Peckerwoods, a white prison gang. The prison had many white gangs, and they all stood for the same thing, the belief their race was superior to any other. From my quick inventory of the gangs in the five days I had been imprisoned, I placed the Peckerwoods on the lower position on the totem pole, the highest being the most violent. The Aryan Brotherhood, Aryan Circle, Nazi Low Riders, Dirty White Boys, and Hammerskins seemed to be more violent - or at least more prone to it.

"My understanding was that I *didn't* want to mark him up. If I did, I thought we'd both go to the hole. I looked at it like I did the disrespectful fuck a favor. So he's saying he whipped my ass?" I asked as I raised my hand to my chin.

As I rubbed my jaw between my forefinger and thumb, he nodded his head.

"I suppose there's a price you pay for making him look like he got his ass whipped, and a price you pay for leaving him looking like he ain't even been in a fight. Depends on which one you're most comfortable with," he said.

"And you're telling me I have to get permission to whip his ass?" I asked.

He nodded once.

"Well, when you go talk to the shot caller, tell him what happened, and tell him I'm going to beat that motherfucker again, for GP. If this is my new home, I'm sure as fuck not going to get off on the wrong foot," I said through my teeth.

"You're a hard case, Killer," he chuckled, "Too hard for the yard."

"And that's another thing. Don't call me that. Tell all the 'Woods, hell, tell everyone in this joint. My name's Jack. Nothing else," I said.

He clenched his fist and held it at arm's length. I clenched mine and pounded it against his.

"Bet," he said.

"Well, I'll go tell Black what time it is," he said as he peered through the cell door, "We got a half hour till lock down."

"It'll take me about sixty seconds to do what I gotta do," I paused and narrowed my eyes slightly as I realized what he had said, "The black shot caller's name is Black?"

He nodded his head, "Ironic, huh?"

I shrugged my shoulders and gazed out onto the cellblock as Deuce walked past me and made his way toward the other side of the run. A group of white men, - all shirtless, covered in tattoos, and sporting shaved heads - stood against the handrail as they watched a group of Hispanic men assembled across the run fifty feet away. As they noticed Deuce walking along the run, one of them nodded his head in Deuce's direction. I shifted my eyes to the right. A group of black men stood talking, studying the white men intently. Tension was just about what I expected - high at all times. The prison reeked of sweat, dirty clothes, and adrenaline. The salty smell of the sweat was so thick I could taste it.

I studied the group of black men as Deuce strutted past them, his chin high and his chest thrust forward. All eyes shifted to him as he walked past. I shifted my eyes to the Hispanics. One tossed his head toward Deuce as he stepped into the cell of who I expected was the black shot caller. As Deuce walked in, a thin black man emerged. Slowly, the group of Peckerwoods who were leaning against the handrail stepped away from it and backed against the wall.

Without a word spoken, it was clear what was happening. News in prison traveled primarily through body language - and it traveled fast.

After a matter of seconds, Deuce walked out, gazed in my direction, and nodded his head once. I shifted my eyes around the cellblock. Batista, the man I had fought with earlier, stood against the wall with a group of four black men. As he noticed Deuce walking toward me, his gaze shifted to where I stood.

Our eyes locked.

I grinned and raised my clenched fists.

"All clear, do what you gotta do, Killer," Deuce said as he stepped between me and the open cell door.

"Jack, god damn it," I growled.

The name Jackson reminded me of my sister and Em, and there was no provision in my heart or mind to allow anyone but those two refer to me by my given name. The name Killer reminded me of my trial, and I had no intention of hearing that road name in prison. The prison guards leaked my name to the prisoners from my file, or *jacket* as it's referred to in prison.

He coughed a laugh and shook his head, "You're a hard motherfucker, ain't ya? Do what you gotta do, *Jack*."

"How long they put us in segregation for fighting?" I asked.

"Thirty days in the SHU," he nodded.

"See ya in thirty days," I said as I turned away.

As I walked down the run, I heard a whistle from behind me, similar to a bird chirping. Immediately following the sound, the group of Peckerwoods began walking toward where Batista stood. My eyes shifted around the commons area. The group of Dirty White Boys who were surrounding the phones along the far wall began walking in the same direction, and as they did, one whistled a similar sound. Immediately, white men emerged from their cells like ants from a mound and assembled along the walls.

I'd always believed if a man couldn't stand up for what he believed in, he must not believe in it with his heart. Fighting a man for suggesting I'd let another man fuck me might seem foolish to some, but as far as I was concerned, it was a matter of respect. If I was going to spend my life living in a place where only the strong survived, I needed to be strong, or be perceived as being strong. Allowing a man to treat me disrespectfully in my first week would only open the door for others to follow.

Although I may have been depicted differently by all who knew me, I doubt anyone ever described me as being weak. And, as far as I was

189

concerned, thirty days in the hole, or Special Housing Unit, was a small price to pay for keeping my pride.

Taking my pride in this particular circumstance would require another man whipping my ass. I didn't know Batista - and really I didn't have to - fighting was something I did extremely well. I started at an early age, growing up in the orphanage. The loss of both parents before I was a teen angered me, and my release of the anger was fighting. Although I wouldn't describe myself as an angry adult, fighting was sometimes an evil necessity.

"Telling the fellas you whipped *my* ass, huh?" I grunted as I worked my way through the crowd.

He bounced up and down on the balls of his feet like he was training for a boxing match. My mouth curled into a shitty little smirk as he pulled his clenched fists toward his chest. From what I could see, this was going to be easy.

"Come and get it white boy," he growled as he tucked his chin into his chest.

Hell, I didn't need an invitation, but it was nice of him to give one. As I positioned my feet and raised my hands, he swung a wild left hook toward my chin. I leaned back, and as his fist swung past me, I hit him with a hard right jab. The punch more than stunned him, and although I could have ended it right then and there, I felt I needed to make a better showing for the crowd who was gathered around watching. If they saw me knock him out with two punches, there was no doubt some might call it blind luck. If they saw what I was capable of, I suspected respect would be in order when I was released from the SHU.

And respect was all I wanted to gain.

I allowed him to regain his wits and come at me again. As he pulled his right arm back in recoil, I swung a hard left hook into his ribcage. He gasped for breath as his hands fell to his sides. Now standing before me a human punching bag, I viewed him as nothing more than an opportunity to earn my much deserved respect.

A very well executed barrage of punches to his mid-section, followed by half a dozen more to his face - all in a matter of seconds - was all it took. As he fell to the concrete, bleeding profusely from his mouth and nose, one of the Peckerwoods behind me gasped his opinion of what he had seen.

"God damn, Killer's got some hands on him."

"Boxer. Heard he was a professional boxer," I heard another respond.

The sound of jangling keys in the distance was unmistakable. In a matter of minutes, the equivalent of a SWAT team would be upon me. As one of the fast approaching officers screamed his command, bodies scattered like roaches.

"Lockdown! Get to your cells!" the officer bellowed as the group of officers rushed into the cell block.

"Inmate!" another screamed, "Get on the ground."

I gazed down at Batista. If I was going to get a reputation, I needed to make sure my message was clear. As the officers worked their way toward me, shields raised, I glanced over my shoulder. Deuce stood across the cell block, beside his cell door. Many others stood outside their cell watching the commotion. As Batista attempted to raise himself onto his elbows, the entire cell block was focused on where I stood.

I swung my right leg back and kicked him in the face as hard as I could. More screaming and the clanking of keys from behind me reminded me I was soon going to be in worse shape than Batista if I didn't stop.

But I had a point to make. If I was going to spend life in prison, I was going to do so being respected by all men. I really didn't give two fucks if they liked me, but respect me they must.

"Don't move, inmate!" an officer in front of me shouted.

I gazed over my shoulder. Behind me, a wall of federal officers with riot gear stood at the ready.

I turned toward my right. Another line of officers with riot shields and helmets stood in front of me. For lack of a more accurate term, I was surrounded. I sighed and gazed down at Batista.

"Inmate…do not move…get on the ground!" the officer demanded.

I swung my leg to the rear and kicked him with all my might one more time. Cheers erupted from the entire cell block. I did it again. More cheering erupted. I fully realized the majority of the men witnessing the beating viewed it as a racial incident. In reality, nothing could be further from the truth. I beat Batista because he was disrespectful to me in a manner that was contrary to my survival in prison - and for no other reason. I gazed around the cellblock and raised my hands in the air as if I had just won the World Championship Heavyweight fight. Screaming, cheering, and beating on the steel cell doors echoed throughout the cellblock.

Although I received a beating from the guards much worse than the one I gave Batista, I did win something on that day, and it wasn't the championship fight.

It was respect.

And that was all I needed to survive.

JACK

June 6, 2015

The changes a man's mind goes through in prison, adapting to the differences between being free and being confined can't be forced. Naturally, over time, the mind makes adjustments, eventually accepting confinement as being a way of life. I suspect no differently than animals adjusting to their surroundings in the wild, man adjusts to his surroundings in prison. The adaptation, at least for me, took roughly a year.

I had accepted prison as being my home, realizing there was no way I could change the situation to be something it wasn't. Accepting it, however, didn't change my mind's inability to process the change. Living in a room the size of a child's bedroom closet with another man, and never having so much as a moment's privacy wasn't easy to adapt to. Initially, the days seemed as if they were hundreds of hours long. The weeks passed like months, and each year resembled living a complete lifetime. I convinced myself with the slow passage of time I was destined to live the equivalent of many lives in prison, watching the clock spin at a rate much slower than it did in the free world.

After a year, something within me changed. In hindsight, I believe although I had become comfortable with being incarcerated, my mind had not. Now, after almost nine years had passed, my surroundings had not changed one bit, but my mind accepted my new home as being the only option I had.

Although many men find God in prison, often praying for change, acceptance, or protection from harm, I was not one of them. God had been in my life, my way of living, and my heart since I was a child. I doubted many people looked at me and categorized me as Christian, but I was and had always been.

When I was free, my family consisted of my younger sister Sydney and the men in the motorcycle club I rode with. Although I had written off the club at the very beginning of my incarceration as being nothing more than a group of men who like to drink beer and fight, casting my sister aside was a difficult decision.

I loved Sydney in a manner differently than most brothers would love their sisters. Growing up, I acted as her best friend, brother, father, and family. We had very little as children, and went from foster family to foster family after the death of our parents. Eventually landing in a foster home where we remained until adulthood, I did my best to protect her from any and all things that would possibly cause her harm. Sydney was the world to me, and losing her had proven to be far more difficult than I could have ever imagined.

But it was necessary.

My only love was also cast aside, which provided her the freedom to live life beyond the walls of the prison I was condemned to spend my life inside. Tying Em to me would have been beyond selfish on my part, and releasing her was not only the hardest thing I had ever done, but something I struggled with each and every day for the eight and a half years I had been incarcerated.

As much as I loved Emily I decided early in my incarceration I must to cut all ties to her. I chose to remove her from my mailing list, visiting list, and force her to proceed living a life without me in it. Asking someone else in the free world to be incarcerated by proxy wasn't something I could bring myself to do. I was required to spend the remaining portion of my life in prison, and from what I could imagine life would be like for her, allowing her to become part of the living hell I was in would have killed me.

I didn't abandon her out of anything but the deepest of love. I loved her then, and I continued to love her more than I was ever capable of loving myself.

Separating myself from Em and my sister allowed them to live life without any attachment to me, and forced them to accept the loss of me from their lives - no differently than if I were dead - and proceed living without the day to day sorrow from having the man they desperately and completely loved dying a slow death in prison.

My only tie to the outside world was the box of letters I had saved from my early years of being incarcerated. I cherished them and read, reread, and read again their contents, reliving the stories and memories they depicted.

"Step out of the cell, Shephard," the officer barked.

I folded the letter, slid it into the envelope, and carefully placed it into the shoe box of letters. After positioning the box under the bottom bunk, I walked out of the cell and turned to face the guard.

"Another fucking shakedown?" I asked as I stepped out onto the run.

"Cell inspection. The new AW wants shit tightened up around here. He thinks your houses look like shit," Officer Turner responded.

The new Associate Warden was an anal retentive prick. He had been relocated from a minimum security prison camp to the maximum security prison I was housed in. Immediately, he changed rules and regulations regarding paint, floor polish, cleaning supplies, and cleaning procedures. As much as he tried, he couldn't change the fact he was in an actual prison and not in a prison camp that resembled a college dorm. I was quite certain his mind was adapting to the changes no differently than mine did.

"You're going to need to get your shoeboxes of letters put up or toss them in the trash, Shephard. Same thing for your cellie. If it can't fit in your locker, it's trash," Officer Matting said as he emerged from the cell.

"You know good and god damned well those boxes won't fit in my fucking locker. Shit, I can't fit my fucking clothes in the little fucker," I paused and gazed past him at the two boxes of letters Sydney and Em had written me, "Sorry, Boss, but I'm not tossing my letters, they're all I've got."

"Having a surprise cell inspection on Monday. Your cell can't have anything on the floor. That's the AW's new rule," Matting said.

I turned around and placed my hands behind my back. "Cuff me and take my ass to the SHU now. I'll take my letters with me. Fuck the AW."

"I'm not taking you anywhere, Shephard. Just get all your shit off the floor," Matting said.

I turned around and focused on Turner. He shrugged his shoulders and grinned. I shifted my eyes to Matting. He shrugged and tossed his head toward the next cell.

"Step out of the cell, Newman," Matting said as he leaned into the cell beside me.

I glanced down at the boxes of letters. They were all I had to remind me that there was a world outside of prison, and my only means of communicating - even if my communication was limited to reading letters I had never responded to. To toss them in the trash would be to walk out on what little life I had left. The letters kept me sane and provided me hope that Sydney and Em would continue living the life I would never be able to. In some respects, I lived vicariously through my thoughts of them. And, although I hadn't written Sydney in over four years, and Emily in almost eight, the letters continued to come, one a week, for eight years.

All of which I refused to accept, open, or acknowledge. The prison simply provided a letter refused chit, stating I refused another letter, and the name of the person who attempted to send it.

"Time for store," Newman said as he stepped beside my cell door.

I nodded my head as I grabbed my mesh laundry bag from on top of my bunk.

"Big order this week, soap and Batteries," I said as I buttoned up my shirt.

Earning $0.23 an hour wasn't the wages I suspected I'd retire on, but there was no changing the work system in prison. Working 6 hours a day in prison earned me $6.90 a week to spend. With a bar of Dial soap costing $1.00, and a granola bar costing $3.00, my priorities quickly became the necessities, and nothing more. I treated myself once a month to a treat of some sort from the store, typically a candy bar. The order from the Commissary went in by filling out a request several days in advance, checking the appropriate box beside the item requested. The inmate placed his prison ID number on the request, and signed his name. The order was then waiting for him at the Commissary, and the money was removed from his 'books' or account to pay for the items purchased.

As Newman and I stepped into our place in line, I gazed down the ranks of men. In my time at Big Sandy, I'd seen men come in, leave, be transferred, and get killed. Although one would suspect someone like me would have no worries after doing eight years, the opposite was true. In prison, a man must always be on guard and attentive to his surroundings at all times. A new inmate attempting to make a name for himself, or someone trying to get his patch with one of the gangs was always a threat. As I studied the men, their movements, and listened to the faint whispers, I relaxed slightly, feeling minimal tension amongst the crowd.

"No talking during movements," the guard bellowed.

After being escorted to the store and waiting in line for my turn, I stepped up to the window and held my ID up for the officer to see.

"Shephard," I said.

"Double A's and Dial?" he asked.

I nodded my head, "Sounds about right."

He handed me the items and printed a receipt. As he handed me the receipt, he nodded his head toward the piece of paper. I glanced down to see my balance, but based on his gesture, I figured my funds had diminished beyond my previous calculations.

$2,542.36

I gazed down at the paper for a moment, wadded it up, and placed it into my pocket.

"You saying that's what I got on my books?" I asked.

He nodded his head once.

"Next!" he bellowed as he peered past me.

I slapped my hand against the counter. "Gimme a jar of motherfucking peanut butter."

"Shephard, you know there's no substitutions. Get it next week. Next!" he hollered.

"Where's my order sheet?" I asked.

He shrugged his shoulders. "In the trash by now, why?"

"Had a peanut butter on it. All I got was batteries and soap. Need that peanut butter, Boss," I responded.

He shook his head and grinned.

"Missed a jar of peanut butter for Shephard," he barked over his shoulder.

The inmate working in the commissary walked up and handed the officer a jar of peanut butter. The officer printed a new ticket and handed me the jar.

"Next!" he hollered.

I stepped aside, peered down along the ranks of men, toward the guard, and twisted the lid from the jar. As I studied the guard, I shoved two fingers into the jar of peanut butter and slid them into my mouth.

I found it odd something as simple as a jar of peanut butter was able to provide tremendous satisfaction to an inmate in federal prison, and be nothing more than a snack to someone in the free world. All of the things I had taken for granted on the outside were now viewed as luxuries.

Being touched affectionately. Listening to a bird chirping. Turning a doorknob and opening a door. Deciding what to wear. Petting a dog. Sitting at a stoplight. Deciding what to eat.

Taking a shit without an audience.

These were simple things I would never do again.

I dropped the peanut butter into my laundry bag and reached into my pocket. After stepping to the side and away from the watchful eyes of the other inmates, I removed the wadded receipt and stared down at the balance.

$2,542.36

Many people over the years had made a promise to place money on my books, but very few ever delivered. Most deposits into my account were in the first few years, and after that, nothing ever came. I had no idea who sent the recent money, but whoever had just changed my way of living, and for that I was grateful.

"You must have long money on your books, buying peanut butter and shit," Newman said as he tilted his head toward my bag.

"Living the dream," I responded.

And for the time being, the statement was true.

I was living the dream.

One scoop at a time.

JACK

July 1, 2015

After almost a decade of incarceration, a person loses all hope for any change to take place. During the first several months, everyone tells themselves they were wrongfully convicted, they hope for an appeal, or they believe someone or something can or will eventually save them from the unthinkable - remaining in prison.

But the appeal never comes, and no one ever emerges to save them from anything. Acceptance of life in prison is difficult, but necessary. Hope, to a prisoner, is like a cancer. Hope eats at your ability to accept life as being what it is. Hope will make a strong man weak, and a weak man dead.

In prison, there is no hope.

"Mail call!" the officer barked from the end of the run.

I stood at the cell door and watched the men gather around the officer. As he pulled the mail from the basket, he shouted the names of the respective inmates. After a few minutes, my gaze became more of a blank stare, and my mind faded to thoughts of Sydney and me as children.

Newman hollered at me, snapping me out of the shallow daydream.

"Mail," he shouted.

"Last call, legal mail, Shephard, Jackson!" the guard shouted.

Legal mail?

"Shephard, right here," I hollered as I walked toward the guard.

He handed me the letter over his shoulder. I gazed down at the envelope and studied the addresses to make certain it was mine. I glanced around the cellblock and turned toward my cell. After walking into the cell, I opened the envelope carefully and removed the letter. After unfolding it, I began to read the typed words.

Jackson,

You don't know me, but my name is Avery. I'm a friend of your sister, Sydney. I work for a law firm in Wichita, and I was initially intrigued by your case when hearing of the ATF and their persistent requests for you to admit to wanting to kill a member of a rival club. After having my first two letters I had written to you rejected and returned, I decided to write you an official legal letter, as this matter is now officially official (sorry, but I laughed when I wrote that).

I'm the Ol' Lady of the President of the Selected Sinners, a Kansas based 1% club. The club is thirty strong in Wichita, and has chapters in Oklahoma and Texas as well. Overall, they're a tight knit bunch of brothers who would do anything for each other, or for the cause.

I'm far too excited to go very long without just getting to the point I would like to make, but for the sake of safety, I'll request you take the time to sit if you aren't already sitting.

Now, I'll assume you're sitting and I will continue with my announcement.

I paused, peered over my shoulder, and into the cellblock. After reassuring myself no one was watching, I gazed down at the desk and continued.

I filed an appeal on your case based on your having been provided an attorney who was incapable of sufficiently defending you, and secondly on your being entrapped by the ATF to commit the crime in question. The appellate court accepted the appeal, and has responded.

I really hope you're sitting down right now.

Jackson, they've accepted your appeal. You're going to have a new trial, and if they find you were entrapped, you'll go free. For what it's worth, the attorney taking your case will be my boss, and he has never (yes, I said never, as in NEVER) lost a federal case.

The cost of the trial, the fees, and the paying of the attorney has all been done in advance, and will be of no cost to you.

Mr. Shephard, breathe easily. Your life is in very capable hands.

I can't pretend to understand what you've gone through, or what you go through on a daily basis, but I have a favor to ask of you. The club placed some money in your account, so I know you can afford to do it. I've done a lot for you, and I want something in return. It will cost less than a dollar, and will take only an hour's time.

Write your sister a letter. Her address has changed and I have attached it in the next page of addresses.

She loves you dearly, and would love to hear from you.

That's all.

Well, I can't wait to meet you in court, and Sydney's looking forward to seeing you as well. She's the Ol' Lady of the club's SAA, Toad. All of the fellas send their best, and Axton (my Ol' Man) made it mandatory for the club to attend the trial, so you'll have the support of the entire club and you won't go through this alone.

I know it's been a long time, but do your best to recall everything that happened through the course of the investigation. We'll have almost no time to prepare, so anything you can remember will be used in your favor.

All my best.

Avery (the bad-ass bitch who got you a new fucking trial)

I dropped the letter onto the desk and gazed down at the neatly typed pages. As my mind swirled into a whirlwind of emotion, the unthinkable happened.

My heart filled with hope.

JACK

Present day

I felt odd sitting in the courtroom. The memories of my initial trial were not good ones, and I believed at the time that I was railroaded through the system and sent to prison on a bullshit charge. Although I accepted it as being part of life and realized I wasn't capable of changing it, I didn't like it then and I didn't like it now.

The attorney appointed to my case was an extremely aggressive man, and was much better prepared than my original attorney. As he asked the questions, I did my best to answer in a manner I expected he wanted me to.

"Did you know agent Blackburn was an ATF agent at this time?"

I leaned toward the microphone and spoke clearly, "No, Sir."

"Did you view the members of your club as brothers?" he asked.

I nodded my head. "Yes, Sir, I sure did."

"Family?" he asked.

"Yes, Sir, I did. They were my family."

"Mr. Shephard, where is your mother today?" he asked.

I hoped he knew the answer, and it seemed odd he would ask even if he didn't know, but as much as I was offended by the question, I suspected somehow it must have had merit.

"She's dead, Sir. She passed away when I was a very young boy," I responded.

"I'm sorry to hear that. And your father?" he asked.

"The same, Sir. He passed at the same time. I grew up in orphanages and eventually in a foster home with my only sibling, my sister," I responded.

"I'm sorry for your losses," he responded as he turned toward the jury and appeared to be wiping tears from his eyes.

Oh, this motherfucker's good.

"Would it suffice to say the club and your MC Brothers were the only family you had?" he asked.

I nodded my head toward Sydney and responded, "Yes, Sir, them and my sister."

"And you perceived agent Blackburn as a brother?" he asked.

I glanced toward the prosecuting attorney's table. Blackburn sat at the table with a shitty grin on his face. The cocksucker had infiltrated our club, and had lied to become a fully patched in member. To me, even though I disliked him, he was a brother, and no differently than I told him on the night in question, I would have taken a bullet for him. Now, I wouldn't piss on him if he were on fire. In my mind, he was marked for death, and living on borrowed time.

"Yes, Sir, I *did*," I responded.

"To the best of your knowledge, were the Shovelheads MC a 1%er club?" he asked.

"Yes, Sir, they were," I responded.

My attorney walked away from his post and slowly approached the witness stand. He looked confused. As he rubbed his jaw in his hand and glanced toward the jury, he spoke, "And Hell's Fury was also a 1%er club?"

"Yes, Sir, we were," I responded.

"When a 1% club who has claimed territory - for this sake I'll call them the parent club -has another club ride into the territory without permission, wearing their colors including a lower rocker claiming the *same* territory, how does the parent club perceive this trespass?"

"As disrespectful, it's considered a threat," I responded.

He widened his eyes as his mouth fell open comically, "A threat?"

I nodded my head and leaned toward the microphone, "Yes, Sir."

"And when a 1% club makes a threat, what might that threat include, generally speaking?"

Oh, I see where you're going...

"Violence," I responded.

"Violence. I see. Let me back up a little bit, to where we were before. This club, the Hell's Fury, these fellas were your *family*, is that correct?"

"Yes, Sir," I responded.

"I see. And when agent Blackburn asked you what you'd do if they came into your territory, wearing a lower rocker claiming Kansas as if it their own, what was your fear, if any?"

"They were a rival club, always causing problems and talking..." I paused and turned toward the judge.

I knew what I wanted to say, but had no idea if I would be allowed to.

"Can I cuss?" I whispered to the judge.

"Yes, son, you can," he responded.

I leaned toward the microphone and continued, "Talking shit. Saying they were going to do this, and do that. If they rode in wearing their colors, I guess my fear was that they'd probably kill us, or at least try."

"So, your eventual response to ATF agent Blackburn was one more of protection than of aggression, was it not?"

"Objection, your honor. He's leading the witness," the prosecuting attorney complained.

"Granted. Rephrase your question," the judge instructed my attorney.

"Why did you eventually respond in the manner you did to the ATF agent? Agreeing that you'd kill members of the Shovelheads if they came to town?"

I'm trying to stay with you, brother. You're shocking the shit out of me. See what you think of this.

"I didn't realize he was an agent. At the time, he was a brother, you know, part of my family. My fear was that the Shovelheads MC might hurt him or some of my other brothers. My thoughts at the time were that I needed to protect my family," I responded.

"Your *only* family?"

"Yes, Sir, my only family," I responded.

"No further questions for this witness, your honor," Kurt said flatly.

I left the witness stand feeling good about my case and the new trial. Win or lose, at least I was being allowed to have my sister, her new friends, and the jury hear the truth. In my first trial I was not asked many questions, and the information projected to the jury was one-sided and left me feeling as if I did something wrong, all the while knowing all I did was respond to a question in a half-drunken stupor.

After a short recess, my attorney began questioning the ATF agent. The questioning was difficult for me to listen to, as his responses reminded me of the 'lost recordings' and what I expected to be bullshit answers - primarily lies - prepared to insure my case was lost and I went back to prison.

I really didn't expect anything less.

I leaned back, gazed toward the witness stand, and studied agent Blackburn.

If I get out of here, I'm going to hunt you down and make you pay, you cock sucker.

"How long was your investigation of the Hell's Fury?"

"Two years and one month," Blackburn responded.

"And in that time, twenty-five months, how many arrests were made?"

One, you piece of shit…

Me.

"One," Blackburn responded.

"One? A twenty-five month long investigation of an Outlaw Motorcycle Gang, and it only produced *one* arrest?"

"Yes," Blackburn snapped back.

"Did the ATF make a decision not to prosecute the other cases?"

"There were no other cases," Blackburn responded.

"Let me get this straight. You successfully infiltrated an outlaw gang of motorcycle thugs for twenty-five months, and produced this as your only case? Seems more like they were a group of good old boys, not an OMG…" my attorney stated.

"Your honor, I object. It appears the defense counsel has chosen to provide his own testimony," the prosecutor howled.

The judge turned toward the jury and raised his index finger in the air, "I'll ask the jury to strike the last statement made by the prosecutor. Counsel, you have been warned."

"In discovery, I requested the voice recording of the conversation on the night of the instant offense. I was advised it did not exist in legible format. Are you aware of the lack of availability of said recording?"

"Yes, Sir, I am. Unfortunately, the recording device did not work properly on that evening, and background noise made the recording worthless," Blackburn responded.

"I was provided recorded conversations before and after the date in question. In fact, I have a few hundred hours of recorded conversations. Almost four hundred hours if memory serves me correctly. Now, my question to you is as follows…" Kurt paused and turned toward the jury.

"Agent Blackburn, how many conversations through the course of the investigation were unintelligible, to the best of your knowledge, that is?" he asked as he continued to face the jury.

"One," Blackburn breathed in response.

"I'm sorry, I didn't hear your response. Can you speak into the microphone?"

Fuck yes, make him repeat it ten times.

Blackburn leaned forward and responded, "One."

"Only one missing, and it just so happens it's the critical one," my attorney seethed.

"Strike that last statement. So, agent Blackburn, I'm curious. During your infiltration of the group of outlaw bikers, did you give them your *actual* name?" he asked.

"No," Blackburn laughed.

Sure as fuck didn't, you chicken-shit.

"Did you make one up?"

"Yes, I did," Blackburn responded.

"Did you give them an accurate history of who you were?"

"No Sir, I provided fictitious information. Information believed to be more acceptable to the type of people I was investigating," Blackburn responded.

"So you lied. You told lies to the bikers to get them to either like you or accept you, is that correct?"

God damned right, he lied.

"I object!" the prosecutor yelled.

"Your honor, the witness stated he provided inaccurate information to the group during his investigation. I'm simply…" he paused and shook his head, "I'll rephrase the question."

"Was the information you provided the bikers regarding your background and your name the truth?" he asked.

"No," Blackburn snapped.

"Was it a lie?" he asked.

"Objection, your honor," the prosecutor hollered.

"I'll allow it, but you shall make your point in a timely manner, counsel," the judge stated.

"Yes," Blackburn said through his teeth.

"Explain your thought process to me on lying to these men during the investigation. Why would you feel compelled to tell them lies?"

"To preserve the investigation, we are taught to give either limited information, or false information. It provides protection to the bureau and to the agent," Blackburn responded.

"You're taught to *lie* during your investigations?" Kurt asked.

Blackburn glanced toward the judge. The judge nodded his head.

"Yes," Blackburn muttered.

"So, through the course of your work, you may tell a lie, but it's not necessarily a lie in a conventional sense, because you're *working*, correct?"

"Objection, your honor, asked and answered," the prosecutor

hollered.

"I'll allow it," the judge said.

I studied Blackburn. This was an interesting approach, making him out to be a liar.

"I'll ask the question again. Through the course of your work, you may tell a lie, but it's not necessarily a lie in a conventional sense, because you're *working*, correct?"

"Correct, we're often required to lie, as you say, to preserve the investigation," Blackburn responded.

"Do you only lie during the course of work?"

"Yes, during the course of my work, and when required for my work," Blackburn responded.

"Are you being paid for your testimony today, agent Blackburn?"

I locked eyes with him and waited for him to respond. He sat motionless with his lips pursed.

"You must not have heard me. You testified that you told lies through the course of your work to preserve the investigation. My question was this: Are you being paid for your testimony today? Are you *working*?"

"Yes, I am," Blackburn murmured.

My attorney raised his finger in the air and spoke. "No further questions, your honor."

Fuck yes, you lying son-of-a-bitch.

After the prosecution rested, both attorneys gave their closing arguments and we were released while the jury went to deliberate. Having no idea whether it was going to take hours, days, or a week, I was thrilled to be taken to the county jail and not back to the USP at Big Sandy - at least not yet. The new scenery and different living quarters might have been temporary, but it was a welcomed change. As the US Marshall loaded me onto the elevator, he pressed his hand to his earpiece as if he was receiving a message.

"Looks like you're going back to court," he said as he released the earpiece and reached for the button to open the door.

"What do you mean?" I asked.

"Jury reached a decision," he said as the elevator doors opened.

"In ten minutes? That can't be good," I said under my breath.

He shook his head, "Hard saying. Might be good, might be bad."

In a slight state of shock, I followed him into the courtroom. After finding my seat beside my attorney, I gazed around the courtroom and eventually fixed my eyes on Sydney and her friends. Win, lose, or draw, I appreciated all they had done for me. If nothing else, Avery had secured Sydney a spot in my life as a pen pal forever.

"Counsel, please stand," the judge said into the microphone.

My attorney and I stood. He turned his head to face me and whispered.

"No matter what the outcome, hold your head high," he said.

I swallowed heavily and nodded my head once, "I will."

The judge cleared his throat and gazed out into the courtroom as he spoke, "I want it understood there will be no outbursts in my courtroom, regardless of the verdict."

The judge turned toward the jury.

"Has the jury reached a verdict?" the judge asked.

The foreman nodded his head, "Yes, your honor, we have."

"In the matter of Jackson Shephard versus the United States of America, what say you?" the judge asked.

I gazed down at the floor.

Your will, not mine, Lord.

"In the matter of Jackson Shephard versus the United States, we the jury, find him *not guilty*; as he was entrapped by the ATF to commit the crime listed in the indictment, your honor," the foreperson responded.

Not guilty?

Not?

I glanced over my left shoulder. Sydney sat between a man and a woman with her hands covering her mouth, crying. I shifted my eyes toward my attorney.

They said 'not guilty'.

Not.

Guilty.

I swallowed the apple sized lump in my throat and tried my best to appear to be level-headed.

"So now what? Back to Big Sandy for a bit? Another appeal on their part?" I asked.

He shook his head and grinned as he patted me on the shoulder.

"In the court's eyes, the government forced you to commit a crime. They entrapped you. You're not guilty, you're a free man, Mr. Shephard," he responded as he reached toward the mound of paperwork in front of him.

My throat constricted. I stood and stared blankly beyond him as the jury walked away. My eyes welled with tears. I gazed down at the floor and stared for a few seconds. Finally, I swallowed heavily and shifted my tear filled eyes upward.

"Free?" I asked, "It's over? That's it?"

"Free to do whatever you want. As a matter of law, you've never been convicted of a felony. Congratulations," he said.

There was really only one thing I wanted. Well, two, but only one I could take care of immediately.

"Can I go hug my sis?" I asked.

"You can do whatever you want, Mr. Shephard, you're a free man," he responded.

Free? How free?

I turned and attempted to stay standing on my shaking legs. Although I fully expected to be tackled and handcuffed by US Marshall's if I continued, I took a few steps toward Sydney. Nothing happened. I continued to walk toward her. She stood beside a man crying. He stood an easy six foot six and seemed to be solid muscle. I wondered if he was her boyfriend. Slowly, I continued walking in her direction, peering over my shoulder as I approached, expecting a guard to stop me before I got to where she stood. I bit my lower lip and continued until I had walked all the way across the courtroom.

This can't be happening.

I released my quivering lip, opened my arms, and grinned. Somehow, I managed to speak.

"Gimme a hug, sis," I said.

She vaulted herself over the handrail and onto the floor beside me, almost tackling me as she did so. As she held me in her arms, she blubbered into my shoulder. Half embarrassed by my emotional state, I leaned into her and wiped my eyes on the shoulders of her jacket. After a few minutes of sobbing, she collected herself and looked up into my eyes.

"We've got a place for you to stay for as long as you want. You'll have your own room. And Cambio's got a bike you can ride. His old Softail, he said you can have it. He said you won't be truly free until you can ride," she said excitedly, wiping tears from her face as she spoke.

I glanced to her left. A man wearing a cut with the Sergeant-At-

Arms ribbon stood at her side. His patch read *Toad*.

I cleared my throat and extended my hand, "You Syd's man?" I asked.

He nodded his head as he reached for my hand, "Toad."

"Jack," I said as I shook his hand.

"Well, you ready to get out of this shit-hole?" he asked.

I glanced around the courtroom. With the exception of us, the room was empty. As hard as it was to believe, it appeared I truly was a free man. The thought of *not* going back to prison still hadn't quite sank in. I turned toward Toad, realized I probably shouldn't try and speak, and chose to simply nod my head once.

"You up for a ride?" he asked.

I nodded my head again in agreement.

The man standing behind him raised his hand in the air. "Saddle up," he said.

Saddle up.

I never thought I'd hear those words again.

Sydney stood beside me, grinning and crying softly. I glanced around the courtroom as all of the fellas began walking toward the door. Normally, hearing my little sis cry would cause me pain, but at that moment it was music to my ears.

I still didn't feel free, and as awkward as it seemed as I walked out of the courtroom, a certain comfort washed over me.

I had a second chance to live my life.

And I intended to do just that.

Live my life.

JACK

Very few men were provided a second chance in life. Having an opportunity to make changes in life, once the time has passed, is procedurally and physically impossible. For some reason, however, I was being given a chance to do so.

And, I intended to make it count.

"So you're telling me I can ride that little softie anywhere I want?" I asked.

Toad glanced up from polishing the tank on his bagger.

"Sure can," he said, "As far as I'm concerned, it's yours."

"It's *yours*, and as soon as I get a few things taken care of, I'll pay you for it. Just really needing to know if I can take it out on the road alone," I asked as I pushed the plug into the top of the oil tank.

"You can do anything you want with it. I realize it's not as road worthy as a bagger, but it'll have to do," he said over his shoulder.

"No disrespect, I see you and a few of the other fellas ride baggers, but I never had much use for 'em. Riding a house on wheels isn't riding as far as I'm concerned. Hell, I've ridden from one coast to the other on a Softail. Anything I need can be strapped down or worn. I'll strap a bedroll to the ape hangers and wash my clothes in a river. That's fucking riding," I said.

"That's old school as fuck," he said with a laugh.

"So, you ain't gonna trip if I take it for a day or so?" I asked, realizing I was still talking in prison speak.

"Take it wherever you want," he said, "I mean it. Consider it yours."

"Appreciate ya," I said with a nod as I turned away.

I walked to the workbench and picked up a clean rag. After several minutes of wiping the dust from areas that seemed to have never been cleaned, I stood back and admired the bike. It was black, covered in chrome, and actually just as nice as the bike I had ridden for most of my life. Many men felt a need to upgrade, buy accessories, and add useless pieces of attached shit to their motorcycles. I, on the other hand, had always felt less was more; leaving my motorcycle as stripped down as possible.

Having only what I needed and nothing more allowed me to truly feel free when I rode. There was never a feeling of need on my part for creature comforts on a motorcycle. A CD player, cruise control, a windshield, and hard saddle bags would cause me to feel no differently than if I was riding in a car, and as far as I was concerned, cages were reserved for my ride to my final destination.

The cemetery.

And I was far from dying.

"Good looking little sled," I said as I admired the bike.

Toad nodded his head and grinned, "It's alright."

He was a man of few words, but from everything I could see, and what little I had heard, he was rock solid. After hearing the story of how he stepped in front of a man who was trying to shoot one of his former Marine brethren, I realized I wasn't the only one who took protecting the ones I loved as a way of life and not a choice. He explained he didn't make a decision to step in front of the gun and get shot, but that it was his natural reaction to a potentially violent situation. Something inside of him caused him to naturally react. No differently, from what he said, than swatting at a mosquito or scratching an itch. In the end, he was shot in the chest, and hospitalized with a collapsed lung, broken collar bone, and comatose.

By the grace of God he pulled out of the coma and recovered fully. He, not unlike me, was given a second chance.

"It's fucking perfect, is what it is," I stated.

"Well, brother, if you're happy, I'm happy," he said over his shoulder.

Almost immediately I felt closer to him than I had ever felt to any of my brothers in Hell's Fury, partially because he reminded me of me. His suffering from PTSD and the fact he was provided with what I perceived to be another chance at living life made me more comfortable accepting him than most of the other men I had met, because I realized I also suffered from PTSD, and I was given a second chance.

Damned near a decade in prison would cause even the most stable of souls to suffer.

I felt I was accepting Toad as more of an actual brother - the one I never had growing up - than a brother in the MC sense. My sister was happy with him, engaged to be married, and so deeply in love that it was almost difficult for me to witness. Each and every time I saw their expressed love for each other, and it was quite frequent, it reminded me of my loss.

"Syd's cooking dinner, should be ready in a few," he said as he wiped his hands on a rag.

I shook my head, "Love to stay, but I have a few things I got to take care of. Might be a day or two, but I'll be back."

He lifted his chin slightly and locked his eyes on mine. "Need someone to roll with ya?"

I shifted my gaze down to my feet.

"No. Just have a few things I need to take care of," I said.

I missed Em deeply. A hollow shell of my former self, I wondered if it would even be possible that I would one day return to the loving, caring man I had once been. Expressing emotion in prison made a man an easy target, and over time, all prisoners became hardened and not only less willing, but less capable of feeling *anything* at all. In prison, letting go of the ability to feel emotion was the only thing that allowed a man to truly survive.

Now, trying to remember how to allow emotion to become a part of my day-to-day activities wasn't difficult, it was proving to be impossible. Although I didn't share my thoughts with anyone regarding my feelings of being insensitive, I hoped one day I would be able to return to the living.

"Sure you don't want to eat first?" he asked.

"Get something on the road," I responded.

"Tell Sydney I'll see her in a couple days," I said.

"Tell her yourself?" he asked, his voice filled with a slight bit of hope.

I shifted my eyes up from the bike and stared at him for a short time.

"Alright. Well, be safe, brother," he said.

I rolled the pair of jeans, clean boxers, and a few wife beaters I had brought into the garage in a blanket and strapped the roll to the handlebars. As he stood and studied me, I started the bike, backed it out of the garage, and offered a nod of my head as I released the clutch and pointed the bike north. My only hope was that I didn't get pulled over by the police, because one thing I didn't have was a driver's license; something on my list, but far from a priority.

The Selected Sinners had all but immediately voted to make me a fully patched member, providing me with a sense of family, brotherhood, and self-worth. For reasons I wasn't able to explain, I hadn't quite accepted brotherhood as being something I was quite ready for. I accepted the patch and the responsibility that came along with it, but accepting a group of men as necessary part of my life wasn't something that was coming to me naturally.

For now, physically, I was somewhat of a loner.

And emotionally, I was alone.

JACK

After a ninety mile ride, I rolled into town feeling alone, nervous, and for the first time I could ever remember, scared. Rolling along so slowly the motorcycle barely stayed upright, I turned each corner without thought. The town had changed very little, no differently than I expected. Finally, I turned the last corner, and came down the small hill.

The car in the driveway was my first hint. The perfectly manicured lawn was my second. As I rolled closer, the sound of the exhaust popping behind me, the name on the mailbox provided all of the confirmation I needed. I killed the ignition, rolled to a stop, and swept the kickstand down with the heel of my boot.

I attempted to swallow, almost choked, and stepped over the seat. The last time I had seen the outside of the house, I was being dragged into a government Suburban by two ATF agents. The memories were more than I was prepared to deal with, and although the majority of them were good ones, it seemed like the life was being choked out of me as I gazed at the front porch. I inhaled a deep breath, tilted my head to the sky, and exhaled. As I sauntered up the sidewalk toward the front door, my heart began to race in anticipation of what I expected was sure to come.

I rang the doorbell and stepped back two steps. After a moment, the door opened.

"Can I help you?" she asked.

I bit my lower lip, nodded my head, and attempted to maintain my composure.

"Yes, ma'am…I uhhm…I used to live here. It's been a bit, say almost ten years, but I was uhhm…I was…I was shipped out in kind of a hurry, and I left someone here. Her name was Emily Stewart. Would you have any idea of where she might have gone?" I asked, fighting against the emotion that boiled within me as I spoke.

She shook her head.

"I'm sorry, I moved in last October. It's just a place I'm renting while I'm working out at the airport. Sorry," she responded.

I shifted my eyes up from the toes of my boots, and nodded my head. As I pointed toward the back yard, I tried to explain my other need.

"I uhhm," I murmured as I wagged my finger toward the fence.

Her eyes widened slightly and she stood waiting patiently for me to continue.

"Yes?" she said, attempting to get me to continue.

I shook my head and lowered my hand to my side.

"Nevermind," I said, "Thank you for your time."

"The library has internet. You might try, maybe you can find something about her there," she said as I turned away.

I glanced over my shoulder and tried my best to smile, "Thank you."

The time I had spent in prison, away from any means of technology had left my mind - and me - in the stone ages. Something as simple and common as the internet had escaped me as even being a possibility. I hadn't stroked the keys on a computer in almost ten years, and as far as I knew, they didn't even exist. Her very kind and sure to be useful suggestion had me feeling like a complete fool.

I sat on the bike and watched as she shut the door. After starting the engine and riding half way around the block, I pulled over, parked, and removed my leather gloves from the bedroll. I pulled the gloves onto my hands, clenched my fists a few times, and walked up the driveway of a home I didn't immediately recognize.

After jumping over their fence and into their yard, I walked confidently to the far side of the fence and lifted myself over it and into the easement. A few more steps and I climbed over the wooden security fence and into the adjoining yard.

I stood and stared.

Right where I had planted it, it remained. Now three times larger than when I had last seen it, the rose bush completely covering the trellis. I glanced around the yard, stooped down, and walked immediately behind it for cover.

After gripping the base of the bush with my gloved hands, I pulled for all I was worth. Although it moved slightly, it didn't uproot itself at all. I bent at the knees, gripped a little tighter, and thought of the day they were screaming at Emily in the living room, guns drawn and acting like the jack-booted thugs they really were.

I straightened my knees, pulled with every ounce of muscle I had worked ten years to develop, and growled from deep within my lungs.

Slowly, the bush lifted from the earth and snapped free of the soil. I set the large ball of roots to the side, leaned down, and dug in the soft soil of the large void. After a few seconds, the green plastic of the box I had buried was right below the tips of my fingers. After I brushed the dirt free of the box, I lifted it from the hole, hoping the rubber gasketed weather-proof box was as good in real-life as the advertisements claimed.

I tucked the box under my arm, walked to the fence, and tossed it over into the easement. After climbing over the two remaining fences, I walked to my bike and removed the tool kit from under the seat. I carefully worked the screwdriver against the dirt-covered latches for a few minutes, and they eventually popped free. Eager to look inside, I shoved the screwdriver into my front pocket, opened the box, and peered inside.

Just the same as the day I left it.

I grinned, glanced up and down the block, and pulled the pistol from the box. It appeared to be as perfect as the day I placed it in the box, which was surprising considering the weather and the amount of time that had passed. I nodded my head in appreciation of the quality of the box I had chosen. I leaned forward and shoved the pistol into the center of the bedroll, removed the magazine, ammunition, and money from the box, and dropped the empty box beside the curb where I was parked.

Realizing I needed to move before I drew any more attention to myself than I already had, I started the bike, pulled from the curb, and twisted the throttle back.

Two more stops, and I'd be ready to hit the open road.

JACK

After a knock on the door produced nothing, I rode to the only other place I knew to go. As the building came into view, my heartbeat increased, and I was filled with all of the emotion which had been absent for the last ten years. As the sound of my motorcycle wasn't anything out of the ordinary, I didn't expect to raise any suspicion, so I pulled alongside the building and parked.

I pressed the pistol into the front of my jeans, pulled my cut down to cover it, and walked around the side of the building and into the parking lot. As I walked up the drive and toward the open door of the shop, eyes widened and jaws began to drop.

"Killer, I heard you were out, the President of the Selected Sinners called and talked to …"

"Shut the fuck up, Bart," I demanded.

Sarge locked eyes with me.

Each member who surrounded him immediately stood to the side, exposing him to my approach without any obstructions. Naturally, his hand slowly hovered over the knife he carried underneath his cut.

"Don't bother," I said as I lifted my cut slightly, showing him the H&K pistol I carried.

"Listen, brother…" he began.

"Don't call me a brother," I said through my teeth as I took the remaining steps which separated us.

"You abandoned me," I yelled, "Each and every one of you worthless pricks abandoned me."

I glanced around the half a dozen members who stood with wide eyes and quickly shifted my gaze to meet Sarge's.

"Not a fucking goodbye, good luck, not a dollar on my books, and none of you pieces of shit took care of my Ol' Lady. Shit, you motherfuckers..." I paused, inhaled a deep breath, and realized I was angrier than I could ever remember being.

As I exhaled, I leaned forward and swung an uppercut into the bottom of Sarge's chin. The punch connected perfectly, and sent him back on his heels. As he stumbled and reached for his cut, I slapped his hand away and swung a left hook into his ribs.

He leaned forward and coughed as he tried to catch his breath. Two more carefully positioned punches into his face while he was bent over were all it took.

He fell to the floor of the garage like the piece of shit he truly was.

I shifted my eyes to the men, back toward Sarge, and bent over him as he groaned and attempted to get up. As I pulled the knife from his belt, I hissed my request in his ear.

"Don't ever let my name pass your lips or I'll come back and kill the entire bunch of you pricks. Not a threat, you fat prick, it's a promise. You hear me? A fucking promise," I seethed.

As I stood up and shoved the knife into my back pocket, I noticed Chili standing wide-eyes and chewing his bottom lip.

"Not a fucking word, you aren't any better than the rest of these pricks," I growled.

"Suh…suh…suh…awwe, shit, Killer…I sent…muh…muh… money. Fuh…fuh…four or fuh…five times. Buh…but…it was huh… huh…hard. The A…A…ATF told us if wuh…wuh…we…muh… muh…made contact…"

I waved my hand in his direction and turned away. Part of me felt sorry for him, yet a bigger part felt disgust. I didn't want excuses or explanations, I wanted satisfaction, and although it might have seemed like a simple solution, I received it.

Chili was one of them, and to me, they were dead. I walked to my bike without turning around. Where I had been for the last ten years, this was the ultimate disgrace. Walking away from a man who challenged you in prison without so much as taking a second glance was perceived as one of the most disrespectful things you could do. It sent a clear message you had not one ounce of fear regarding his ability to harm you.

Although neither Sarge nor the men would understand, I felt satisfied I had said all there was to say. I started my bike, tossed Sarge's knife in the weeds beside the shop, and pulled out onto the road.

As I twisted the throttle back, I grinned into the wind. It felt great to release my tension. I glanced at my right hand and gazed blankly past it as the wind blew the blood back along the back side of my clenched hand. I twisted the throttle a little further and smiled a smile I hadn't smiled in years.

It felt good.

And I only had one more stop.

JACK

I pressed the tips of my fingers against the keys of the keyboard and pressed 'enter'. It seemed awkward using a computer and I felt an odd guilt, checking over my shoulder as I waited for Google to produce the results of my search.

The search of 'Emily Stewart' produced page after page of people, men and women, but none of which were the Emily was searching for. After feeling like an idiot, I narrowed my search with a more specific request.

Emily Stewart restaurant.

Again, Google produced pages and pages of worthless articles, documents, and web pages. I sighed, stared down at the keyboard for a moment, and grinned as I had a revelation.

I pecked at the keyboard, making an even more specific search, placing the quotation marks before and after the phrase I was searching for.

"Emily Stewart's Restaurant"

My heartbeat increased to steadily as the page opened with the results. I clicked the first option, and fought against every emotion within me as the new page I had opened revealed a photo of Em.

I glanced over my shoulder into the empty library, and upon satisfying myself I wasn't going to get into trouble for proceeding, turned toward the computer. My throat clenched as I read the article, and breathing became almost impossible. As I listened to my choppy breathing while attempting to keep from losing my complete composure, I read the article.

Albuquerque Sentinel

"Is something wrong?" my lunch companion asked as we sat together enjoying our first visit at Albuquerque's newly opened Jackson's, a restaurant owned by a rather eccentric Emily Stewart. The establishment, a fine family dining experience with a few strange twists, sits at the corner of Candelaria Road NE and Highway 85.

I was elsewhere, floating above the clouds, my mouth filled with Dijon mustard infused rosemary-sprinkled chicken unlike anything I had ever had the opportunity to experience.

Yes, experience.

"You look like you've seen a ghost," he chuckled.

In many respects, he was right. Emily had just happened by, checking on us, wearing a white apron secured to her waist by a white belt tied in a simple knot. Atop her head, a white chef's hat with the name "Em" embroidered on the front, she could have passed for a ghost. I pointed down at my plate, and quickly realized I had all but offered him to sample my food. As his eyes did their very best to focus on my plate, I quickly pulled it away and covered it with my forearm.

"What's wrong?" he asked.

I shook my head and carefully selected my next bite, a small sautéed whole new potato.

"Do you find it odd she serves the salads last?" he asked as he placed the menu beside his plate.

Incapable of response, and having had witnessed the establishment's signature dish first-hand prior to him even attempting to begin his meal, I now knew better than to dismiss anything the breathtakingly beautiful owner chose to do as odd.

I reached for my glass of water...

My heart racing, and filled with pride for Em, I eagerly scanned through the article to see the conclusion of the review.

Determining the tone for a new restaurant can be complicated. As construction expenses increase and ambitions continue to rise, so do the complications. The tone, however, at Jackson's reveals the ambitious nature of the owner and chef very well.

A meal not to be tasted, but experienced.

Five forks up.

My eyes were welled with tears. I gazed around the library, read the article once more, and stood from the leather chair. Albuquerque was roughly 650 miles away, and would take ten hours on the bike.

Growing up as an orphan, I had never anxiously waited for a birthday or Christmas as a child, and, as a result, waiting had never been a strength of mine. In my former life, waiting ten hours would have killed me.

Having just spent the last ten years in prison, however, provided me with much more patience than I had ever believed I was capable of possessing.

The ten hour ride would be a blessing.

And maybe, just maybe, the ten hours of hot summer wind blowing past my face would dry the tears of pride which were beginning to roll down my cheeks.

JACK

As I exited highway 85 on Candelaria road NE, my heart sank. The only restaurant at the intersection was clearly marked Ruby's. I sat at the traffic light, exhausted, hot, disappointed, and still slightly hopeful. As the red light switched to green, I released the clutch and rode along the access road and into the parking lot.

I parked the bike, stretched my legs and admired the scenery. In the bottom of a valley, Albuquerque sat at the base of the mountains surrounding the city, and from where I was standing, was quite beautiful. I found it as no wonder Emily had chosen the area for her restaurant.

As I walked toward the restaurant, it dawned on me that although I had made no advancements in my life, the clock in the world of the civilians had continued to tick at the same pace the entire time I was away. Emily had lived a life of almost ten years, and it was quite possible anything could have happened in her life; marriage and children included.

Prepared for any and all things I exposed myself to, I opened the door and walked inside. I was immediately met by a Hispanic woman in her mid-thirties wearing a colorful apron and a huge grin.

"One?" she asked.

I began to speak, and instead changed my mind and nodded my head, "Yes, one."

I glanced around the rather small and extremely colorful restaurant and tried to imagine Emily gracefully walking about, her brown hair confined inside a hair net, wearing a chef's hat and feeling as proud as a peacock.

"Follow me," she said as she grabbed a menu and turned away.

"Sit anywhere you like," she said as she waved her hand toward the empty restaurant.

My stomach told me it was time to eat, but my watch confirmed it was only 10:30 am, certainly not a time most people were prepared to eat lunch. I graciously accepted the menu, ordered a glass of water, and began to scan the menu for something I recognized. After a few moments, she returned with a small pad of paper and a pen.

"Ready?" she asked, her voice carrying not so much of a hint of accent from her ancestry.

As I began to wonder if she may be American Indian, she grinned and shook her head.

"Not ready?"

"What do you recommend?" I asked.

"Tacos al pastor are really good. The molcajete is good, the…"

"Sounds good, bring me one of each," I said.

She gazed at me as if I was on fire, staring at my extremely dark and rather sunburnt skin, dirty sweat-stained wife beater, and raccoon-like eyes from wearing my sunglasses for what ended up being twelve hours on the road.

"You want the tacos, and the molcajete bowl?" she asked with wide eyes.

"Sure," I responded as I handed her the menu.

"Okay…" she said as she turned away.

After a short wait, she brought a bowl fashioned from volcanic rock filled with a tomato soup based dish of shrimp, vegetables, and pieces of hominy. She slid another plate with three tacos filled with small diced pieces of pork beside the large bowl.

"Anything else?" she asked.

I raised my finger in the air. "There is one thing. Wasn't this place called something else a while back? Jackson's or something like that?"

She nodded her head. "We've been here almost two years."

Show respect, get respect.

"She had a pretty good chicken dish, but I bet it's nothing like this," I said as I nodded my head toward the bowl of soup.

"You have your work cut out for you. You're big, I hope you're hungry," she said with a smile.

"Just passing through again. Been on the road for twelve hours, so yeah, I'm hungry," I said as I reached for my spoon.

As she turned to walk away, I continued.

"Do you know what happened to it? The other place?" I asked as I dipped my spoon into the bowl.

"She moved to Sante Fe and opened a new place," she responded.

"Ahhh," I said as I lifted the spoon to my mouth.

I knew little about New Mexico, but I was well aware Sante Fe was north of the city; I had passed it an hour or so before reaching the restaurant. As excited as I was to try to find Emily, I figured the least I could do was finish my meal.

I never really cared much for Mexican food, but the lava rock bowl filled with soup and my empty stomach were quickly changing my mind. After enjoying each and every drop of the soup, I ate the three tacos and all of the garnishments spread artistically around the plate.

As I relaxed in the booth and slowly slipped into a light sleep, the sound of a set of car keys jingling caused me to jump from my seat. I glanced around the restaurant, muscles tense, prepared to run.

A lone Hispanic man with a cowboy hat sauntered in and sat at the bar.

A sound I doubted I'd ever again become accustomed to, keys jingling were the tell-tale sign of being approached by the guards in prison. Partially worn on the utility belt as an audible warning of their approach, and more than likely used as a deterrent to violence, the keys rattled with each step the guard took toward the cellblock, warning the inmates to run like roaches and return to acceptable behavior before the arrival of the prison's only policing force.

I wiped the sweat from my face and gazed around the restaurant. The waitress grinned as she walked toward me with a pitcher of water.

"Sleepy man," she said.

"Guess so," I responded as I moved my empty glass toward the edge of the table.

"You done, or you want more?" she asked.

"Done," I said.

"How long you been out?' she asked.

I wrinkled my nose and stared, "Excuse me?"

"Out of the joint. How long you been out?" she asked.

I shrugged my shoulders, "Ten days? How'd you know, the shitty tattoos?"

She shook her head. "The way you ate, like someone was going to take it from you. And when Emilio came in, you jumped out of your skin. The keys, huh?"

I nodded my head and chuckled lightly, "You a part-time cop?"

"No, my brothers are locked up more than they're home. Well, good luck," she said as she placed the ticket on the table.

"Appreciate it," I said.

I paid the tab in cash, and left a healthy tip. As I walked out to the bike, I realized that nothing more than an hour's time separated me from seeing Em, but as eager as I was, I needed to be presentable when we met, regardless of her marital status. I gazed across the street at the motel and decided to pay whatever I had to for a shower, use of their washing machine, and a short nap.

And then I would make my appearance.

JACK

"Well, some say she went to New York City, and others said Los Angeles, so I can't rightly answer for sure," he said.

"A year you said?" I asked.

"Give or take," he responded as he tugged against the brow of his straw hat.

He was thin, approximately sixty-five years old, and wore faded jeans, a cotton pearl snap shirt, worn leather boots, and a cowboy hat. Emily's restaurant had been beside his jewelry store in a long strip of businesses which lined the streets in a part of Sante Fe reserved more for the tourists than the local residents.

"She had the best damned chicken I ever ate," he said as he extended his hand, "Earl."

"Jack," I said as I shook his hand.

He cocked one eyebrow slightly and shifted his eyes up and down my frame.

"Jack, huh?" he asked.

"Yes, Sir," I responded, disappointed that Emily had gone, but excited that he knew at least a little bit about her.

"Hmmph," he huffed as he studied me for a moment, "But not Jackson?"

241

I swallowed heavily and nodded my head, "It's…uhhm…yeah, I'm Jackson."

He lifted the brim of his hat over his wrinkled forehead, looked down his nose at me for a long moment, and studied me as if I were a ghost.

"*The* Jackson?" he asked as he continued to push against the underside of the brim with the tip of his thumb, lifting his hat even more.

I nodded my head, wanting to know what he knew, but not wanted to make him uncomfortable. He seemed to be slightly more skittish than me, and I had my doubts that he just got out of prison.

"Yes, Sir, I suppose so," I responded.

"Doubt that," he said as he turned away.

"What do you know about Em?" I asked excitedly as I stutter-stepped toward him.

He stopped, turned around fully, and took off his hat. As he ran his hand over the top of his head and pressed the thinning gray hair against the tanned skin of his scalp, he pursed his lips and inhaled through his nose. After a several second long wheezing sound emitted from his nose, he coughed a few times and pulled his hat down covering his brow fully.

"I ain't tellin' you a damned thing about that little girl unless you're him, Jackson Shephard, that is. Show me your driver's license," he demanded as he pointed toward my pocket.

As my heart raced, I reached for my pocket, pulled out my wallet, and before I even opened it, realized I would come up short if I did.

"I don't have one," I coughed, "What'd she tell you about me?"

"I ain't tellin' you shit," he said, "Men all the time was a coming by and tryin' to get that poor girl's money."

"I'm Jackson Shephard, I really am," I said, "I'm not after money, I just need to find her."

"Did she describe me?" I asked, realizing if she had left only a year prior, and had taken the time to tell him about me - including my name - there was still hope.

"You look like every other biker who passes through these parts," he responded.

"She's five foot six, brown hair, the deepest brown eyes, and the cutest little hands you've ever seen..." I said.

"When's your anniversary?" he asked, interrupting me as I spoke.

"Excuse me?" I coughed as my knees went weak.

I shoved my wallet into my back pocket, grinned, and realized my lower lip was shaking from nothing more than sheer excitement. For him to even ask such a question meant that Em had at least told him about us, and was proud enough of the fact that we were once together to tell him when our anniversary was. Either that or she still wore the necklace. My mind began to race as I fought to come with something to say. One thing I felt I had to know was whether or not she was still single.

"Is she still single?" I asked as I rubbed my palms against the thighs of my jeans.

He turned away, and began to walk behind the glass jewelry display case. I realized in the excitement I hadn't answered his question about our anniversary.

"June 21st, 2006," I responded, "And if she ever showed you the necklace I made her, it's a...it's a hand-stamped piece of sterling silver...the uhhm...the letters are all upper case...the date is in roman... in roman numerals," I stammered as he walked away.

He stopped in his tracks and turned around.

"Well I'll be go to hell," he said as he lifted the brim of his hat.

"And show it to me? Shit, son, she wore that damned thing every day. Never took it off. Ask me, I think it looked down right stupid, but she sure liked it. You know, she swore one day you'd reappear, in fact she was adamant about it. Drove most men crazy that she went on and on about ya the way she did, but I never minded much. Just never really knew if she believed you was coming back one day, or if she just said 'cause *she* wanted to believe it. I figured it mighta been because she just wanted the locals to leave her be," he paused and tugged against the brim of his hat, "In fact, I found the entire mess to be pretty damned interesting. Now how's a man, if you don't mind me askin', go about breakin' out of a federal penitentiary?"

I shook my head and looked for a place to sit. Feeling like I was undoubtedly on the verge of a heart attack, I gazed down at my shaking hands.

"It's a long story, but I won an appeal. I'm a free man," I responded.

"I'll be dipped in shit," he said flatly, "Is that a fact?"

I nodded my head, "Yes, Sir."

"Telephone number. You got her telephone number?" I asked.

He shook his head as he slowly shuffled toward me.

"Strange thing about her. She didn't have one. Hell, in this day and age, everyone has one, but not her. Damned girl hated the government for what they did to ya, and was afraid they'd come after her someday. Had some odd notion they'd track her through the phone or somethin'. Might be why she moved around so much, hell, who knows?" he said.

"New York or Los Angeles, huh?" I asked as I wiped the sweat from my brow.

"Sorry I can't be of much help," he said as he shook his head and lifted his hat.

"You've been a great help. I'll find her. Somehow, some way…" I said as I gazed around his shop.

"I'm sure you will, son," he said as he reached out and patted me on the shoulder.

I gazed out the storefront window toward my motorcycle. There was little in my life that meant much to me, but my Em was sure at the top of the list. By the time I got home, I'd have been gone three days, and if I was going to find her, I would no doubt need some help. From what the fellas had said, the Selected Sinners gun business went without any harassment by law enforcement because Slice had the local police on his payroll.

If anyone could find Em, a cop would sure be that person. And my only way to get a cop to help me would be through Slice.

"Sorry, I gotta go," I said.

"Alrighty, then," he said with a laugh.

I extended my hand, "Thank you."

"Good luck," he said as he shook my hand.

If Emily didn't have a phone, and didn't believe in them, finding her would take more than luck, it would take determination.

And that was something I knew a lot about.

JACK

"Goes without saying, and no disrespect intended, Boss, but as far as I'm concerned, I really don't want anyone knowing about this but you and me," I said.

"No shame in loving a woman," he growled.

"Didn't say I was in love," I said under my breath.

He leaned back in his seat and tilted it up on the rear legs as he studied me.

"Didn't have to," he said, his mouth curling into a smirk as he spoke.

I nodded my head once and stared past him as my mind slowly drifted to thoughts of Em. As he began to speak again, I shifted my eyes to meet his.

"Listen. The decisions we make in life that we *don't* have to think about? They're always the right decisions. And the decisions we contemplate, mull over, and ask the opinions of others?" he paused, dropped his chair onto the floor, and leaned forward.

"There are two rules I try to live by. Well, actually there's a whole fucking book of 'em, but I like these two the most. One, don't ask a question if you already know the answer. Two, go with your gut," he leaned his chair rearward again, as if he'd made the point he intended to.

"You go with your gut on this?" he asked.

247

I pursed my lips, clenched my jaw, and nodded my head.

"Well, your decision's the right one. Plain and simple. I'll keep it to myself; you have my word on that. Sure as fuck not much to go on, but let me see what I can find out. Might take a while," he said as he stood from his seat.

I stood, nodded my head once, and gave my parting remarks, "Appreciate anything you can do."

"Before you get out of here, let me ask you something. You alright?" he asked.

"I'm solid, Boss," I responded as I turned around.

He locked eyes with me and glared. "I know you're solid. There's no doubt you're one stand up motherfucker, Jack, but I want to know if you're alright. Toad says you barely sleep, and I can vouch for the fact you're pretty fucking skittish around some of the fellas. Just making sure you don't need anything."

Having a president like Axton was much different than having Sarge as a president. Having never been in another club, and really having no exposure to other presidents and not knowing how they acted, I always assumed Sarge was as good as a man could be. Seeing how Axton handed his men and knowing he perceived their problems as his problems made me feel like I had finally found a place I could truly call home.

"Just hard to adjust," I responded with a shrug of my shoulders, "You know, I wasn't locked up for a year or two; I damned near did a dime."

He glared at me for a moment, making me slightly nervous that maybe he didn't care for my response. Axton was a hard man to read, and rarely showed any expression short of angry. After what seemed like an eternity, he spoke.

"Good point. Corn Dog did a nickel in state, but that damned sure doesn't come close to dime in the Pen. If you need anything, you come to me, understand? And I mean anything," he said.

"I'll let you know, Boss," I said.

I started to turn away, and paused.

"Got one more thing, Boss," I said as I turned to face him.

"Let's hear it," he said under his breath.

I gazed down at my boots and tried to decide if what I was going to ask would be perceived as disrespectful. I'd already asked who put the money on my books, and thanked Biscuit for doing so. I had not found out who paid for the attorney fees, and after giving some serious thought to the matter, decided someone had to, especially after I reread the letter Avery sent me while I was locked up.

"Well, I got a box of stuff from the joint the other day, and I was digging through it. Read that letter your Ol' Lady sent me about my trial again. Then I read it again. Guess what I wanna know is this: who paid all of the fees and shit associated with my trial?" I paused and crossed my arms in front of my chest as I waited for his response.

"He'd rather remain anonymous," Axton said flatly.

"Any promises made?" I asked.

"What?" he snapped back as if I had no right to ask.

"Any of the fellas give their word they'd keep their mouth shut about it, or is it just something the Good Samaritan would rather I didn't find out?" I asked.

"More the latter," he responded.

I gazed down at my boots, held it for a short time, and shifted my eyes upward.

"Well, we've all got our pride, and it's hard for me to keep from swallowing mine with all of these people helping me out. Fuck, I'm riding that Softy outside and it ain't even mine," I complained.

"I'd appreciate if you'd tell me, so I can thank him and try and pay him back. It'd sure help me out. You know, about that skittish shit you were talking about earlier. Might help me deal with coming back to the free world, Boss," I said.

"Well, I can tell you right now, he won't accept a cent in return. Don't know the man real well myself, but your soon to be brother-in-law does, and I know of him well enough to say he won't be interested in your money," he paused and rubbed the stubble on his face with his fingertips.

"Let's say this. How about you agree to thank him in private, they'll be up here in a month on a little visit. They're heading up to a rally in Wisconsin," he said.

"Agreed," I said, "Who is he?"

"He's actually the Heavyweight Champion of the World in boxing. Shane Dekkar. His Marine buddy is the one that Toad took a bullet for down in Austin. The Marine is originally from here, and him and the rest of his ratty little do-gooder MC will be riding up to a rally in Wisconsin next month. They're stopping in to see Toad, should be about month give or take a day or two. I'll keep you posted, how's that?" he asked.

"Heavyweight Champion, no shit, huh?" I asked.

"One strange motherfucker, but tough as fuck," he said with a nod, "I'm guessing you didn't keep up on that shit in prison?"

I shook my head and laughed, "Didn't let us watch fights, said they'd evoke a riot."

"Figures," he said, "That it?"

I nodded my head and extended my hand.

He shook my hand and hugged me, which made me feel a little more comfortable about everything. It made me nervous speaking to Axton without someone there to witness our conversation, but I knew I had to talk to him alone - at least about this particular subject. Still stuck in my prison way of thinking, I feared talking to anyone of authority without a witness. In prison, any time an inmate talked to a cop about anything, another inmate would be asked to witness it. If an inmate went alone, it was automatically assumed his conversation was a secret, and he was labeled a snitch.

I walked out through the shop, glanced around for any of the fellas, and after seeing no one, started my bike and rode home.

With Sydney at work and Toad gone doing whatever it was he did all day, I went into my bedroom and pulled my box of letters out from under my bed. Within a few minutes, I had all of them spread out on the floor. My life, so to speak, for the last ten years, was in front of me in a pile. It seemed strange now that I was out of prison, but ten years of my life was able to fit in two shoe boxes.

And I felt empty.

JACK

I stood in the shop nervously sipping my beer. It had been two weeks, and I hadn't heard a word about Em. I'd spent considerable time on the internet searching for her name and any association with a restaurant named *Jackson's* and all I was able to find was the restaurant in Albuquerque. All but convinced she had moved away to some secluded area with a man, I recalled that I never got a response from the old man regarding whether or not she was single.

I began to feel weak from my feeling of necessity. After doing a reasonable amount of reading on the internet about being released from prison, I decided I was institutionalized, and no differently than any other prisoner, had to focus on something to keep my mind under the false belief that I had a routine.

I had been taken to breakfast, lunch, and dinner for ten years at the exact same time every day. We were locked down for count at the same exact time every day and locked down at night at the exact same time every night. Lights out at the same time, every night, for ten years.

In prison, my entire life was a routine. I didn't have to think, all I had to do was survive.

And now, living in the free world, I was obsessed with finding Em. Partially, I suspected, because I needed to focus on something. And more so because I was truly in love with her and would never be able to live my life fully unless she was in it.

If I had never met her, things would have been totally different.

But having had her in my life and realizing what love actually was prevented me from living every moment without yearning to have that feeling again. A feeling that only Em could provide.

As Toad and Otis stood and talked, I stared blankly at the floor and tried to assemble a routine to provide my day with a little structure. I was already working out with weights for an hour and a half a day, and almost an hour and a half was taken up with meals, leaving sixteen hours of unscheduled activity in my day after my five hours sleep.

A set of keys on the shop floor beside a Wide Glide caught my attention. After glancing around the shop nervously, I bent down and picked them up. A short study of the keys made the hair on the back of my neck stand up. I glanced around the shop, studied each of the men individually, and didn't recognize anyone.

I tossed the keys right back where they were.

"We need to go talk to the boss," I said, interrupting their conversation.

"Alright, gimme a minute," Otis said.

I shook my head, "Right now."

"Well, just go in there if you need him right now," Toad said.

I shook my head. "Need someone with me. So both of you want to go in there with me?"

Toad glanced at Otis, shifted his eyes to me, and shrugged. "If you really think we need to."

I swallowed heavily and nodded my head. "Same as going to talk to the cops in the joint far as I'm concerned. You never go alone to talk to the man. Always go in pairs, that way nobody can start the *he said she said* shit. I just want witnesses."

Otis tossed his head toward the office. "Come on."

I followed them in the office and as they sat down, I began pacing the floor, half afraid to say anything, but more afraid not to. Part of me wanted to hop on my bike and ride to a secluded place where no one would ever find me, but I'd never avoided a good fight in my life and I didn't think now was a time to start. As I stared at the floor and paced back and forth, Axton's voice caused me to glance up.

"You alright, Big Jack?" he asked.

"Be fine, Boss. Just thinking," I responded.

I pulled out a chair and sat down.

I locked eyes with Axton and spoke. "Permission to speak candidly?"

Axton broke my gaze, shifted his eyes to Toad, then Otis, and back

"What the fuck's going on?" Axton asked as he stood from his seat.

I stood nervously.

"Sit the fuck down, you pricks are making me nervous. What the fuck's going on here?" he asked.

"Sure, whatever. Speak freely," he snapped.

I inhaled a deep breath, exhaled, and said what I had to.

"Think we've got a cop in the club, Boss," I said flatly.

Axton narrowed his eyes and glared. "What the *fuck* are you talking about? There ain't a cop patched in in *this* MC, I can guarantee you that much. Now why the fuck are you saying this, you nervous motherfucker? What the fuck happened?"

I stood from his seat and began pacing.

"Sit the fuck down," Axton demanded.

"Sorry, Boss. I got to stand. Hear me out, okay?"

"Fuck it, I guess you can walk. And I'm fucking listening," he said.

255

"Well, when I was in the joint, we had cops that took us to the hole in the elevator when we got a write up. They had this special key, it looks like one of them round keys for a soda machine, but it's about half inch longer. Elevator repairmen have 'em too, but that's about it. It lets you stick the key in the elevator, turn on an override, and make it go to the roof or the basement or whatever. Now when I was in court the first time, and the second time for that matter, I saw the same thing. The US Marshall and the ATF fellas that took me to court in the beginning, and again the other day, they both had 'em. They had to put 'em in the elevator to get down to the basement to their cars. There are only a couple of elevator manufacturers, *Dover* and *Otis.* Most of the keys say one of those two names on 'em…"

"God damn it, Big Jack, get to the point," Axton interrupted.

"That fella they call Gunner, Boss. He's got one of them keys on his key ring. It says Dover on it for sure, I looked at it. And unless he's repairing elevators on the side, he's probably a fed or a prison guard," I said.

Toad jumped up from his seat, clenched his jaw, and began to walk toward the door. "I fucking knew it. Phony ass piece of lying shit. Motherfucker says he was in the shit, I never trusted his phony ass."

"Sit the fuck down, Toad. God fucking damn," Axton bellowed, "Hell, he's been here for years, he can't be a cop. Who vouched him in the club?"

"Don't need the book, Slice. I can tell you who vouched him in," Otis said.

"Who?"

"Hollywood," Otis said.

"Fuck!" Axton screamed as he kicked the table.

Axton exchanged glances with each of us, sighed, and kicked the table again.

"Fuck! Fuck! Fuck!" he seethed as he turned around, "Who's that cock sucker run with?"

"Ran with 'Wood. Well, till 'Wood committed suicide," Toad sighed.

"Fuck!" Axton screamed.

He turned around and locked eyes with me. "You God damned one fucking hundred percent sure he's got an elevator override key? One fucking hundred, not ninety-nine. You sure?"

"Wouldn't be here if I wasn't, Boss. Hundred percent," I responded, thinking of the keyring with the name Gunner stamped on a brass tag.

"Fuck!" Axton shouted.

"Let's talk about this, what are we going to do?" Otis asked.

"Torture his ass, get him to admit it, and kill the fucker. Pretty simple shit," Axton responded.

"I'll do it," Toad growled.

Axton shook his head, "*I'll* fucking do it."

"Hold up, Boss," I said, "You kill this fucker now or you even kill him later, fed's will be on this club like shit on a shoe. Whoever sent him knows he's *here*. He comes up missing or turns up dead, we're fucked."

"Well, what the fuck do you suggest?" he growled.

"I say we kill the prick," Otis suggested.

"ATF will be here in a quick minute," I said as I shook my head.

"What's the answer?" Axton asked.

I responded slowly, thinking as I spoke. "Well, he's gonna be wearing a wire, you can bet on that. So we need to get him where we can talk to him and the wire ain't any good. Won't be easy, him being a cop and all, but we'll have to do it. Anybody got a swimming pool?"

"A what? A fucking swimming pool?" Axton snarled.

"Yeah a pool. Make his ass get in the pool. Water will ruin the wire. Only way I know for sure, other than stripping him down, and then you still don't know. Fucking things can be in their hair, ears, hell some of the fellas in the joint said they even had 'em sewn into their clothes. So if you make him strip, and he tosses his clothes in a pile beside him, he can still be listening," I responded.

"Biscuit's got a pool," Otis said.

"Alright. I'll get with Biscuit. We'll need to get Gunner over there without making him nervous. How in the absolute fuck are we going to do that?" Axton asked.

"Have Biscuit tell him we've got some pussy over there?" I said, "But don't tell him there's a pool, fed's hate being around fucking pools. He'll know what's up for sure and he'll call in the troops."

"I hope you're wrong," Axton sighed as he fixed his eyes on me.

"Ain't wrong Boss," I assured him.

"You fellas go out in the shop and act like nothing happened. Is the fucker out there now?" Axton asked.

"Was a minute ago," I responded.

"Fuck!" Axton growled as he kicked the table so hard he almost tipped it over.

"Where's Biscuit?" Axton asked.

"Fucking the girl from the bar," Otis said.

"Alright, I'll call him. Stay out in the shop, and just follow my lead. I'll be out in a minute," Axton said.

The thought of an ATF agent or a cop in the club made me nervous about even being in a MC, but I knew I had no other choice. The MC way of life was my only shot at ever having a family, and what little I'd seen of the Sinners, their way of doing things was right in line with what I believed to be best.

"Big Jack?" Axton said as Otis opened the door.

"Yeah Boss?" I responded over my shoulder.

"Your cut looks good on ya, and this is damned sure where you belong. And about this…" he paused and pointed at the floor, "Good lookin' out, Jack. Good lookin' out."

"Just doin' my job, Boss," I responded as I stepped through the door.

As far as I was concerned, I had an obligation, and the men in the club expected me to fulfill it no differently than I expected them to do the same. Backing away from a situation like this one wasn't an option, and as much as I hated the thought of an ATF agent or any kind of cop infiltrating the club, I had a responsibility to stand up and do everything in my power to protect the men in the club from going through what I went through.

Even if it meant I'd have to do it all over again.

JACK

Being right all the time is impossible. I made it a point to never give my word on something unless I was convinced I was right, or at least that I believed deep down inside that I was standing up for something I believed in with all my heart. Obtaining confirmation on my belief was always something that made me feel as if I was receiving a pat on the back from the man upstairs.

"You've been my field assignment for two and almost one half years. There's no one else on this investigation. I swear to you. I had a meeting a few weeks ago with the director, and he's pissed because I claimed I wasn't ready to testify before a Federal Grand Jury..." Gunner stammered as he tried to keep his head above water.

We had been at Biscuit's pool for some time, and Axton was interrogating Gunner, waving a gun in his face the entire time. Participating in the fiasco was satisfying in many respects; knowing I was right about Gunner being a cop wasn't necessarily all I wanted, but it was all I needed. This was Axton's club, and his decision, regardless of what it was, would be supported by me.

"What in the fuck does this have to do with anything? Let's get one thing straight. I don't like cops. You're a fucking cop. If I took a vote right now, at least four of these fellas would agree to kill you. My math skills aren't too damned shabby, and that's eighty fucking percent, excluding you. Damned sure a majority," Axton growled.

"Look," Gunner pleaded as he tried to continue to tread water.

"I started investigating the Sinners on guns. In the last two years, you really haven't done anything contrary to law. Might be a stretch, but possibly selling guns to a prohibited person is all I can come up with. To indict you, I need to testify and turn in my reports. Reports come first. If I don't, there's no case. Period. End of story. I'll agree to not testify, how's that?" he begged.

Biscuit stood beside the swimming pool with a long aluminum pole. As soon as Gunner spoke, he swung the end of into his head, cutting his face alongside his nose.

"You've got to be fuckin' shittin' me…" Biscuit grunted as the pole came down on Gunner's head.

"You no good son-of-a-fuckin'-cop-bitch," Biscuit howled as he raised the pole again, "I'll just beat you to death if they won't let me shoot you."

Axton raised his hands in the air and screamed. "God fucking damn it, Biscuit. Put the pole down."

"Ain't happenin', Slice. These fuckin' cops, you can't trust 'em. Probably got a Smith and Wesson .44 Magnum shoved up his ass as a backup piece. I'm keepin' the pole," Biscuit responded as he held the pole over his head, ready to strike again.

"Well, don't hit him with the fucker again unless I tell you to," Axton said, laughing as he spoke.

Axton shifted his eyes to where Gunner was treading water in the pool. "I don't trust you any further than I can throw you, you fat son-of-a-bitch. Don't think I can agree to that."

"You've got two options," Gunner explained, "Kill me, or let me go. That's it."

"Fuck this motherfucker, Slice. He's tryin' that cop psycho-babble mind game shit on us," Biscuit grunted.

Axton raised his hand in the air, "Put it down, God damn it, Biscuit."

"Man's got a point, Boss," I said, "We've only got two fucking options. Kill him, or let him go."

"Well, what the fuck do you four fuckers want to do?" Axton growled as he tossed his hands in the air.

"Kill him," Biscuit snapped back.

"Same. I say we kill him," Toad agreed.

I exhaled and nodded my head as I turned to face Axton, "Want to kill him, Boss, but it ain't too practical. Soon as he doesn't report in, they'll come to the clubhouse."

"Hand me the gun," Otis said.

"We need to talk about this, my fucking head's spinning," Axton said as tossed his hands in the air, still holding the gun in one hand.

"Hand me the fucking gun," Otis demanded.

Axton took a step rearward and narrowed his gaze. Otis shook his head in apparent disgust, walked to the table where Gunner's gun was sitting, grabbed it, and stomped to the end of the pool.

"Shut the fuck up. Every fucking one of you. Just shut the fuck up, especially *you*," Otis yelled as he pointed the gun at Gunner.

"God damn it, Otis," Axton bellowed.

"Shoot the motherfucker!" Biscuit hollered.

"Otis!" Axton growled.

"Every god damned one of you, shut the fuck up!" Otis yelled.

Otis jumped in the pool, grabbed Gunners head in one hand, and pushed the barrel of the pistol in his eye with the other.

"Listen to me, motherfucker, and listen *good*. I'm not like these other four fuckers. I'm the quiet one you need to worry about. You've been here two and a half years, so you know I'm the protector of this fucking MC, regardless of who wears the SAA patch," Otis seethed, "You've got one opportunity to answer each question I ask. *One*. If you don't, I'll pull this fucking trigger."

"Otis!" Axton yelled.

Otis didn't flinch.

I hadn't had much exposure to Otis other than a few drinks in the bar, but from what I was seeing, he was a no nonsense type of fella. Immediately, regardless of the outcome of the fucked up situation, I had more respect for him.

"What's your God given name?" Otis asked through his teeth.

"Allen. Allen Pintler," Gunner murmured.

"Current place of residence?"

"Wichita. Right here in Wichita," Gunner responded.

"Got a wife and kids?"

"Uhhm. I uhhm, yeah. I have a family," he cried.

Otis nodded his head and pushed the pistol deep into Gunner's eye socket. "You've got one option and one option only, and I'm going to explain it to you. You're going to get out of this pool, dry off, get dressed in some of Biscuit's clothes, and you and I are going to go to your house in Biscuit's truck. You're going to prove to me that it's your house by showing me your fucking mail, pictures of you with your fucking wife, and pictures of you with your kids. Your kids old enough to have laptops?"

What the fuck?

"What? Laptops?" Gunner muttered.

"Easy question, motherfucker. Do your fucking kids have laptops?"

"Yeah, they both do," he responded under his breath.

"Alright, again, listen carefully," Otis explained, "You're going to allow us access to their laptops, and we're going to put a LoJack on them, just to make sure you don't try and run anywhere. We'll track your kid's whereabouts, and we're going to put one on your bike and your personal car as well. And we'll track you. You either refuse to testify to the Grand Jury, or I'm going to kill your wife and kids. It's that simple. This isn't a threat, it's a solemn promise. If I'm going to spend life in prison, it isn't going to be on your terms, it's going to be on mine. You agree to these conditions?"

"Don't hurt my kids, just don't hurt my kids," Gunner cried.

As I saw the fear in Gunner's eyes, it was pretty obvious Otis had hit a soft spot with him in regard to his kids. Something he undoubtedly held sacred, the one thing he loved more than he loved himself. To him, his kids were what Em was to me. I nodded my head in an understanding manner, satisfied Otis was going to get exactly what he wanted from Gunner.

Good work, Otis.

If there was a way to stop Gunner from proceeding with his investigation, and, in turn, prevent anyone from going through the hell I was forced to live in through my arrest, incarceration, trial, and prison, I was all for it. If Gunner crossed the line by getting one of the Sinners drunk, begging them to say something, and arresting him for doing so, I would vote his fate be much different.

As I gazed down into the pool, I thought of agent Blackburn and what his fate should be now that I was available to administer the punishment I felt fit *his* crime. The only sufficient punishment was a decade in prison, and as that wasn't going to happen, I felt killing him was the only *real* option.

"It's all up to you, Special Agent Allen Pintler. It's all up to you," Otis said as he extended his arm over his shoulder, handing Axton the pistol.

Otis climbed from the pool and turned toward Axton. "Sorry, Slice. It was the only thing I could think of."

Axton shook his head. "LoJack's? Where the fuck did you come up with that?"

"Got one on my car and another on my laptop. They work pretty damned good, you can track them in real time on the internet," Otis said.

One more thing I must have missed in the last ten years...

"Get out of the pool," Axton demanded as he nodded toward Gunner.

"Toad's going with you. Toad, if he tries anything, and I mean *anything*, do whatever a war torn Marine thinks is best," Axton explained.

"You got it, Slice," Toad responded.

I turned to face Axton. He reached out and patted me on the shoulder. After a short hesitation he extended his hand. I reached for it, shook his hand, and as I did, he pulled me into him, and hugged me. As he held me, he whispered words that meant more to me than anything I'd heard in years.

"Love ya, brother," he said.

"Just doing my job, Boss," I responded.

And I meant every word I said.

A-TRAIN

Once a Marine, always a Marine. I had said it before and I would undoubtedly say again: I took an oath to protect the citizens of the United States of America from terrorists on our soil and abroad. The oath had no expiration date, and I've never had as much as an ounce of admiration for a man who couldn't keep his promises.

Terrorists come in all shapes, sizes, ages, colors, creeds, nationalities, and religions. A master of what they do, they're often camouflaged so well that an untrained eye isn't able to identify them. I, on the other hand, have years of experience, and believe my ability to recognize a terrorist for who he is and what he represents is second to no man's, and therefore have no reservation acting on my instinct in providing my continued protection to the men and women I took an oath to protect.

I am not so shallow that I believed all police or factions of the police were assembled only by men who were corrupt. As with all men in general, there were good cops, and there were bad cops. When an officer who gave an oath similar to the one I gave, and then chose to abuse his power, manipulate the system, and lie to convict an honest citizen of a crime that was never committed, he quickly identified himself as the enemy. The camouflage, so to speak, was removed, and who he truly was stood exposed for all to see.

He becomes a terrorist.

And my solemn duty was to the men and women of this United States, which I had sworn to protect, who relied on me and those like me to prevent them from being preyed upon.

I leveled the rifle on the parapet of the roof and slowed my breathing. From my short study, I had less than five minutes before he would be walking across the street. The distance of 600 yards was almost half a mile, an extremely long range for most men to shoot something the size of a Boeing 747, but for me it was a walk in the park.

I realized the report from the rifle would be heard from anyone within earshot, but the area I had chosen was surrounded by homeless people, and at least for the time being, I looked no differently than they did.

As my training and experience required, I blended into my environment well.

The target stood at the crosswalk, waiting for the light to turn green. With the early evening sun at my back, I peered through the scope, inhaled, exhaled slowly, and squeezed the trigger. The 660 grain bullet traveled the distance in less than a second, but, no differently than any of the other similar shots I had taken, seemed to travel in slow motion, providing sufficient time for me to recover from the recoil and see what I needed to see.

There was no doubt the target was eliminated.

Mission accomplished.

I quickly disassembled the rifle, placed the components in my backpack, then pulled my wool jacket over my shoulders and my hood over my head. After picking up the can of beer I had placed beside the pack, I opened it and took a drink. I gargled the warm beer, poured my hand full, and splashed a little on my jeans. I dumped the remaining beer on the hot roof and placed the empty can in my pack, and slipped my arms through the straps. Now, I would smell to anyone who passed my on the street no differently than the hordes of homeless gathered below.

I walked across the roof to the fire escape of the abandoned building and climbed down and onto the sidewalk. Within five minutes, I was a block away, amidst a dozen homeless. In five more, I was on my bagger traveling a comfortable 65 miles per hour down the interstate.

And the world was a better place to live in.

JACK

I watched in amazement as the man balanced on ice skates while he pummeled the man in front of him. With his left hand holding the jersey of his opponent, and his chin tucked to his chest, he swung wildly but effectively, hitting the other man in the face with no less than half his punches. The referees stood to the side and watched as the two players fought until completely exhausted. As the man getting hit the most finally fell to the ice, the referees skated in between them and stopped the fight.

"Can you fuckin' imagine if they let 'em fight in baseball? Motherfuckin' first base coach kickin' the shit outta the umpire for a bad call. Whippin' the piss outta him until one of 'em fell on the ground? Gotta love a fuckin' hockey game," Ripp growled as he stood and clapped.

I clapped my hands and cheered. I'd never been to a hockey game, and as much as I protested going, the fellas from Austin all but demanded it. Now that I was actually experiencing it, I was glad I agreed to attend. The thought of hockey always fascinated me, but going reminded me of Em, as she always spoke of her love of following the playoffs.

It was the least I could do to repay the man who paid for my freedom.

On my left, the heavyweight Champion of the World sat quietly and humbly, probably hoping no one would notice him. A few had, and it was pretty exciting to me to be sitting with a true celebrity. Having an entire career of undefeated matches was not only an accomplishment, but spoke clearly of what type of a man Shane Dekkar was when it came to devotion.

"Sit down, Ripp," Shane sighed as he shook his head.

"Fuck, Dekk. Did you see that shit? Put some skates on your ass and see how long you keep the title. These motherfuckers are brawlers. I need to get me some skates and practice up. We got a team in Austin?" Ripp asked as he lowered his oversized self into the small plastic seat.

Shane nodded his head. "Texas Stars in Cedar Park. I'll buy the skates if you'll try out."

"Soon as we get back," Ripp said over his shoulder.

Otis leaned forward and got my attention. "Look at the goalie. He's going to slap the shit out of number 22. Each time he skates by, he slashes at him with his stick."

I shifted my eyes to the goalie. As soon as 22 skated around the goal, he swung his stick, slapping it against the back of the skater's legs. I knew very little about the fast-paced game, but it sure appeared the goalie was off-limits when it came to people making contact with him, and 22 had been coming close all night.

The previous fight was all because the other skater had knocked the goalie over when trying to rush in for a goal. As I did my best to pay attention to everyone skating back and forth, the buzzer sounded, ending the period.

"Holy shit, fellas, this is some exciting shit," I said as I glanced to my left and then my right.

Toad leaned forward, resting his elbows on his knees, and peered past Otis and Ripp.

"One more period, then it's over. Fucks me up how they count the time backwards on the clock. I think when they let those two out of the box, they'll go at it again," he said.

I nodded my head. "Hope so, pretty fucking exciting shit."

Being at the game allowed me to enjoy myself for the first time since I had been out of prison. I had not thought about anything but what was in front of me since we arrived at the game, and spending time with the fellas from Austin was pretty damned entertaining. Ripp was a comical fucker, always talking shit to Shane, and joking about everything he found amusing. Personally, I'd put him up against the MC's practical joker, Biscuit as far as story telling abilities go. Shane was quiet, and although he kept to himself, was extremely respectful and quite humble.

A-Train was the Marine who served in the entire war with Toad, and saved his life during one of his many tours. Toad, while in Austin, returned the favor by taking a bullet intended for his Marine brother. Although so far I wasn't able to spend much time with A-Train, he was a man who immediately made me comfortable to be around. He listened far more than he talked, but when he took time to talk, he didn't do it for attention or recognition. He spoke because it was necessary.

Immediately, and without thought, I admired him for it.

They had been in town for almost a week, and were scheduled to leave in the morning, going back to Austin after their trip to Wisconsin for a rally. Disappointed that A-Train wasn't able to make the game, but grateful that he provided me the ticket, I sat anxiously waiting for it to continue.

"What do you think they pay that dumb fuck to drive that deal on the ice and polish it?" Ripp asked.

"Five bucks an hour?" I shrugged.

He wrinkled his nose and stared, "How long was you locked up? They pay a motherfucker at McDonalds eight bucks."

"Shit, I don't know, eight bucks then," I chuckled, "And ten years. I was locked up for ten fucking years."

"God damn, brother. Better man than me. I woulda hung myself," he said as he shook his head.

Although I saw a few people commit suicide in prison, the thought never crossed my mind. For some reason, suicide never seemed to be an option for me. I felt my only way of leaving this earth would be the same as my entry, one God decided, not me.

When I was sixteen, Johnny Kilgore was seventeen. He and his twin brother, Jacob, spent almost every waking hour together, and were friends first, and brothers second. One weekend, while on a date, Johnny was driving on a county road, and attempted to cross an unmarked railroad track.

The investigation produced very little information from what I could recall, but there was no alcohol involved, nor were there any drugs present in either his or his girlfriend's bloodstream. The train hit his truck broadside, and when it did, the truck exploded. It didn't explode into a fiery ball of flames, it disintegrated. The dismantling of the truck was immediate, and parts of it were strewn along the track for a mile.

Both Johnny and his girlfriend were killed immediately. It was the second time in my life I had to deal with death, but the first, my parents, was when I was too young to understand it fully.

One thing I will never forget was that there was pair of shoes dangling from the telephone line thirty feet in the air above the crash site. Although some viewed it as a hoax, and others truly believed they were Johnny's girlfriend's shoes, I never really thought it mattered. The shoes hung from the line for a year as a symbol of what happened, and just how immediate death can be.

Every time I passed that intersection, I saw the shoes before anything. I always looked both ways before I crossed, which was something I hadn't always done in the past. I perceived the shoes as somewhat of a warning or maybe even a reminder of the permanency of death.

Jacob wandered around town in a fog for roughly a year before he took his own life one day. He did so at the crossing where his brother had died, shooting himself in the head with his father's pistol. It was the third time I had to deal with death, but my first suicide. Something inside of me broke that day, and I always believed it was a result of witnessing someone so young who was once full of life decide to take his own life. The decision wasn't something that could be reversed later, nor was it something he could recover from.

At his funeral, I made a decision.

I spent an entire Saturday afternoon shooting at the shoes with a friend's .22 caliber rifle until I literally cut the shoe strings in two, causing the shoes to fall to the ground. Although I had reservations at first, feeling almost as if the shoes were sacred, I eventually walked over and picked them up. I later took them to the grave of Johnny's girlfriend and placed them in front of her headstone.

A few weeks later, they added a warning light at the intersection. A little too late to save the lives lost, it was my first experience with the indecisive nature of a bureaucracy and how it could - and would - have an effect on society.

"Well, if I woulda taken that option, I wouldn't be here watching this, would I?" I asked as I jumped from my seat.

Number 22 was in an all-out brawl in front of the goalie. The player from the penalty box had immediately skated toward him and challenged him to a fight as soon as he was released. As we stood and cheered until one man hit the ice, I was grateful for a lot of things in my life.

And the first was that I was alive and well.

"Well, glad you didn't," Ripp said as he slapped my shoulder, damned near knocking me down the rows of seats.

I initially glared at him, and then fully realized that he didn't mean it. He was just big, strong, and full of life himself. As he screamed at the referee and eventually threw his remaining cup of beer into the rink when the referee kicked the player out for instigating a fight, I slapped him on the shoulder equally as hard.

"Me too," I said.

Me too.

JACK

Toad called me in to see the news, which left me feeling slightly relieved, and, at least initially, a little scared.

Agent Blackburn was executed while walking to his office from court late Friday, at approximately 7:10 p.m., the result of a sniper's .50 caliber bullet. The shot, according to authorities and ballistics experts with the bureau, was taken from approximately a mile away, a distance that made and will continue to make apprehension of the suspect or suspects difficult at best.

Agent Blackburn, who had been with the bureau for 18 years, was best known for spearheading the case against an Outlaw Motorcycle Gang, and later writing a book about his experiences while in the gang, which was entitled The Eagle's Nest.

Our thoughts and prayers go to the family of the deceased.
Jim?

I stared at the television.

"That your guy?" Toad asked as he turned down the volume.

I swallowed the lump which had risen in my throat. Although I fully intended on paying Blackburn a visit, it felt odd knowing that he was dead, and not by my own doing. It appeared I wasn't the only one who viewed him as an enemy and a threat to society.

I pursed my lips and nodded my head.

"Probably a good thing you were at that hockey game last night," A-Train said as he turned to face me.

I stared blankly, eventually shrugging my shoulders.

"They said it happened at 7:10. Hell, you've got a rock-solid alibi. Plenty of witnesses, one a damned celebrity," A-Train paused and tilted his head toward Shane, who stood a few feet away.

"And from what I can recall, that new arena is full of cameras; probably got you dumb fucks on film. It's a shame about that agent, though. Well, if nothing else, it'll make sure you don't go right back to the joint for doing something stupid," he said.

I stood and stared, partially in shock, but not enough so that my mind wasn't working overtime to digest what had happened.

We were all scheduled to ride out of town with the group, seeing them to the state line, and returning to the shop afterward for a small party of our own. Toad's home was filled with men, Axton and Otis included.

"Got a minute?" I asked A-Train as I tossed my head toward the door leading to the garage.

"Got a lifetime," he responded as he turned toward the garage.

As he followed me into the garage, my mind attempted to assemble the pieces of the previous day. I never considered myself a stupid man, but I also hated to make assumptions. But as men often did, my MC brothers had told stories of A-Train before his arrival, many of which were stories of war, his life in Austin, and some tales of the time when he lived in Wichita. One thing each of the stories had in common was a body.

A *dead* body.

Never a witness, and from what they said, he never admitted to anything.

But I couldn't help but wonder.

As we stepped down the stairs and into the garage, I glanced around at the various the motorcycles. I felt slightly nervous, but not so much that I was afraid to speak. I suspected part of my apprehensive nature was a result of Blackburn actually being dead and my mind attempting to place that piece of my puzzle aside.

"So, where were you last night?" I asked.

He gazed toward me, but it was as if he was looking through me, or maybe even into me. As I stood, feeling as if he was peering into my very soul, he reached into his pocket, pulled out a pack of cigarettes, and lit one. As he flicked the Zippo lighter closed against the leg of his jeans, he took a long drag from the cigarette, and answered as he exhaled a cloud of smoke.

"With an old friend. A local doctor," he responded, "Why?"

"Just wondering," I responded.

I gazed down at my boots for a moment, glanced up, and hesitated. As I stood wondering how to proceed, he exhaled another cloud of smoke, lifted his cigarette even with his face, and studied the smoking tip.

"Something you need to say?" he asked.

"I don't know for sure, I was just wondering…"

He clenched the butt of the cigarette between his teeth, closed one eye to protect it from the rising smoke, and while peering at me with his open eye, began to speak.

"What's on your mind, Big Jack?" he asked as he pursed his lips around the cigarette.

The end glowed as he took another long drag. Standing there talking to him didn't make me nervous, but I was far from being in my comfort zone. He seemed different. Distant. His eyes looked like they were deeper in his skull, and they seemed almost three dimensional in color, like a hologram.

In short, he seemed like a walking ghost.

"I uhhm…"

"You want to know if I killed that man?" he asked.

My constricting throat prevented me from responding. I nodded my head as I fought to swallow.

"Ask me," he said as he opened his mouth and dropped the cigarette to the floor.

As he pressed against it with the tip of his boot, I did just that.

"Did you?" I asked.

"Let me ask you this. If I told you yes, would you shake my hand, or would you turn around and walk away?" he asked.

I shrugged my shoulders. "I don't know."

He shook his head, bent down, and picked up the cigarette butt. As he pushed it into the pocket of his jeans, he continued.

"Never ask a question unless you're fully prepared for the repercussions of the response," he said as he slapped his hand against the side of my shoulder.

As he turned and began to go up the steps, I responded truthfully.

I lifted my chin slightly and focused on his rising shoulders. "I'd shake your hand."

He stopped, turned to face me, and after a short study of my eyes…

He extended his hand.

JACK

"Shit, okay. I appreciate it," Axton said as he scribbled on the note pad he carried with him at all times.

He glanced toward me, nodded his head, and continued, "I'll make a fucking donation to the Fraternal Order as soon as I get back to town. We're stopping for a beer. Appreciate the call," he said.

He shoved the phone into his front pocket, pulled the sheet from his pad, folded it, and handed it to me.

"What's this?" I asked as I glanced at the sheet of folded paper.

He glanced over each shoulder, and leaned toward me.

"Your girl. That's her address, and the address of her new restaurant," he said under his breath, "Said she just opened it, like she *just* opened it. And he said for what it's worth, he's sorry it took so long. She was a tough one to find. Said she doesn't even use fucking credit cards."

I could feel my pulse beating in my ears.

He glanced at Avery and after studying her for a moment, shifted his eyes toward me, studied my shaking hands, and grinned.

"Just go. I'll tell 'em something," he said as he opened his arms.

We embraced like brothers. As much as I had to say, and as deeply as I appreciated all that he had done, I couldn't speak. It had been almost a month since he called in the favor, and I had all but began to lose hope.

As I released him and gazed into the bar my eyes began to itch.

"Hit the road, Jack," he chuckled.

I nodded my head and lifted the sheet of paper slightly.

"Devil looks after his own," he said as I walked away.

As I walked to my bike, clenching the paper in my hand, I realized Axton and the Selected Sinners were right.

The Devil does look after his own.

EMILY

"Miss Stewart, does the name of the restaurant have anything to do with the roman numerals on your necklace," she asked.

I nodded my head and smiled as I reached for the necklace.

"Call me Em, please, and yes, it's got everything to do with it," I responded.

I had named my new restaurant *Six Twenty-One*. I liked the name much more than *Jackson's* and the other name I had used, *J&E's*. Both names brought too many questions, and over time it became much too difficult to continue to tell the stories over and over. Each time I told them I filled with pride, but later, when I was home and alone again, my nights seemed to last a lifetime.

"Care to share? And call me Tina," she said, her fork still hovering over the plate.

"Finish your meal, I'll come back in a few minutes and check on you," I said as I pushed myself from the table.

"I'm finished," she said as she lowered her fork to her plate and picked up the napkin.

I felt offended. I paid more for a month's lease on my restaurant than she probably paid for her Mercedes-Benz. Las Vegas wasn't a place many people were able to succeed in, but I was determined to do so, and

I needed her review to establish myself early.

I turned to face her and relaxed. As I did my best to bite my respective lip, I inhaled a shallow breath through my nose, opened my mouth slightly, and exhaled.

"Was there something wrong?" I asked as I nodded my head toward her plate.

"You're from the Midwest, aren't you?" she asked.

You fucking bitch. You didn't have to come here.

I forced a smile and did my best to add a little Midwest accent with my response.

"Yes ma'am," I said with a slight note of sarcasm.

"Your voice," she said with a light laugh, "It reminds me of my mother's sister, my aunt. She is from Nebraska, and she sounds just like you."

I nodded my head and glanced down at her half-eaten meal.

She leaned forward and smiled, "I rarely do this, but I'm far too excited not to. My review will be posted in the *Las Vegas Review Journal*, the *Time Out* publication, and the little magazines you see in all of the casinos, well, at least the ones owned by MGM Grand. It will be a few weeks before it's in the magazines, but it will be in the newspaper next week. Friday."

She paused as she glanced over each shoulder.

"Five stars. Tell me, Em, how do you do it?" she asked.

My heart raced. I wiped my sweaty hands on my pants and fought not to cry. This was it. I had finally made it to the big leagues. With her favorable reviews, I would be noticed by each and every person who frequented the Las Vegas Strip.

"Thank you," I whispered, "And I don't know. Passion, I suppose."

"Now, the name, I'd love to include something about it," she said as she reached for my hand.

We were seated on the patio facing the strip. The front side of the restaurant had large glass doors similar to garage doors which were open, leaving the restaurant open to the outside and the patio open to the restaurant. I sat facing the restaurant, and she faced the strip. The evening was warm, but it was late enough in the season that it wasn't ridiculously hot. I leaned back in my chair, inhaled a deep breath, and gazed beyond her at the palm trees lining the street.

"Ever been in love?" I asked.

She nodded her head and grinned. Still cupping the top of my hand in hers, she responded.

"Frank. He passed two years ago June. But, to answer your question, yes. And very much so, I might add," she said.

She was in her mid-sixties, very well-dressed, and adorable. Dressed in a light blue pants suit, and with perfectly placed short gray sprigs of product-infused hair, she could have easily doubled for a retired movie star.

I closed my eyes and thought of the day Jackson kissed me the first time, at the coffee shop.

"Well, I don't know if Frank was a kisser, but Jackson is. And the first time he kissed me…well, let's just say it was one of those kisses that made me go weak in the knees, lose my hearing, and realize without a doubt, all at the same time," I paused and opened my eyes.

"That he was the one. There would never be another soul to challenge him, take his place, or fill the void he left when he was gone. God graced me with his presence," I said as I reached for the necklace.

"The date is our anniversary," I said.

"Oh how sweet," she said as she released my hand.

"And his name?" she asked.

The sound of a passing motorcycle caused me to pause, but it seemed they always did. My choice for the previous two restaurants was based primarily on the lack of motorcycle traffic alone. It was one thing I certainly wouldn't be able to change about the Las Vegas strip, and would take some getting used to, but a sacrifice I told myself I was willing to make.

"Jackson," I said.

"The name of your first restaurant," she said.

I nodded my head and fought to smile.

After an apology, she scribbled a few notes onto her pad, and sighed lightly as she finally finished. As she shifted her eyes upward, I gazed past her. As I studied the inside of the restaurant from the outdoor patio, focusing on anything proved to be difficult. The interior of the establishment appeared to be much darker when looking in from the outside, but I watched curiously as a man who had entered resembled Jackson so much it caused me to shiver.

After I forced myself to tear my eyes away from him, I turned my head slightly to the side and shifted my gaze to meet hers. She sighed again and smiled. I glanced once again toward the restaurant. He stood staring back at me. I felt guilty for returning the stare; it was almost as if I was cheating on Jackson.

And that was something I would never do.

I tried desperately to force myself to look away, but I wasn't able to do so. For a moment I simply wanted to admire him, all the while telling myself it was Jackson, and not some stranger. As my eyes went in and out of focus and my mind drifted into a distant past, he began to walk my direction.

I blinked and forced my eyes to focus.

It appeared he was crying.

He walked onto the patio. Dressed in dark jeans, a black button down shirt, and black dress boots, he could have passed for Jackson's twin. My eyes filled with tears. Embarrassed, I turned away and faced the street.

"Em," Tina said.

I turned to face her as I wiped the tears from my eyes, fully realizing I was being rude.

"Em…" the man's voice was filled with emotion, but unmistakable.

I glanced upward and attempted to stand as I responded in an almost inaudible tone. The response took no thought whatsoever, but was something I had not said to a man in almost a decade.

"Yes, Sir?" I squeaked as I stood.

Our eyes met. My legs didn't go weak, they collapsed. As I fell, it was as if I was caught by an angel, and in looking back on it, I really was. As he lifted me into his arms and held me against him, my heart raced, my eyes filled with tears, and I even questioned my sanity.

But he was real. He was holding me. And he finally came home.

"I love you so much," he said.

Tears ran down his cheeks.

"I love you," I said, my mouth forming the words, but my voice incapable of making a sound.

He lifted me by my waist and held me in front of him. He looked no differently than the day he left, and as he absorbed me with his eyes, his mouth curled into a smile revealing the dimples I yearned to see.

And, as ridiculous as it sounds saying it now, I knew one day he'd return.

Because he made me a promise that he'd eventually *always* come home.

And Jackson Shephard never breaks a promise.

www.ingramcontent.com/pod-product-compliance
Lightning Source LLC
Chambersburg PA
CBHW050712180626
46814CB00002B/392